The
Six Hundred Thousand
Dollar Club

Carol S. Trevillion

The Six Hundred Thousand Dollar Club

Copyright © 2010 by Carol S. Trevillion

This is a work of fiction. Names, characters, places and incidents are either the product of the author's imagination or are used fictitiously, and any resemblance to actual persons, living or dead, business establishments, events or locals is entirely coincidental.

To all of my friends, family and writing buddies who have been so supportive during my writing of The Six Hundred Thousand Dollar Club, I give you all a big hug. And to my son, Mike and grandson, Andrew, thanks for your technical help. Daughter Lysa, the 'grammar queen', tons of thanks to you.

An extra big thank you hug and kiss to my very patient hubby, Robert, for living on endless leftovers that he scrounged from the fridge so that I could spend time writing my novel. I love you.

Thank you, thank you and thank you all.

Six hundred thousand dollars. That's what's in the pot. The last one to outlive the others will get it all. Only ten members left. Who will it be? Each aging member keeps close check on the other nine's health. "How are you feeling?" has become the official weekly greeting of the club for the past ten years.

Since its beginning in 1953, only one member has passed away. And only one has dropped his membership because of the lack of finances to pay the thousand dollar yearly dues. Both dropped members' dues remained in the pot to be added to the lucky survivor's purse.

Because the club has a good number of members and other people involved, I feel it is only fair to you to provide a bio and a bit of history of each character. You will meet the members of the club at its beginning. You will note that the ages of each are much younger than depicted in the cast of character listed below, which shows their ages at the time of the mysterious happenings begin to occur. You may wish to refer to their bios as you follow us along on our journey through The Six Hundred Thousand Dollar Club.

The Cast Of Characters In Alphabetical Order:

Ardon Steris: Age 73. Retired President of Flashing Financial Institute. He and his wife, Verina Steris, founded the Six hundred Thousand-Dollar Club in 1953.

Bibi Mercille: Never married. She still has high hopes of finding a husband. She is the giddy type and finds humor in things that are not always humorous. She is now 69 years of age, still in her prime, if you ask her.

Doralene Drake: Age 69. Divorced from Fredrick Drake. Loves sexy clothes, expensive jewelry and perfume. Charter member of the club since its beginning in 1953, when she, her ex, the Roms and the Sterises formed it. Fredrick's monthly alimony checks are the highlight of her life. She eagerly waits by her mailbox on the first of each month just to be sure the postman has an envelope from Fredrick's attorney.

Fredrick Drake: Age 70. Married to Doralene. Retired real-estate broker. Charter member of the club. He continued his membership until Doralene and he divorced, forfeiting his share of the pot because of the lack of financial stability after the divorce. He hates paying alimony to Doralene.

Charles Rom: Age 66. Charter member of club. He and his wife, Hazel, and the Drakes reluctantly helped Ardon and Verina Steris form The Six Hundred Thousand Dollar Club over dinner in 1953.

George Imimes, Attorney of Law: Age 26. Hired by the members of The Six Hundred Thousand Dollar Club to write up the contract and to oversee the money of the club. He was chosen because of his young age. The club members hoped he would still be alive when the last survivor was to get the money.

Gladys Grey: 38. Married to Landis Grey. Could stop Landis in his tracks with one look, though they were in love. She refused to let Landis join the club. Even up to her death, after losing the battle with cancer, she was still giving him the, "You better not even mention it" look.

Hazel Rom: Age 66. She has been a member of The Six Hundred Thousand Dollar Club since 1953 when she and her husband, Charles, the Drakes, Fredrick and Doralene, and the Sterises, Ardon and Verina formed it. She also has high hopes of out living every one else in the club.

Landis Grey: Age 72. Joined the club several years after it was formed. Married years ago, but his wife, Gladys never joined The Six Hundred Thousand Dollar Club. She has been deceased for six years before Landis reconsiders his option of joining the dub. Occupation: retired schoolteacher.

Meeno Max: Age 40. Driver for the Sterises. Single. Lives on premises of Sterises' estate. Hates his job, but it's easy and it provides an income to help pay for his needs and habits. He thinks all the club members are a bunch of crazy, old coots.

Nellie Wheeler: Age 37 when she and husband, Owen, joined the club in 1953. She developed a heart condition in her later years.

Owen Wheeler: Age 70. Widowed. He and wife, Nellie, joined at beginning of the founding of the club. His wife's share of dues stayed with club after her death.

Pearl Preston: Age 65. Joined shortly after The Six Hundred Thousand Dollar Club formed. Her husband, Roy, never joined the club. He just finished his fight in Korea. He remained in the military until his death in 1964 in Vietnam. Pearl joined the club just to have a social life while her husband was away. Being the youngest of the club members, she is almost positive she will be the lucky beneficiary of the pot.

Richard Long: Age 40. Private Detective. Hired by Shana Willow to investigate suspicious deaths of club members, mainly the death of her grandfather Ardon Steris.

Shana Willow: Age 36. Granddaughter of Verina and, Ardon Steris. Suspects foul play in the death of her grandfather and other members of the club She is concerned about the safety of her grandmother.

Tracy Eager: Age 37. Assistant to Richard Long. She is helping him solve suspicious deaths of the club members. She spends much of her time looking up "interesting facts" on the computer.

Verina Steris: Age 72. Married to Ardon Steris. Co-founder of The Six Hundred Thousand Dollar Club. She has been confined to a wheelchair since falling off of a horse in 1962. She enjoys the finer things of life. Her main interest is The Six Hundred Thousand Dollar Club.

Rules of The Six Hundred Thousand Dollar Club: are quite simple: "Pay the thousand dollar annual fee and outlive all the other members".

The mission statement is just as simple: "Live the longest and prosper."

Chapter One: 1953

"This is the craziest idea you've ever come up with, yet," Charles said to Ardon. "This is crazier than the "Make wine in your basement" idea. I am not going to get caught up in any of your get rich pyramid schemes. I work hard for my money and I want to keep it. And besides, my new bride here would never agree to such a ridiculous idea, would you honey?" he said as he looked at Hazel. "We have big plans for our money and it doesn't include giving it to you to lose for us." He reached over and squeezed her hand.

"But you won't be losing any money, unless of course, you die first. Then your money and Hazel's will stay in the pot and who knows, if Hazel outlives us all, she will have a very fine pot o' gold at the end of her rainbow."

"I don't know, it still sounds like a pyramid scheme to me."

"How can you lose? You're just setting aside money for your old age, if you outlive us all of course. Plus you'll get everyone else's money, too, if we die before you. See, nothing to lose, everything to gain."

"Except a thousand dollars a year. I wouldn't exactly say that's nothing. Remember, Hazel and I are just starting our lives together. We want to buy a house. Maybe have some kids in a couple of years."

Hazel reached over and patted him on the arm.

"I'm glad you put that cart and horse in the right order, sweetie."

Verina let out a long sigh.

"I would have liked to have maybe one child, but no more than one. I don't think I could stand all that pain. And the dirty diaper business is definitely not my idea of pleasure. I would definitely have to hire a nanny."

"I'm sure when the time comes dear, you'll be able to handle it just fine," Ardon said. "So what do you think, Charley? Are you in or not? And what about you, Hazel? You in?"

"I'll do whatever Charles says. My money is his money and his money is mine. My job is to spend it. His job is to keep track of it and to replenish it when it gets low."

"Hey, I like that plan," Verina said. "But as far as Ardon's proposition of a money club, I think he has a great idea. I could see where money stashed for twenty or thirty years could add up to a pretty big sum, don't you think? Of course, there would have to be some kind of contract written up with specifics, so no one gets greedy or off scoffs with the lot. Do you have any idea about how that should be handled, Ardon? I'm sure our best friends would feel more comfortable knowing their money is protected, though I'm sure they trust us and we trust them."

"I haven't said I'd agree yet, remember?" Charles said. "What do you think, Hazel, dear? Should we let this idiot friend of ours take our money or should we just tell him where to go with his harebrained idea?"

"I'll do what ever you think is best, Charles. You are the money manager, remember?"

"Well, I think Hazel and I need to think on this awhile, don't you Hazel?"

Hazel smiled and nodded her head.

"OK, fair enough," Ardon said as he reached for his martini. "You think on it and let me know tomorrow."

"Tomorrow? That doesn't give us much thinkin' time," said Charles.

"So why don't we hear more about these specifics of this contract we need to write up, so Hazel and I can make a better decision. And I'd like to know who's holding onto our hard earned cash and where is it being kept until the next to the last guy or gal kicks the bucket? I wouldn't want it to just suddenly disappear."

"OK, well let's write up a contract right here and now, tonight. It can be signed and notarized tomorrow, when you say yes."

"Wait a minute, who said I was going to say yes?"

They all laughed as they leaned forward, moving glasses and silverware out of the way to make room for writing up the contract. Arden motioned for the waiter to bring another round of drinks.

"And would you bring us a pad of paper and a pen?" Ardon asked the waiter. "And please take some of these dishes out of our way."

When the table was cleared and the round of drinks, pad of paper and pen were brought, they all moved closer, so that they could see exactly what Ardon was writing.

"First, we need to establish some rules," said Ardon. "Then we need to decide who and how many others we need to get to join to make this profitable."

"Whoa! Whoa!" said Charles. "What do you mean others? You never said anything about others."

"Well, if we want to keep the pot growing, we will have to invite others."

"So, this is a pyramid scheme," Charles said.

"No, not really. With a pyramid scheme, you make money off of other people you bring in. What we would be doing is just holding everyone's money for them, like a savings account. Only the interest paid out is a whole lot more than any bank interest could ever pay."

"OK, but it still sounds like a pyramid to me. And when you look at it, you are technically making money off of other people, are you not? But, go on, let's hear about this wonderful contract," said Charles.

"Well, I think our first rule should be, no one takes the money out. It stays until there is only one person left to collect. Just think, if three of us live to be a ripe old age of, say seventy or eighty, that's what, two hundred, three hundred thousand dollars? And if we get, say eight or nine other people to join us, well that's near six hundred thousand dollars at least. Pretty good retirement income for someone, I would say. See, it's not a pyramid, it's a very ludicridous investment, same principal as life insurance."

"Yeah, with only one beneficiary. And my money will be paying for it," Charles said.

"Not if you outlive us all, Charley, ol' buddy."

"OK, what else is in this great plan of yours? What else do I have to do to take up your offer to make me a rich old man?"

"Well, that's about it, except putting in your thousand dollars every year. Maybe suggest a friend or two to join on. Other than that, I don'tsee any other thing, do you? How about you ladies, can you see anything we need to add? If not, that's it, plain and simple!"

Neither Hazel nor Verina had any suggestions. They both seemed more interested in obtaining a dessert menu and one more round of drinks.

"OK, then why don't we meet here tomorrow night for dinner and you and Hazel can give me your answer.

Verina and I will need to think this through, also. Verina, honey, you haven't said much about what you think of the plan. Do you think it's a good idea or not? We will be investing our thousand dollars a year, each, too, you know."

"I like the idea of getting all of that money, if I outlive you all, but how does an old woman spend that kind of money?"

"Who knows, honey, we all may meet our maker at a very young age and then you'll have all that money to blow on fancy dresses and expensive jewelry while you're still young and beautiful. Not that you won't still be beautiful in your twilight years."

"Wait a minute, maybe I'll out live all of you and I'll be wearing those fancy dresses and expensive jewelry," Hazel said.

They all laughed as the waiter appeared with the dessert menus.

"Why don't we call it The Six Hundred Thousand Dollar Club, since that's about what we should have saved up in about fifty years?" Hazel suggested. "You know, so we have something to refer to when we talk about it to our children and grandchildren years from now."

The other three agreed it sounded like a proper name for their new venture.

"Besides, having a name like The Six Hundred Thousand Dollar Club may draw more interest when recruiting other members in," thought Ardon.

The rest of the evening was spent joking about how they would each out live the other and what they would spend the inheritance on if they were the sole survivor of The Six Hundred Thousand Dollar Club.

Ardon and Verina chatted excitedly all the way home about the promises of a great future for the club. They both agreed that it was amazing that no one else had ever thought of it before.

Charles and Hazel discussed the club on their way home, also, but not with as much enthusiasm as Ardon and Verina. Charles was still sure this was just another one of those schemes his friend had cooked up to con him and Hazel out of their money. He was willing to think about it some more, weigh all the options, and try to find any loopholes that his friend may have slipped in without his knowledge. He remembered several times during their college days when Ardon had pulled the wool over his eyes more than once to get his hands on his money or his latest girlfriend. Charles was not going to fall into Ardon's trap again. He loved his best friend, but he was not a fool.

Chapter Two: The Beginning

Ardon woke up at six. He was really surprised, since he hadn't slept very well. He was so excited about his newfound club that he tossed and turned all night. He had gotten up around three, went downstairs to make a sandwich. He made and devoured the entire sandwich in less than two minutes. He had to do something to calm himself down. Maybe a glass of warm milk would help. At least that's what his mother used to say. "Warm milk is like being at the mother's breast." He smiled to himself, because he could hear her voice in his head. He thought of other things his mother used to say as he reached for the milk. Pouring it into a pot on the stove to heat, he wished his mom were still alive to see what a great idea he had about forming the club. He may have even talked her into becoming a member if she were alive. She was always so tight with her money. He doubted she would even consider it. "You need to watch every penny, because you never know when it will be your last", he could hear her say, again, her voice from his days when he was a young "spend freely, save nothing" youth. He poured the milk into a glass and looked into the cabinet to see if he could find something else to snack on. For some reason, he found himself craving something sweet.

"Sweet, like the money I will have when everyone else kicks the bucket," he thought. "I only hope Verina is alive to share it. Of course if she is, I may not be the one to claim the money. This is a community property state, though, so what is hers is mine and what is mine is hers."

Finishing his milk and wiping the crumbs from his chocolate chip cookies off of his pajama shirt, Ardon slowly climbed the stairs to go back to bed to try to get a couple more hours of sleep. Today he would go to the First City Bank and open a savings account for the club. He was sure his friends Charles and Hazel would agree to form the club. Today he would also sit down and make a list of other friends that he could approach with the idea of The Six Hundred Thousand Dollar Club.

"Of course, I still have to convince Verina that they should invest her money into the club. That should be easy, though, since she thinks I am the financial wizard of the family", he thought. Sighing, he said, "But right now I need to get some sleep. This is definitely going to be a busy day." Turning off the lamp by his bedside, he rolled over and closed his eyes. "Sweet dreams, Ardon," he said to himself.

Whether it was the warm milk or the sweet dreams of the club, he slept peacefully through the rest of the night. When he awoke he heard Verina in the shower.

"Hmm..., maybe I should join her," he said. "Only, I really want to get to the bank early and get started on the list of potential members. Maybe I'll even have time to make a few calls before our dinner date with Charles and Hazel tonight. The more interested people I have, the better the chances Charles and Hazel will agree to join. As they say... money is time and time is money."

He climbed out of bed. Going into the second master bathroom, he brushed his teeth while he was waiting for Verina to get done with her shower. When he heard the shower turn off, he quickly turned the water on in his shower. Humming, he quickly showered, shaved and got dressed. By the time he was dressed and downstairs Verina was standing at the stove frying scrambled eggs. The aroma of the coffee smelled extra good this morning.

"Would you like some scrambled eggs and toast this morning, dear?" Verina asked. She poured his cup full of coffee and handed him a glass of orange juice.

"That would be nice. Thank you, love," he said. "Have you thought any more about the club?"

"Oh, yes, as a matter of fact, I have. I think it's a bit risky, but what in life isn't? I think, if nothing else, it would be a very interesting sort of game. Sort of an "I win you lose" kind of game. And, dear, you know how I do enjoy games, especially risky ones. You can definitely put my thousand dollars in the pot. Just think, even if you and me are the only members, and you die first, I still double my money," she laughed.

"And that goes the same for me if it turns out the other way around, *dear*," he said.

They touched their orange juice glasses together, calling it a touché.

"Here's to us!" Ardon said. "May the best one live"

"I'm going to the bank this morning to see about setting up an account for the club. Then I'll come home and make a few calls to see if I can create a little interest in the club to a few friends of mine. Do you have anyone in mind that you could invite to join?"

"Well I could ask my friend, Bibi. She is a little dingy, so she should be an easy one to convince. She's always joining some kind of group. I may have to tell her that several eligible young men are joining, though. She has her antenna alerted for single men all the time. Do you remember her?"

"Is she that chatty one from your bridge club?"

"Yes, that's the one. I'll call her this morning and invite her over tomorrow to play bridge and then I can talk to her about it then.

"Good. I don't know how you ever get to play cards, with her yakking constantly. I hope you are able to get in a word or two about the club."

"Don't worry, dear, I'll work it in before she has time to start telling one of her, "The man who got away" stories. I'll invite Pearl over to play bridge tomorrow, too. She has been joining us for bridge a lot lately. She is always looking for something to do while her husband, Roy, is overseas. I'll talk to her about it, too, when she comes tomorrow.

"OK. Well, I'd better get going before the line at the bank gets long. I don't want to have to wait too long to get to see an officer to set up the account. I'll see you in a couple of hours. I love you," he said, as he kissed her on the cheek.

Verina heard the door of the garage close. She wished Ardon had time to sit and talk this morning. She wanted to tell him about the dress she saw in the window at James Taylor's yesterday.

"It is an expensive dress, but it would look so good on me at the Rider's Ball in a couple of weeks. After I call Bibi and Pearl, maybe I'll go by and try it on. I wonder if they have it in emerald green? Emerald is definitely my color. It will bring out the green in my eyes. Ardon always says he fell in love with my green eyes."

"What do you think of Ardon's crazy club, Hazel?" Charles asked. "What do you think he is up to?"

"I think it could be great for a very healthy person or a person that never leaves his bed. Do we really want to give up a thousand dollars every year, hoping we outlive everyone else? I don't particularly like the idea of just sitting around waiting for my friends nor my husband to die so I can be rich."

"Well, I don't particularly want to sit around waiting for someone to die, either. But, you have to admit, it does sound interesting. I wonder how Ardon came up with such an idea? I tell you, he has a mind like no other. He always was a weird duck. A duck that swims against the steam. While everyone else is swimming downstream, he's swimming upstream. I guess that's why I like him. He always makes life interesting."

"Charles, if you want to invest your money into this crazy scheme, I'll go along with you. We could probably save up a thousand dollars in a year."

"You mean two thousand dollars. Remember, we each have to put a thousand in, that is if you want to do it, too."

"Of course I will if you do, Charles. You don't think I want to loose all the money you put in when you die, do you?"

"No, but who said I was going to die first?"

"Well, let's just hope we both outlive everyone else."

"OK. Are we in agreement that we tell Ardon yes, when we meet the Sterises for dinner tonight?"

"I guess so. It is kind of exciting when you think about it, don't you think?"

"Yes, it is. Since we don't have to work today, shall we go out for breakfast this morning? I feel like I need to get some fresh air and some fresh eggs. Maybe even a few slices of bacon on the side."

"OK. Sounds good to me. I could use a break from cooking. No dishes to wash…life is good, my love, life is good," Hazel said as she grabbed her sweater and headed toward the door. "Last one in the car buys breakfast," she shouted over her shoulder.

"You're on, lady!" Charles shouted back as he ran past Hazel, nearly tripping over the neighbor's cat stretched out on the step.

"What are you doing here? Scat you lazy cat. Go sleep on your own step."

Hazel took advantage of the situation and ran past Charles. She sat in the car with her arms crossed over her chest waiting for Charles.

"OK! You owe me a breakfast, Mister! Let's see, I think I'll have steak and eggs for breakfast and maybe a nice slice of chocolate cream pie on the side."

"Chocolate cream pie, for breakfast? Yuck! That doesn't even go with steak and eggs any time, especially at breakfast."

"We agreed that you would buy if I beat you to the car. Well here I am, waiting for you. We didn't say what had to be ordered. I could have said, Brussels sprouts and pumpkin pie and you would still have to buy."

"OK, OK, I get it. But I am not waiting for you to throw up after you eat that stuff. You are not pregnant, are you? I mean it would be fine with me if you are…but are you?"

"No, I'm not pregnant. I just like steak and chocolate cream pie. Is that all right with you? Or are you trying to weasel out of buying me breakfast? Because, if you are it's not going to work."

"No, I was just wondering, that's all. Onward to Yucks' Ville. One steak and one chocolate cream pie coming up for the lady."

Chapter Three: Four For The Money

"Where are they?" Ardon asked Verina for the third time in the last ten minutes. "They should have been here by now. We said we would meet here at seven o'clock. It's now twenty past and they still aren't here. I just hope they haven't decided that they don't want to form the club with us. We already have the savings account opened."

"Don't worry, dear. They will be here. If they were not coming, they would have called us. Even if they have decided against joining the club, they still would have called to say so. Watching the clock just makes the time go slower. Sit back and enjoy your drink. They'll be here soon."

"OK. I guess you're right. I guess I'm a little nervous that's all. I know this will work, if we have enough members."

"I know, dear. Remember we still have other prospects even if Charles and Hazel back out. Aren't you having lunch with your friend, Fredrick, tomorrow? And Bibi and Pearl will be by to play bridge tomorrow. I'm almost certain Bibi will jump on the chance to join any club that gives her the chance of meeting her knight in shining armor. Pearl probably will be willing to join for the social benefit of it, too. Which reminds me, we do need to think of the social aspect. Socializing is always important in any club if you want to keep active members, don't you think? And we also need to think about a place to have our meetings and social events. I think we need to choose a nice upscale dinner club with lots of good food and little noise. Maybe some place like The Red Carpet Cuisine on Lilac and Vine. Their pheasant is wonderful and the atmosphere is perfect for socializing. I'm sure we could ask for a private room for our club."

"That sounds good, Verina. What ever you say. Where are they? Maybe I should call them to see what's happened."

Just as Ardon started to go find a phone to call the Roms, they walked in arm in arm.

"Where have you been?" said Ardon. "I was beginning to get worried."

"No, he *was* worried!" laughed Verina. "He's been on pins and needles worrying you wouldn't show up. I told him not to worry that you would be here. Is everything alright?"

"Yes, everything's fine," said Charles. "We just needed to stop by to pick up some things at the office. Since we didn't have to go to work today, I needed to get some papers to be signed by a client first thing in the morning, so it was easier to pick them up tonight so that I can run by and have them signed on my way to work tomorrow. Sorry we are late. We didn't mean to make you worry, Ardon. I guess we should have called to tell you we were running late."

"Don't worry about it," said Verina. "You're here now, that's what's important. We had a drink while we were waiting. Ardon, shall we call the waiter over so Hazel and Charles can order? You look lovely tonight, Hazel. Is that a new dress you are wearing. I just love the color. You look so good in blue." She was hoping someone would notice her new emerald green dress and say something about how it brought out the beautiful green of her eyes.

"Thank you, Verina. No, I've had this dress since Charles and I took that cruise to Mexico last summer."

Disappointed that no one mentioned either the dress nor her eyes, Verina just smiled across the table at Hazel.

"Oh, yes. I remember when you took that cruse. You were so nervous about being on a boat while a war was going on. I do hope that Korean thing gets settled soon."

"Actually, it was a ship. And I must admit, I was a bit scared. Every time someone dropped something I thought for sure it was a bomb."

"I've never seen anyone so upset over something that should have been a pleasure," Charles said, as he gave Hazel's hand a squeeze.

After they had ordered their meal, Ardon, clearing his throat said, "So, have you come to a decision yet? About the club, I mean?"

"Yes, as a matter of fact we have," said Charles. "Hazel and I talked about it a lot this morning, didn't we, dear? We decided that it was a little too risky for our blood. Sorry, chum."

Arden could feel his heart drop all the way down to his socks. "But... But..." he stammered.

"Oh, I'm just kidding," chuckled Charles. "Don't have a heart attack, at least not until we've made this club official. Hazel and I are in, but we want to go with you to see a lawyer to make sure that everything will be done legally, not that we don't trust you, o'l pal. You know, just good business practice, that's all."

"You won't be sorry in a few years, when you see how much interest has accumulated. Of course, we expect you and any other members that join to go with us to see the lawyer to get thing drawn up, legally, as you put it," Ardon said as he wiped his sweaty palms on his napkin.

"I won't be sorry in fifty years, when I'm the only one living you mean," said Charles. "Who else have you asked to join our get rich club?"

"I have a luncheon meeting with a friend tomorrow. His name is Fredrick Drake. You may know him. He's a real estate agent across town. I think he and his wife will be interested. I also plan to invite another friend, Landis Grey. He is a history teacher at the high school. I think his wife may join too, though I haven't talked to either of them yet. I plan to stop by the school tomorrow."

"And dear, don't forget Bibi and Peral."

"Oh, yes, and Verina's bridge club friends, Bibi and Pearl." What about you two? Do you have anyone in mind to invite? We don't want it to be just our friends."

"We could talk to The Wheelers, Owen and Nellie," said Hazel.

"Yes, that's a good idea, Hazel. Maybe we could invite them over for dinner Saturday evening and talk to them about it then. I just hope we aren't all embarrassed when this thing falls through and we all lose our money." Charles couldn't help but to throw in as many jabs toward his friend as he could. "So when do we hand over the money and go see a lawyer?"

"I think we should see how many of our friends will join on and then we can all go together. Until then, I don't see any reason to go to a notary, do you...I mean since we are going to hire a lawyer? Well, on second thought, maybe we should say why the money is being deposited in the savings account at the bank. We can probably have it notarized right there at the bank. Which reminds me, once we do that, I think we need to find a young, but experienced lawyer to handle us. We don't want some old coot that will die in three years and leave us floundering on our own. Do you have anyone you could recommend, Charles?"

"No, but when we get everyone signed on, maybe we can come up with someone, if we all put our heads together. It would look better if everyone had some input, don't you think?" said Charles.

"That's a good idea," Ardon agreed.

"And I think we need to decide on a really nice place to have our meetings and social events, too," said Verina. "I'm thinking someplace like The Red Carpet Cuisine, but maybe we should wait until we all come together to decide that. Oh, this is going to be such fun."

"I agree," said Hazel. "I can hardly wait until this gets off the ground. We can plan all kinds of fun events."

"Leave it to the women to want to turn everything into an *event*," said Charles.

The rest of the evening was spent in jovial conversation and rich desserts, which suited Hazel and Verina just fine.

Chapter Four: The More The Merrier

"Hello, Fredrick, this is Ardon. How are things going in the real-estate business? Good, good. Can you believe how fast housing is growing in this city? Good business for guys like you, I guess."

"Yeah, helps to keep my wife in expensive clothes and perfume. So what's up?"

"Well, I have something I'd like to talk to you about. Could we meet tomorrow for lunch? I think you'll be very interested in what I have to say."

" I have a client I need to meet with to show a house at ten, but I should be free by noon. We could meet then."

"Great. Where do you want to meet?"

"Are you buying? If you are, I like Rose's Garden on Seventh Street. They have excellent lobster there. If you aren't buying, then The Hamburger Shack is fine.

"Rose's Garden it is," said Ardon. "I'll see you tomorrow at twelve o'clock."

When Fredrick arrived at Rose's Garden at eleven forty-five, Ardon was already there sitting at a table near the back of the restaurant. He didn't want to sit near a window or entrance because he didn't want any chance of distractions to interfere with what he was about to present to Fredrick. He had already ordered Fredrick's favorite drink, a straight whiskey, and no ice. He wanted to make sure Fredrick was in a good mood when he explained the benefits of the Six Hundred Thousand Dollar Club. He was starting to really like saying the name of the club.

"Hazel had a good idea by coming up with that name," he said to himself. "It's so catchy and will draw the attention of a lot of people, besides. At least people who can afford to invest a thousand dollars a year."

"Hello, Ardon. Have you been waiting long? I thought I'd be here before you. So, what's up?"

"No I just got here a few minutes ago myself. Sit. Sit. I ordered drinks already. I hope you don't mind. I know how you like your whiskey, straight, no ice. Why don't we take a look at the menu then we can talk?"

"OK. But I already know I'm going for the lobster. Thanks for ordering my drink. This must be something serious for you to buy lunch *and* drinks. I don't know if I can wait to hear this," Fredrick said.

"Well it will be worth the wait," said Ardon. "I know you will like what you hear."

Fredrick heartily enjoyed his lobster, while Ardon barely touched his prime rib. Fredrick ordered cheesecake with fresh strawberries on top. Ardon skipped dessert altogether. He felt a nervous rumble in the pit of his stomach. Though he didn't mind paying for the expensive lunch, he wished Fredrick would hurry up so he could get to the reason for inviting his friend to lunch in the first place.

"OK, now what's this all about, Ardon?" Fredrick asked as he licked the last remains of strawberry that had slid off the end of his fork.

"I have a very promising proposition for you, my friend," Ardon began. "How does a club called The Six Hundred Thousand Dollar Club sound to you?"

"What's The Six Hundred Thousand Dollar Club?"

"It's a group of people, say ten or so, putting, say... a thousand dollars a year into a pot or savings account, for the rest of their lives, then the last one to outlive all the rest gets all the money. Sort of a challenge to take care of your health and get rich at the same time."

"Are you kidding? Who came up with this nutty idea? Don't tell me you've gotten involved in a crazy thing like that."

"Actually, it was my idea. Verina is in on it, too. You remember Charles and Hazel Rom? Well, we met last night and we wrote up a contract to get it started and when we actually put our money together, we are going to get it notarized and maybe sent to a lawyer for legal advice. Hazel came up with the name, since our goal is to save up at least six hundred thousand dollars by the time we are all seventy or eighty."

"Or dead!" said Fredrick. "So you're telling me you want me to give you a thousand dollars a year for as long as I live, hoping I out live a bunch of other people, so I can take their money? And if I die before the last guy, I loose my money and I'll never know who the lucky sucker is?"

"You make it sound so negative, Fredrick. It's really a good thing when you think about it. Don't you do the same thing when you buy life insurance? You give some guy your money every year, knowing that some day you are going to kick the bucket and you, personally, will never see your money again. With my plan, you at least may see your money pay off, plus a good sum of extra cash as well."

"*May pay off* are the key words here. It may not pay off if I get hit by a bus in a couple of years or worse, if I'm the next to the last survivor and my wheelchair suddenly slips off of the sidewalk and rolls under a semi truck and I'm splattered all over Pleasant Street. I gotta say, that would not be very pleasant, for me at least."
Ardon laughed as he thought about his friend in a wheelchair rolling under a rig.

"No that would not be to pleasant for you or the city workers who had to clean up the mess. They probably would have to change the name of the street from Pleasant Street to Bloody Avenue," Ardon chuckled. "At least you would have street named in your honor."

"Very funny, wise guy."

"Alright, I guess that was a bit of a sick joke. But you have to admit; your chances are as good as anybody's, that you'll live a long happy life."

"I don't know, a thousand dollars a year adds up to a lot of dough."

"Yes, but think of what it could mean to you in a few years. Besides, you said your real estate business is booming right now, so you can probably put a little cash away to invest in something that may pay off in the long run. Right?"

"I'll have to think about this for a while. You said there are others investing?"

"Yes, the Roms, Charles and Hazel. They and anyone else who joins the club will sign a contract, so no one can take off with all the money. We will then go to an attorney that will be decided up on by the group, and have everything legalized, so there are no loopholes or funny business from any of us. Verina has a couple of friends that are interested, also. If you have anyone you would like to invite into the club, bring them, or their names at least, to our first meeting. We are thinking of making it a weekly dinner meeting, so we can all stay in close contact and really make it feel like a club. More like a social club."

"More like to keep tabs on your money, don't you mean?"

"With everything taken care of by a lawyer, we shouldn't have to worry about keeping tabs on our money," said Ardon. "I can assure you your money will be completely safe."

"I'm still not sure, besides I'll need to talk to Doralene about this. She may not see it as such a great idea."

"Sure. As a matter of fact, why don't you see if she wants to join, too? I'm sure she would enjoy showing off some of her sexy clothes and expensive jewelry that her loving husband has bought her. The dinner meetings would be the perfect place to do it."

"Yeah, she does enjoy dressing for attention. I'll think about it and let you know in a couple of days, but I'm not making any promises."

"That's understood. Just don't take too long, because we want to get things rolling with the lawyer and put the money into the savings account. The sooner the better as far as interest dividends are concerned. Every quarterly interest dividend we get means more money in our pot and more money for some lucky person."

"Say, why don't we have another drink, since you're paying? Then I need to get back to the office before my boss sends out a search party."

"Sounds good, but why do I have the feeling you are taking advantage of my kind offer of lunch?"

When their drinks arrived, Ardon suggested they make a toast to the possibilities of the club and to the certainty of Fredrick's answer of yes in a few days.

"If Fredrick and Doralene plus Verina's two friends, Pearl and Bibi, join and Charles and Hazel, Verina and myself, that will be quite a start to our venture. Eight thousand dollars in the pot and it hasn't even been a week yet. This could turn into something really, really big." He couldn't help feeling proud of himself for coming up with such a smart idea.

Now he had to go home and share the good news with Verina about the possibility of two more recruits. He wanted to call his friend, Landis Grey, as soon as school was out today. He hoped Landis didn't have a staff meeting. He thought about going by the school but had second thoughts about it. He didn't want to interrupt Landis's history class or any meetings with parents. He wanted Landis to be open about the offer to join the club, so he must stay on his good side and showing respect for the teacher's job was one way to accomplish it. No, he would call him later when he got home, when he was sure Landis was home, had his dinner and in a relaxed mood. Maybe he would ask if he could come by later in the evening and talk to him. Gladys would probably be there, so he could try to talk her into joining as well.

"If Landis and Gladys join, that would mean we would have another two thousand dollars and a total of ten members for the club. Ten thousand dollars and we haven't even seen the lawyer yet. I can't believe it. This is the best idea I have ever had!" he said.

He found himself singing along with the car radio all the way home.

"Yep, a very good idea, if I do say so myself."

Chapter Five: The Bridge Club

"Hello, girls. I'm so glad you both could make our bridge club today. Thelma will be here in a few minutes. She had to do some errands. She called to say she was running late. Come in. You can help me set up the table, if you don't mind. I'll go get the snacks. What would you two like to drink? I have sodas, coffee or tea, with or without sugar." Verina said as she started toward the kitchen.

"I'll have tea with as much sugar as you'll allow me to have," said Bibi.

"Tea is fine with me, too," said Pearl. "Only go easy on the sugar for me. I need to lose a few more pounds before Roy gets home from his war games. I swear, that soldier boy loves to play with the big guns. He probably volunteered to lead the troops right up some hill on the front lines. I can hear him now. "Charge!"

"When will he be home?" Bibi asked. "I know you miss him. I know if I had a husband so far from home, I'd be worried sick everyday just wondering where he was or what he was doing. If he was alive or if he was with some foreign floozy making ... well, you know what I mean."

"Well, I do worry, Bibi. Every morning when I wake up until I finally fall asleep at night. I don't think I need to worry about Roy and some floozy, though. I don't think they have too many floozies in his foxhole in Korea. Not with bombs flying over his head. He told me in his last letter that two more of his buddies were killed. I do wish this war would end soon. I thought it was supposed to be a cold war. If it's such a cold war then why are our men dying? But, thanks a lot for reminding me to keep worrying. I was hoping to forget the war for a few hours this afternoon and concentrate on bridge."

"Oh, I am sorry, Pearl. I didn't mean to upset you. I guess I have a tendency to stick my big fat foot in my mouth. Here let me help with that table leg. There! All set for a fun worry free afternoon of bridge."

"Here we are," said Verina as she returned with a tray of tea, crackers covered with thin slices of cheese and blueberry muffins that she had baked this morning especially for her guests. She knew blueberry muffins were Bibi's favorite and she hoped Pearl would enjoy the cheese and crackers. She wanted to make her friends feel welcome before she brought up the subject of the club. She wasn't so sure Thelma would even consider being part of the club, but she was pretty sure Pearl would and even more certain that Bibi would jump right in, especially if it meant meeting a prospect for a future husband. She definitely could afford the thousand dollars a year investment. " After all, a thousand dollars a year is a small price to pay for a husband for Bibi," thought Verina.

"Oh, yum," said Bibi. "You do know what I like, don't you, Verina?" How many muffins are we allowed? If Thelma doesn't get here soon, I get dibs on her share."

"Thanks for the crackers, Verina. I think I better stay away from the muffins, though. Bibi can have my share. OK, Bibi?"

"Yes, Pearl was just saying she wanted to lose a few more pounds before Roy gets home. I don't know where she thinks she needs to lose another ounce, though. Roy would probably be running AWOL if he knew he had such a beautiful thin wife waiting at home for him," Bibi said. She thought the compliment would make up for her blunder from a few minutes ago, about the floozy and Roy. Maybe Pearl had forgiven her since she did offer to give her the muffins. Bibi hoped so. She really liked Pearl and enjoyed playing bridge with her and the other ladies.

"Thanks for setting up the table. Here are the cards. Now all we need is Thelma. Help yourselves to the refreshments, ladies."

The three sat down to chat while they waited for Thelma to arrive. Verina wondered if now was the time to bring up the club, or would it be better to wait and do it during the game. If she waited until they were in the middle of the game, it would take some of the chitchat that Bibi always provided. "What a welcoming thought," Verina thought to herself. "My ears could use a rest. I think I'll bring it up during the game, after Bibi has downed a few more muffins."

"Excuse me," Verina said as the phone rang. "Let's hope that's not Thelma saying she is going to be even later."

" I may have to go bake more muffins if she's much later. I can't believe Bibi can down so many muffins in such a short time. No wonder she can't find a husband. Once they see her eat, they probably take off running as fast and as far away as they can," she thought.

"You really do like those muffins, don't you Bibi?" Pearl said. "No offense, but if I ate that many muffins, I'd be as big as a barn."

"Um, yes I do love my muffins, and these are really good ones. I'm glad Verina thought of baking them. Are you sure you don't want to try one? They are really, really, gooood," Bibi said as she poked the last bite of her fourth muffin into her mouth.

"That was Thelma. She said she's not going to be able to make it today. Her errands are taking her longer than she had expected. She said to tell you that she is sorry. She promises to be the first one here next week and said she will bring the refreshments."

"Oh, that's too bad. I was all ready to have an afternoon of worry free bridge with my friends," said Pearl.

"Yeah, me too," said Bibi. "I hope she brings muffins next week."

"So, what shall we do, if we're not playing bridge? We can't very well play with only three people," said Pearl. "And the muffins are practically gone, thanks to Bibi."

"Well we could just hang out here. We don't usually have much time to just sit around and chat. I have something that I would like to share with you ladies anyway."

"Are you sure we have enough muffins to keep Bibi here?" Pearl joked.

"Well, I'm sure she will stay to hear what I have to say, once I get started telling you about this wonderful idea my husband and I and a few friends have come up with that could be very profitable. I told Ardon, that you two ladies would be just the right people to take part. Would you like to hear about it?"

"Sure," said Pearl. "But is this going to cost me money? Because if it is, I'll listen, but I won't guarantee that I'll go for it."

"I want to hear about it, Verina. You know I always like to hear about new ideas. Like when they came up with that new idea of Swanson and Sons for frozen T.V. dinners. Actually, I think the real name is TV Brand Frozen Dinner. Who would have thought we could eat our dinner out of a little T.V. shaped aluminum tray right in front of the T.V. That was a great idea, especially for girls like me who have no one to cook for except myself. You just have to pop it in the oven for about twenty-five minutes at four hundred and twenty-five degrees, and you have your dinner. No dishes to wash or pots to clean. All for about ninety-eight cents. The turkey, cornbread dressing, peas and sweet potatoes taste just like Thanksgiving. I hope they come up with one that has macaroni and cheese. Have either of you ever tried that one yet? It's really good. It almost tastes like homemade. You should try it."

"No, I haven't tried any of those T.V. dinners. Ardon will only eat real food. I can't imagine him eating his Thanksgiving dinner out of an aluminum tray. Anyway, here's the idea we came up with. I hope you'll hear the whole plan before you form an opinion. As I said there are several people already interested, so if you want to be a part, I wouldn't wait too long to decide. Not just anyone will be invited to join. Since you two ladies are my best friends of course I thought of you first, before Ardon fills it up with all of his friends."

"Well, well, what is it, Verina? We want to hear," said Bibi.

"OK, here goes. It works like this. Well, first let me tell you what the name of the club is."

"Oh, so it's a club. I might be interested," said Pearl. "I can always use some social contact with Roy gone so much of the time."

"Yes, it is sort of a club. Anyway the name of the club is…are you ready? It's The Six Thousand Hundred Dollar Club! Doesn't that sound exciting? Anyway, where was I? Oh yes…"

"A what?" said Pearl.

"The Six Hundred Thousand Dollar Club. Anyway, as I was saying, it's a group of about eight or nine people who put one thousand dollars together every year for as long as they live. It stays in the pot even if they drop out or if they should pass away, and the last person to out live all the rest gets the whole pot, probably about six hundred thousand dollars at least in seventy years or so. We will have a contract and an attorney to over see the whole thing, so no one can take off with everyone's money or cheat in any way. It's all a safe investment. It's really like an insurance policy, except only one person is the beneficiary. And, Bibi, it may be an opportunity to meet some single men while you're at it. We don't know exactly who or how many we let join the club yet. We plan to have a regular weekly dinner meeting night, so you never know who may b show up at whatever restaurant we decide as our official meeting place. So…what do you think?"

"I've never heard of such a thing in my life," said Pearl. "Leave it to your husband to come up with something like that. I like the dinner thing, but I'm not too sure about the money part. A thousand dollars every year? Doesn't it sound sort of morbid to put money on your friends dying before you? I can just hear us now. "Hello, friend. You look a little sick today. I hope you're *not* feeling better".

"My, my," said Bibi. "Six hundred thousand dollars is a lot of money. It's not that I can't afford the thousand dollars a year, but Pearl is right when she said it was a little morbid. I guess I have never thought of myself or of my friends dying. And I don't know how I would feel about taking all their money."

"You wouldn't have to worry about taking everyone's money unless you were the last to die, Bibi!" exclaimed

Pearl. "You may be giving your money to someone else, remember?"

"Oh, yeah," replied Bibi. "Of course the social part does sound interesting like you said, Pearl. Do you really think there will be eligible men folk involved, Verina?"

"Well, I can't guarantee it, but as I said, it's a possibility. You would be helping us to decide where we hold our meetings, so you could be checking out places where single men hang out. Not a bar, but an upscale place where we could have a nice dinner and do business. But as I said, you'll need to make a decision soon because we want all of us to go together to see the lawyer. Ardon says that the sooner the better, because we can add to the pot with the interest at the bank where the money will stay until it's given to the last survivor."

"I don't know. I need to think long and hard on this idea of yours, Verina.. It's a bit to swallow all at once," said Pearl.

"Me too," said Bibi.

"OK, but don't wait too long. Remember what I said about getting in and getting the club started as soon as possible. You know how Ardon is when he gets something on his mind that he wants to do. He wants it right now!"

"I say, we should go home and think about this, Bibi. Haven't you had enough of those muffins? If we join this club, the way you are putting away those muffins, you'll probably be the first to croak!" said Pearl. "I'll think about it and let you know later in the week, after I've done some checking around to see if other people think this is a good idea or if it's as crazy as I think it is. Thanks for the refreshments, Verina. I'll call you later this week, OK?"

"Me too," said Bibi. "I really can't think straight right now. I'm so full of blueberry muffins. I don't even know if I can walk without falling down. Thanks, Verina. I'll call you later in the week, too."

After giving goodbye hugs, both ladies left.

"Well, that went pretty well," thought Verina. "I'm glad Thelma had so many errands to do today. I doubt if she would have even stayed to listen to hear about the club. She would have wanted to just play bridge and go home. I don't know why she even comes anyway. She never likes to socialize. The only time she says a word is to say "deal, or pass". Anyway, I can hardly wait until Ardon gets home so I can tell him the promising news. The girls didn't say no, so that was promising, wasn't it?"

Chapter Six: Growing ... Growing... Growing...
 Or Not?

"How did it go with Fredrick, dear?" asked Verina when Arden walked through the door. "Is he going to be a part of the club? And what about his wife, what's her name, Darline?"

"Doralene. Her name is Doralene. Well, I presented it to him and he presented me with a very expensive lunch tab. He said he wants to think about it, too just like Hazel and Charles. He said he would talk to Doralene about it, also. His real estate business is doing pretty well, so I know he can afford the thousand dollars. He just has to be convinced that it's on the up and up is all. I told him about the interest of the other people we've confronted, and he said he still wants to think about it for a while. I think he will come around eventually, when he sees others are committed. I'll give him a couple of days and then I'll call him back. I'm not sure I want to spend a lot of money on buying him lobster, if he isn't going to put out. What about you? Did your bridge club girls think it was a good idea?"

"Well, I'm pretty sure Bibi will agree. Pearl, I'm not so sure. They both said they need some time to think about it, just like all the others did. Goodness, that Bibi can eat the muffins. She ate almost the whole dozen by herself. Thelma didn't show up, because she was out doing errands, so Bibi ate her share as well as Pearl's, since Pearl didn't want any because she's trying to lose weight before Roy gets home from Korea. I think she is getting anxious for him to come home."

"It may not be too much longer. I've heard that there's talk about a treaty with Korea. We'll see. You never can trust what the newspapers say."

"What's for dinner, Verina? I'd like to call Landis Grey after dinner. I want to talk to him about the club. If he isn't doing anything tonight, I'm going to ask him if I could come by to talk to him and his wife, Gladys. Would you like to come along?"

"No, you go ahead. I think I would like to just sit her and read for a while. After listening to Bibi all afternoon, I have a splitting headache. If it doesn't go away soon, I may just skip the reading and go to bed instead."

"Dinner is almost ready. I made baked chicken, rice and broccoli, is that ok with you? I also have peach pie alamode for dessert. I waited until Bibi went home before I put the pie in the oven to bake or else you may be having just the chicken, rice and broccoli. The table is already set, so go wash up and I'll put the food on the table."

Ardon helped clear the table after dinner and Verina washed the dishes and left them to dry in the dish rack. He went to the phone and dialed Landis's number.

"Hello, Grey residence, Landis speaking."

"Hello, Landis, this is Ardon. How are you and Gladys doing this evening?"

"Oh, fine. What's up?"

"Well, I was wondering if it would be alright if I came by to speak with you about something this evening."

"Sure. Come on by. Is your wife coming, too?"

"No. She would like to but she has developed a terrible headache and is going to bed early.

"Sorry to hear that. What do you want to talk about? Anything that I should be worried about?"

"No, just something that I think you'll want in on. A proposition of sorts. It shouldn't take too long to explain. I hope Gladys will be available to hear it, too."

"I'll tell her you'll be coming over. She will probably want to put on a fresh pot of coffee and offer you some of her delicious homemade custard pie. She just made it this afternoon. I was too full to have a piece for supper. I guess I'll be having some when you get here though."

"OK, then. I'll be over in about an hour. Tell Gladys to get that coffee going", he said. "Maybe I shouldn't have had a second slice of Verinas' peach pie tonight," he thought.

"Honey, I'll be leaving in a few minutes to go over to the Grey's house. Is there anything I can get you before I go?"

"No, dear. Just drive safely and good luck with Landis and Gladys. I'll leave the light on in the hall for you. Love you!"

"OK. I love you, too. Good night," he said as he reached for his car keys.

The porch light was on when he arrived at the Grey's house. As he reached the front door, Ardon could already smell the coffee. "I don't know where I'm going to put another bite of pie tonight," he thought. "But, the coffee does smell good."

"Come in, come in!" Landis greeted him at the door before Ardon had time to knock.

"Gladys, Ardon's here. Is that pie and coffee ready yet?"

"Yes, dear. I'm bringing it out right now. Good evening, Ardon. Sorry to hear about you wife's headache.

I know how headaches can make you feel. I get them a lot. What do you use in your coffee? Cream, sugar?"

"Thanks Gladys. I'll just have mine black."

"I hope you like custard pie. It's one of Landises' favorites," she said as she handed him a plate with a slice of pie that was big enough for two people. Ardon unconsciously put his hand on his already too full stomach.

"Um, this looks delicious, Gladys. I hope you saved some for Landis. I wouldn't want him mad at me for eating all of his pie."

"Oh, no. There is plenty left for Landis. You go right ahead and enjoy. If you want a second slice, you just let me know."

"So, what did you want to talk to us about, Ardon? Some sort of proposition, you say? Sit down Gladys, so our guest can tell us what he has on his mind."

"Well it's actually a club. It's called The Six Hundred Thousand Dollar Club. The members are all friends and what we will do is put one thousand dollars a year each in a savings account and let it draw interest. We hope to get nine or ten people to join, so the investment grows bigger and faster. The money stays in the account until everyone passes away except one person. That person, the last survivor, will get all the money, which we hope will be around six hundred thousand dollars in about fifty years or so. It's kind of like insurance with only one beneficiary. We will have a contract and everything will be handled by an attorney. We already have several member and we only have room for a couple more."

"So I stretched the truth a little," he thought. "We will have several in a few days anyway."

"Well, in all my days. I've never heard of such a thing," said Landis. Who started this club? How come I've never heard of it?"

"I actually thought up the idea, but as I said we have several members already."

"Four is several, right?" he thought again.

"Whew! That's some idea you have there, Ardon. You're sayin' you want Gladys and me to join this club of yours? You do remember that I'm just a schoolteacher, don't you? I can see where some guy makes out like a bandit but the other poor saps get nothing."

Well, they do get something. It's going to be a social club too. We plan to have a weekly meeting at some fancy dinner club and regular events. So, you see you are paying to be a member of a fancy club and possibly get paid for it in your old age…if you outlive all of the rest of us members, that is. But in the mean time you still have a great time and have a group of nice friends in your social circle."

Ardon could tell by the look on Gladys' face that she was not going to buy it. She hadn't taken a bite of her custard pie since he said, "thousand dollars a year".

Landis looked over at his wife. She shook her head and poked at the pie on her plate. Landis knew that look. He had seen it enough during their marriage to know it meant, "Don't get me involved."

"I don't know, Ardon. It sounds a little strange to me. I think we need to think this one over for a while. You say there are several others already members?"

"Yes, several now and more are joining all the time," he said as he almost chocked on his pie. "Think it over and I'll get with you later this week and you can let me know what you and Gladys decide. I'll tell the others that you are considering, but need time to think. How about I call you around next Friday to get your answer?"

He thanked Gladys for the pie and coffee and stood to leave. He was sure Gladys had already made her decision. He hoped she hadn't made Landis's decision also.

On the drive back home he could feel the two kinds of pies fighting over who was not going to give up their place in his belly and who was going to be left along the side of the road.

When he got home, he headed straight toward the medicine cabinet in his bathroom. He needed something to settle his stomach. He found the bicarbonate and reached for the glass sitting next to his razor. Filling it, he dropped the fizzing crystals into the water and waited impatiently for them to dissolve. Gulping down the liquid, he looked at himself in the mirror.
"You better start paying more attention to your diet if you want to be the lucky devil that collects all that dough, Mister," he told himself. He let out a loud burp and rubbed his stomach. "Ah, that's better," he said. "No more pie for me for a while."
He decided a quick shower might help him sleep better. He definitely was not going to have anything that looked like food tonight.

Verina turned over to face him as he got under the covers.
"How's the headache?"
" Much better. I think the sleep helped. How did it go with the Grey's?"
"I doubt if Gladys will have anything to do with our club. I don't know about Landis. I saw Gladys give him a "No way" nod. I hope Landis listened to what I said and decides that it's a good idea. He is kind of thinking about the thousand dollars. He reminded me that he " is just a

teacher", I think were his words. I told him he would be paying for membership into a social club and so he would be getting something for his money, even if he did not out live us all. I'm not sure I convinced him though. I told him I would call him back next Friday to see what he had decided."

"That's good, dear. I think we need to get some sleep now. I don't want to wake up to another splitting headache in the morning. Good night."

"You're right. I only hope I can get some sleep. I know I shouldn't get so keyed up, but I'm just so excited about this, that it's hard to not think about it day and night. Goodnight, love. I'll see you in the morning."

Chapter Seven: And Two More Makes Six...

"I hope you like linguini with crab sauce," said Hazel. "Charles and I are so glad you and Owen could come to dinner tonight. We've been looking forward to this evening all week. Do you like Italian Rum Cake? I picked one up from the Italian bakery this afternoon. I thought it would be nice with coffee after dinner."

"Yum. I love Rum cake. The linguini sound delicious, too. I haven't had it since Owen and I had our anniversary dinner at Louiegies' last year. I wish I knew how to cook Italian, but my sauce never turns out right, so we just go out for it. Is there something I can do to help? Everything smells scrumptious."

"No, not really. We're just waiting for the linguini to boil. It should be done in a couple of minutes. Oh, you might put the wine on the table. Everything else is in place. The garlic bread is warming in the oven and the sauce is all ready."

Just as Hazel finished draining the linguini, Charles and Owen walked into the kitchen. Charles walked over to Hazel and gave her a hug around the waist.

"Um, everything smells good. Do you need any help?"

"No. Everything's under control. You gentlemen could go ahead and get seated in the dining room though. Nellie already put the wine on the table, so you could go ahead and pour, if you like, Charles. Nellie, do you mind putting the garlic bread in the breadbasket? Go ahead and seat yourself, too. I'll be right in with the linguini."

Hazel took the antipasto salad out of the refrigerator and the added oil and vinegar dressing. She hoped everyone liked the anchovies she had carefully arranged on top of the Italian meats. She had decided to add extra provolone cheese, since it was her favorite.

"If someone doesn't like the anchovies, I'll put this little saucer on the table so they can place them on it," she said as she reached in the cabinet to get a small blue saucer that matched the linen napkins she had chosen to use tonight.

"This is delicious," said Owen as he had a second helping of linguini and a third piece of the garlic bread.

"Here, let me refill your wine glass, Owen. You need something to wash that bread down with."

"Are you saying my garlic bread sticks in the throat?" Hazel said. "If that's what you're saying, you ate enough tonight to choke a horse."

"No, no, dear. Your garlic bread was wonderful. I guess I didn't phrase that right, did I? Would you like more wine to go with your delicious garlic bread, Owen?" he said. "Was that better, dear?" he chucked. "What about you ladies? Should I pour a bit more for you to go with your delicious garlic bread?"

"Yes, please," they both said as they held their wine glasses toward Charles.

"Here's to a good meal and a wonderful cook," said Charles as he held up his glass and looked at his wife.

Nellie and Owen followed his lead and gave a toast to Hazel and her delicious meal.

The Six Hundred Thousand Dollar Club

After enjoying coffee and Hazel's rum cake, Charles said, "Why don't we all move into the living room where we can sit back and share in a little lively conversation?" He thought this would set the atmosphere for bringing up the club. He had been hoping that Hazel would have brought it up to Nellie while they were in the kitchen preparing dinner. Apparently she had not because neither Hazel nor Nellie had said a word that gave a hint of anything relating to it. "Oh, well, I guess it's up to me to start the ball rolling," Charles thought to himself. "How can I work it into the conversation?"

"So, what's new?" asked Owen as they all made themselves comfortable. "How's married life treating you two?"

"We love it, don't we honey?" said Hazel as she looked over at her husband. "You had better say yes!" she teased.

"You bet! Life couldn't be better...married life I mean," said Charles as he smiled back at Hazel.

"Why don't you tell Owen and Nellie about our new club we belong to, Charles? They may want to join with us."

"What a good idea," said Charles, thankful that Hazel cleared the way for opening the subject. "Wait until you two hear about this. Hazel and I just joined and can hardly wait until our first official meeting."

"Oh, boy," moaned Owen. "Just what we need to hear. Another club for Nellie to get all excited about. She already belongs to a sewing club, a quilting club and some kind of club where they make pots. We have enough quilts and pots to last us for the rest of our lives and the lives of our great grandchildren's great grandchildren."

"Well this is not like any of those clubs. This one you both can belong to and the only pots involved is one that someone will get that's full of money at the end. Like a pot of gold," said Charles. "Nellie are any of your pots big enough to hold, say...six hundred thousand dollars?"

"Six hundred thousand dollars? What kind of club has six hundred thousand dollars?" Owen shouted. " I don't think I have ever heard of any club like that! Wait a minute. Is this one of those pyramiding scheme things? I've heard about those popping up all over the country lately. I don't want to get involved in anything like that. That's for darn sure. You sell stuff and then you get a bunch of your friends to sell stuff and then they get their friends to sell stuff and on and on it goes until the guy at the top gets rich and the guys at the bottom get stuck with a bunch of junk. Sorry, friend, but if that's what it's about, you can count me out."

"I have to agree with Owen," said Nellie. "I do enjoy my clubs, but I'm not into selling things or asking my friends to help sell things. I don't even like those Tupperware Parties because I hate asking my friends to buy things. And I am not even good at selling tickets to friends for the church bazaar."

"This is not that type of club. It's more of an investment. You don't even have to ask anyone else to join unless you want to. Hazel and I just thought of you, because we didn't want our best friends to be left out and find out later that you wanted to join up and were never asked. Why don't I explain how it works and then you can decide. If you are not interested after hearing me out, then just say "No, thanks". No pressure, no sales pitch, no nothing. OK? Besides, there's really nothing to sell or buy."

"OK. But just remember, I'm not getting into something that I don't like and neither is Nellie. Understood?"

"Understood," said Charles.

The Six Hundred Thousand Dollar Club 43

"OK. Then. Let's hear about this Six ...what did you call it?"

"The Six Hundred Thousand Dollar Club. Here's how it works. But first, Hazel could you get us some more coffee? Thanks, hon."

"Why, is the rum cake sticking in your throat, too, Charles?" she teased. "Excuse me, folks. I'll be right back with the coffee. I'll hurry. I wouldn't want my husband to choke while he's telling you about the club," she said over her shoulder as she headed toward the kitchen to get the coffee.

"No more for me," said Owen.

"Me neither," said Nellie. "But I could use your bathroom before we hear what Charles has to say."

She excused herself. Returning a few minutes later, she folded her hands in her lap, anxious to hear about this new club.

Hazel returned with the coffee. Pouring a cup for Charles and her self. "Are you sure neither of you want more coffee?" she asked.

"No, thank you," both of her guests said in unison.

"OK. I think we're ready now, dear," she said to Charles.

"As I was saying, Hazel and I just joined a few days ago. But we are convinced we did the right thing by joining. There is no way we can lose."

"Lose? Is this a gambling thing? Because Nellie and I are not into gambling either," interrupted Owen.

"No, no. Owen and I have never gambled in our lives. Not even when the church held that raffle for that basket of fruit last year. We didn't buy one ticket, did we dear?" "No. It's not gambling. Not in the traditional sense, anyway," Charles said. His patience was wearing thinner by the minute. He was beginning to think that

asking these two people to become club members might have been a mistake and a waste of his time, not to mention the linguini, wine and rum cake. Was he ever going to get to the part about the thousand dollars before he tossed them
both out on their butts? Taking a deep breath and letting it out slowly, he began again.

"What I meant was, it is a plan that has a big benefit at the end and ongoing benefits as well. Here's how it works. I'll use Hazel and myself as an example. We join by signing a commitment contract, which will be handled by an attorney. We add a thousand dollars each, every year into a savings account along with say, eight, nine or so other people. Also handled by the attorney. We leave all the money plus the interest gained until there is only one person left alive. That person gets the whole pot of gold. We figure if the last survivor lives to be oh, maybe eighty or so, he or she should wind up with about six hundred thousand dollars, hence the name of the club, "The Six Hundred Thousand Dollar Club". It's more like the winner takes all concept, not really gambling, but a wait and see game."

"But, besides the grand prize at the end, everyone of us gets to participate in social activities and events," said Hazel, looking in Nellie's direction. "It would be like paying for a yearly membership in a social club like Golfing or some other club like that, but you would also be putting money into a pot like a savings or insurance and possibly get your money and nine or so other people's money besides…and the interest collected, too," said Hazel. "I'm really excited about the social side of it, myself. And if I should outlive everyone else…well that's OK, too. But I'm not even thinking about that right now. I'm looking forward to the weekly meetings and the dinner gatherings with my friends."

Owen and Nellie sat with mouths open and eyes wide, staring at Hazel and Charles. No one said a word for several seconds. Charles squirmed slightly in his chair.

"Why doesn't some one say something?" he thought. "I don't know what else to say." He was hoping Hazel would rescue him again by adding something… anything more to the conversation. The dead silence was deafening. Either the wine or the rum cake was taking an effect, because he was developing a headache. He couldn't stand the silence any longer. He had to come up with something encouraging and convincing to say.

"So you see, it's one of the most promising clubs anyone could ever think to join." "Well, that sounded pretty stupid," he thought to himself. "What next? Wanna join? Yeah, that would sound even more stupid."

"Well what do you think? Doesn't it sound like a terrific idea?" he finally heard himself say. "See, there's not really much risk and a lot of potential."

"It sure doesn't sound like one of Nellie's quilting clubs. That's for sure," said Owen. "I hardly know what to think. Is this for real? People really do this kind of thing? Invest money in hopes that their friends die before them? This beats the heck out of one of those pyramid schemes."

Nellie just sat pinching her fingers together. "Nothing like a Tupperware party, either," she finally said so quietly that she could barely be heard.

"Maybe you better explain this again," said Owen. " I can't believe what I thought I heard the first time."

Charles repeated what the club was about and how it would work one more time to the Wheelers with a little more excitement in his voice this time, hoping some of the enthusiasm would rub off on Nellie and Owen. His excitement drained just a little when he saw in their eyes no more enthusiasm that there was the first time he told them the details of the club. He had all but given up on trying any longer to convince the couple when Nellie spoke.

"You know, Owen? It does sound like a unique idea. You do pay a lot of money on that golf club of yours. And all you get out of it is a shoe full of sand and a sore back. And all of that money you pay for lost balls and bent up clubs? We probably could save at least a thousand dollars in medicine you have to take after your games, alone. Maybe we could think it over and let Charles know later in the week. Did you say we have to sign a contract, Charles?"

"Yes, but we would all go together to the lawyer to do that. Like I said, it will all be done legally and there is no way any one person can cheat the others out of the money in the bank. I would consider it a pleasure to give you time to think it over. Hazel and I waited a few days to check it out ourselves. No one could expect anyone to make snap decisions about such a commitment of this magnitude."

"I guess we could consider it, Nellie. I don't think we should jump in the boat until we make sure there's no hole in it, though. It's just a lot to take in. And I don't think I lose as many balls as you imply, dear."

"Great. I'm glad we shared the information with you two. I can't think of any better friends that I would like to be a member of our club than Nellie and Owen Wheeler," said Charles. At last he started to relax. He got up and went over to Owen and shook his hand and gave Nellie a big hug and a kiss on her cheek. Then he went to Hazel and gave her a kiss and a hug, too.

"Well, anyone for another glass of wine to toast the prospect of accepting our two best friends into "The Six Hundred Thousand Dollar Club"?"

"Prospects, but not members, yet," Owen reminded him.

Hazel went to get fresh wine glasses. When she returned, Charles felt himself smiling as he poured the wine into each glass.
"A toast to long friendships and long lives," he said.
"And to two more *prospective* members of the Six Hundred Thousand Dollar Club," said Hazel as they all touched their glasses together in the toast.

Charles helped Hazel collect the wine glasses and coffee cups from the coffee table in the living room. As they carried them to the kitchen sink, both Hazel and Charles felt exhausted. It had been a long and busy day for Hazel. Going shopping for the food for the dinner, going to the bakery to pick up the rum cake and garlic bread, then bringing it home, cooking and getting the table ready took most of her energy. She wished she had taken time for a short nap before their guests had arrived, but she knew there was no way to fit a nap in today. She felt extra sleepy. Maybe it was the wine and rum cake that made her drowsy. Wine usually made her feel a little like that anyway. She was sure the tension of tonight was part of the reason she just wanted to hit the sack and forget everything that went on tonight. She could still smell the aroma of the garlic bread, even as she walked down the hall toward the bedroom. She chuckled as she thought of Charles' face when she reprimanded him for his comment about needing more wine to wash down her garlic bread. She had to admit, he was quick to fix his blunder. That was partly what had attracted her to him when they had first met. She loved the way he always seemed to know how to get his foot out of his mouth quickly. And she knew he had plenty of practice at doing it since they have been married.

"You were an excellent hostess tonight, Hazel. Your linguini was the best ever. Where did you get that rum cake? It was wonderful. Do we have any left?"

"Thanks, Charles. I'm glad you enjoyed the meal. I bought the rum cake at Louiegies'. There is a piece left for you in the refrigerator. You can have it tomorrow for breakfast if you like."

"For breakfast? I think it wouldn't be such a good idea to show up at work with rum on my breath. My boss may not look so kindly on that."

"Did I say breakfast? I meant after dinner tomorrow. I guess I'm a little tired. I don't even know what I'm saying," she yond.

"Me, too. I thought Owen and Nellie were going to spend the night. I almost wish I hadn't offered them another glass of wine. But at least I have hopes that they may join the club. I don't want us and Ardon and Verina to be the only members of this thing. Some profit that would be." He bent over to kiss Hazel goodnight but she was already snoring softly. "Goodnight my bride," he said.

On the drive home Owen and Nellie could feel the effects of the wine and rum cake, too. Nellie kept drifting off. Owen tried to keep his eyes on the road. He realized that he also had drifted off a couple of times.

"I have to stay awake," he told himself. "Maybe I shouldn't have had so much wine tonight. That rum cake was out of this world. Maybe I can talk Nellie into getting one for us sometime. I'll have to have her find out where Hazel bought it," he thought.

Nellie woke up just as they reached the driveway. She yawned and stretched her arms above her head.

"Are we home yet? I am so tired. You may have to carry me upstairs to bed."

"We are here. I don't think I can even carry myself up those stairs tonight. I may just stay here and sleep in this car tonight," Owen teased. "You go on in and I'll put the car in the garage. I'll say good night right now, because you will probable already be in bed, asleep by the time I get in the house."

"OK. But, no sleeping in the car. Goodnight, dear. I'll see you in the morning."

After turning off the motor of the car, he went into the house and locked the front door. Owen climbed the stairs to the bedroom. He was right about Nellie being asleep when he got into the house. She was snoring loud enough to wake the neighbors.

He wanted to think more about the club offer, but tonight was not the time to think of anything. All he wanted to do was get undressed and get into bed and get some very much needed sleep. He barely got under the sheet when he could feel his eyes closing and his head spinning off into dreamland. The last thing he remembered was picturing himself on the golf course standing next to his golf bag full of money and a sand trap full of golf balls. He would have to share that thought with Nellie in the morning. "I know she will find the humor in that picture," he thought. "But for tonight, just sweet, sweet dreams."

Chapter Eight:: Will Bibi Bite?

Verina was at the neighborhood grocery market, The Real Deal Supper Market, getting milk, bread and was just about to hit the vegatable and fruit aisle to pick up a few pieces of fruit, when she thought she heard Bibi on the next isle. "That must be Bibi," she said. "I could recognize that voice anywhere. Only Bibi would talk to the vegetables and fruit. What a goofy woman she is. For being so young, I swear she acts like a senile old lady, sometimes."

"Hello, Bibi. How are you this morning?"

"Why, hello, Verina. Nice to see you. Are you buying fruit or vegetables today? The lettuce looks wilted, but the carrots look good. I am going to buy a few of these grapes. They look pretty good. Oh, and I think I'll get some of the cauliflower, too. Maybe you should take a look at those blueberries…in case you decide to make some more of those delicious blueberry muffins again."

"Maybe I will," said Verina. " We'll see." "How can one simple "Hello" cause a person to go off on such a tangent that made your ears hurt?" she thought.

"Have you had time to think about joining our club, Bibi?"

"Well, I have been thinking about it. Yesterday I was visiting my neighbor and I was telling her about it. She said it sounded interesting to her. She was kind of staring into the distance while I was talking, though, so I'm not sure she heard the whole thing."

"I can't imagine that," thought Verina sarcastically. "Bibi's yakking can hypnotize anyone after a while."

"So what did you decide?" She thought she may as well get it over with then she could at least be relieved of Bibi's talking and be able to go about her shopping, leaving Bibi to conversing with the fruit and vegetables.

"Well, after a lot of thinking, is it a "yes" or is it a "no", I finally decided to make a list of positives and a list of negatives and see which list was longer. Then I would know which way to go. It took me all evening. I kept thinking of more reasons to join and then I'd think of more reasons for not joining. By the time it was time for me to go to bed, I nearly had a headache. "I can't go to bed until I get the right answer," I told myself. So, I cut up all of the "yeses" and all of the "no's" and put them in a cereal bowl and drew one out."

Verina's head was beginning to spin. "So what did you pull out, Bibi? A "yes" or a "no"?"

"Oh, first I pulled out a "yes", but then I wasn't sure that was what was meant to be, so I pulled again. This time I pulled out a "no". Since it was a draw, I thought I better try again. This time I pulled out a "Yes", so I guess the "yeses" win. I was going to call you yesterday and tell you, but I thought I would give it one more day, in case I changed my mind. But since I've told you yes already, I guess I'll stick with my decision. Yep! It's a definite Yes!"

"That's wonderful, Bibi. I'll call Ardon when I get home and tell him to save you a place on the list of members. Now, you won't change your mind, will you? Because once your name is on the list, it's pretty final," she lied. "Anything to get Bibi on the list and me out of this market."

"Oh, no. I won't change my mind. You can count on that. Once I make up my mind, I don't let anything or anybody change it. So when is our first meeting? Will there be refreshments?"

"We haven't set a date yet. I'm sure it will be in the next few weeks though, and I'm sure we can arrange to have refreshment available."

"Oh, I was hoping it would be sooner. Do you think any of those eligible young men will be at the first meeting?"

"I'm not sure who all will be at the first meeting, Bibi, but I'll let you know as soon as I find out."

"I hope so, because I want to get my hair done if those fellows are there."

"I'll be sure to call as soon as I know, I promise, Bibi. In the meantime, I guess I had better get my shopping done so I can get home and call Ardon to let him know the good news. I'll tell him to work on getting those eligible young men in for you, too, while I'm at it. Good-bye, Bibi. I'll see you later."

"Good-bye, Verina. Tell Ardon he can invite more than one eligible man, if he wants," she heard Bibi yelling to her as Verina rounded the corner to get to the check out counter before Bibi came running after her with something else to say.

As soon as she got home Verina called Ardon at his job. She would put the groceries away as soon as her ears stopped ringing. Right now it was more important to let Ardon know to add Bibi to the membership list, before Bibi backed out. What a blessing in disguise to have met Bibi at the market and get her to agree to join. The not so good part of the blessing was the headache she was getting because of the sound of Bibi's voice that kept ringing in her ears. "I hope Ardon appreciates what I had to endure for him and his club…our club," she corrected herself. I do hope he finds some unsuspecting bachelor to keep Bibi occupied and away from my end of the table during dinner meetings."

"Hello. Flashing Financial Institute, Ardon Steris, speaking."

"Hello, Ardon. It's me. I was just at the market and I ran into Bibi. She has decided to join us. I told her you would try to get a few eligible men to join the club. I hope you do try. She's about to run me crazy with her yakking constantly. Can you believe she was even carrying on a conversation with the fruit and vegetables in the produce aisle? A diversion would be nice if you can arrange it, dear. My ears are ringing so loudly, that I'm getting a headache."

Ardon laughed out loud, "I'll try dear. I'm glad you were successful at getting Bibi to join. I know it was a difficult mission for you. I'll make it up to you when I get home. How about I take you to dinner tonight and maybe we can take care of that headache."

"Are you talking about Bibi or the real pain in my head? Dinner out would be nice. I'll go see if I can ease the ringing in my ears and pick out something special to wear tonight. Bye, dear, I love you."

After putting the groceries away Verina decided the only way to get rid of her headache was to take a little nap before Ardon got home. "What shall I wear tonight?" she thought as she drifted off to sleep. She could still hear Bibi talking to the vegetables in her dreams.

Chapter Nine: All Aboard!

Ardon still had not heard from Fredrick. "Should I call him or give him a couple more days?" Ardon asked himself. "I don't want to rush him. That would make him think I'm desperate. But, I do want to get everything in place soon, before people start backing out. If I don't hear from him by this afternoon, I'll call him at his home. Maybe I'll save myself from buying him another high priced lunch. "I don't think I can stand to look at another lobster for a long time without seeing dollar signs."

Maybe a nice dinner out was a good idea. Maybe it would take his mind off of the club for a few hours any way. "I'll just wait until tomorrow to call Fredrick," he decided. Tonight he was just going to relax and enjoy the company of his beautiful wife. He snickered to himself as he thought of her standing in the produce aisle, trying to convince Bibi to join the club all the while Bibi was standing there talking to the squash. If nothing else, Bibi would add a little humor to the club...if his wife didn't kill her first. He thought of all the male friends that would he might invite for Bibi's sake, but none came to mind. Besides who does he hate so much that he could punish them by pawning Bibi off on them?

Ardon decided to stop by the florist on the way home to buy a bouquet of yellow roses for Verina.

"Maybe I'll stop at the sweetshop and get her a box of those chocolate nutty things she likes. Nothing is too good for my wife tonight," he thought. Again the image of her standing in the market with Bibi came to his mind.

"Honey, I'm home!" he shouted as he walked into the living room.

"I'm in here," Verina called from the bedroom. " I'm just finishing getting dressed. Where are we going to dinner?" she asked. "I hope someplace quiet. I still have just a wee bit of a headache. I'll take a couple more aspirins before we leave. Maybe it will be gone by the time we arrive at the restaurant."

"I thought we could try that new French Restaurant down on Flower and Main. Speaking of flowers…for you my dear," he said as he drew the bouquet from behind his back.

"Oh, Ardon, these are beautiful. And my favorite color too."

"Beautiful roses for a beautiful lady," he said as he kissed her on the cheek. "And delicious sweets for my sweet lady," he said as he handed her the box of chocolates.

"Wow! What did I do to deserve all of this?" she asked.

"It's the least I could do for what you did for me today, don't you think?"

"Don't forget, I did it for me, too. I just hope Bibi is the first to go. Oh, I guess I shouldn't have said that."

"Well, that was sort of mean, but I know what you mean. I'll not tell her you said that."

"Did you think of anyone for her among your friends? I think that's the only reason she is joining the club, you know."

"Not yet. I'm still thinking though. When I do find someone, or should I say if I find someone, we won't introduce them until the contract has been signed, OK? Or at least we won't tell either of them that the other is single."

"Agreed," said Verina. "I'm ready. Do you want to shower and change before we leave? I'll go put these flowers in water and try one of these chocolates while you are getting ready."

"Only one? I can't believe that," Ardon said as he began to undress for his shower. "I'll need to shave, too, but I won't be long. You and your chocolates go sit and relax until I'm ready." He kissed her again and headed for the shower.

"Hmm..., he's sure in a good mood," Verina thought as she arranged the roses in the vase. "Roses and candy? Ardon really is getting into this club of ours. I wonder what he will bring me if I get Pearl to join, too? Hum, let's see what hints should I drop? I could use a few more new dresses and a few pairs of new shoes. I may as well go for a new purse and a few pieces of jewelry, maybe a string of pearls, while I'm at it. Speaking of pearls, maybe I should call Pearl tomorrow. I can't collect beautiful things from my husband if I don't get working on Pearl. I'll call her right after Ardon leaves for work tomorrow. This way if she agrees, he will have time to stop by the jewelers on his way home. Maybe I'll just mention some pearls or that lovely gold necklace and earring set in the window at More Gold Jewelry Store on Second Street and Broadway while we are having dessert tonight. He's always in a good mood when there is dessert to be had. Yes, this club is starting to become more profitable everyday," she said as she devoured her third piece of the gooey, nutty chocolate. "These are delicious. Thank you my handsome husband," she said as she popped one more chocolate into her mouth.

"Hello, Fredrick, ol' boy. How are you doing? I thought I would give you a call to see if you have thought anymore about the club I was telling you about over lunch the other day, and to let you know that the membership list is getting longer by the day. I don't want to rush you, but I wouldn't want you to miss out by waiting too long to give me an answer. You know what I mean?" Ardon tried to sound upbeat and positive as he anxiously awaited an answer from the other end of the line. "Please, please say yes," he thought.

"I'm glad you called," said Fredrick. Doralene and I had a long discussion about it after we had lunch. We spoke to several other people. Some said it was nuts and a few said it was the best idea they have ever heard of. I think Doralene and I will give it a try. I know you said we can't back out without forfeiting any money we have invested, but I don't see any reason we would need to drop out anyway, other than biting the dust, that is," he said. "And neither Doralene nor I plan to do that very soon. Do you know when we will be meeting with that lawyer, yet?"

"No. We thought we would have a meeting when everyone is signed on and decide on a lawyer then. Keep you eyes opened for a good one. Maybe someone that's young enough to outlive us all, when the final reward is presented, if you get my drift. So glad to have you and Doralene join us. Verina will be excited to hear. She was hoping to meet some new people." Ardon was so excited himself that he felt he needed to get off the phone and run to the men's room. He didn't want to sound like he was trying to get rid of his new recruit, though by ending the conversation abruptly.

"So how is the real estate business doing this week?" he asked. He couldn't think of anything else to say. "Have you sold many more houses this week?"

"Well, as a matter of fact, I did sell one house near your neighborhood a couple of days ago and one on Splinter Drive yesterday. If things keep up like this, I may be retiring before I'm fifty."

"That would be nice. I think I'll be working for a lot longer than that...unless of course all of my friends decide to meet their maker and I'm left holding the bag of ... you know what," he chuckled. "But, I doubt that's ever going to happen."

"Yeah, after I just agreed to invest my money into your club. I plan to be the one holding that bag, if you don't mind, friend," Fredrick shot back. "Just think with my millions I'm going to earn from my real estate business and all the money I'll get from the club...well, that should make a very nice retirement income, I'd say."

"Well, you're right about that. That would be a lot of loot, all right. Well, I guess I had better get back to work or I won't have any income if my boss catches me socializing on the company telephone. I'll talk to you later. When we decide when and where our first meeting will be, I'll call you. Don't forget to keep your eyes peeled for a good lawyer. Talk to you soon."

"I'll just do that. Goodbye."

Hanging up the phone, Ardon nearly danced down the hall to the men's room. And not just because he was happy about his two new recruits.

Chapter Ten: Let's Ask Them Again

Owen and Nellie sat at the breakfast table sipping their morning coffee when the phone rang. Putting his cup down, Owen let out a sigh. "Who could be calling us so early this morning?" he said as he got up to go answer it.

"It's really not that early, dear. It's already nine thirty," Nellie said as she started to gather the breakfast dishes and carry them to the sink.

"Hello, Wheeler residence," he said as he yawned and leaned against the wall.

"Hello, Owen. This is Charles. I hope I didn't wake you. You sound drowsy."

"No, I have been up for a while. Nellie and I were just sitting having our coffee. What's up?"

"Sorry to interrupt your morning coffee, but I was wondering if you have thought anymore about joining the club? The list is getting pretty full." He thought he would try that approach again since it seemed to work with Bibi. "I don't want to rush your decision but I thought I'd check with you anyway."

"Nellie and I did talk a little about it. We haven't really made a definite decision yet, though. How about we discuss it a little further and let you know this afternoon?"

"OK, that sounds fine. I'll be waiting for your call or should I call you?"

"I'll call you around five tonight, but if you don't hear from me, give me a call. Just in case I forget to call you.

Nellie may keep me busy all day today with repairing the broken vacuum. She says she can't keep the house clean if the vacuum is broken. What ever happened to brooms, anyway?"

"OK. I'll talk to you later then. And good luck with the vacuum repair. You better watch out or Nellie will want you to show her how it works. Goodbye, Owen."

Charles was disappointed that he had not gotten a definite answer from Owen, but he was willing to wait, if it meant a better chance of getting his friend and his wife to join the club. He decided that he would wait until around five thirty before calling Owen if he had not heard from him by then. "This way, I will not sound like I'm desperate and Owen will have plenty of time to get Nellie in a better mood just in case he is not able to fix her vacuum. I'd fix it and even do the vacuuming myself if I was over there. Maybe then their answers would be a definite yes," he said as he leaned back in his chair. "I'm sure Ardon is anxious to hear something, too."

At five thirty-five, Charles was just about to reach for the phone to call Owen back since Owen had not returned his call at five o'clock as he had promised, when it rang. Charles jumped, nearly knocking his coffee cup off his desk.

"Hello, Charles, speaking," he said hoping it was Owen on the other end.

"Hello, Charles this is Owen. Sorry for not calling you at five o'clock. I fixed the vacuum for Nellie and then she found a few other things she needed me to fix, "since I had my tools out" as she said. I guess you know how that goes. Find one thing that needs to be fixed and five more things just show up that need fixing too. Anyway, about that club, Nellie and I hope we are making the right decision, but we have decided to put our thousand dollars each into this thing and see what happens. We are just hoping it's not some sort of scam. As long as we aren't going to loose more than that, since we were going to donate about that much to the Geriatrics in Need Charity anyway. I guess we will still be donating to the old people, just different old people, if this is a scam. I guess we should know that before the next year's fees are due. You are sure there will be an attorney involved to oversee that everything is on the up and up? I wouldn't want to have to hire a lawyer of my own to go fight for my money."

"Great! I'm glad you and Nellie have decided to join us. Yes. I'm sure about the lawyer. As a matter of fact, we will be choosing one soon. Ardon suggested that we all start checking out a young, but experienced one. He said we should choose a young one, so that when we all get old, maybe he will still be alive, too, so he can handle giving the inheritance to the rightful owner. He also said that it would be a good idea, if we all go together to have an official commitment contract written up and signed. That way no one can say they didn't have a say in how it should be worded or that something wasn't done right. I think he's right in suggesting we do that. You never know when someone decides to be a trouble maker or complainer."

"I'm glad someone has thought this through. I feel a lot better now that I'm sure this is really going to be overseen by a professional. I'm sure Nellie will be relieved, also. So do you know when we will be going to a lawyer?"

"No. Not yet. Remember, we all need to be looking for one that we can bring to the other members for approval. I think we will be having some kind of informal meeting soon though, just so we all know what's going on and to choose the lawyer. I'll let you know as soon as I find out, though."

"Alright. I'll be waiting to hear from you. I'll tell Nellie to start thinking about a lawyer, too. I'm sure she's looking forward to some of the club activities. I heard her talking to her mother on the phone this afternoon about how she would like to start doing more social things with friends. I don't know if she was talking about the club or just social activities in general. I hope she's not planning some kind of big hoopla that's going to include me wearing a tux and tie. I'm still stiff from the one I had to wear for our wedding. I don't like those monkey suits any better than I like getting my molars pulled."

"Why is it women always come up with these ideas that men should dress up like penguins and dance around a crowed floor anyway?" laughed Charles.

"Oops! Speaking of women, I hear my woman calling me right now. I hope this means dinner is ready and not something else needs to be fixed. I'll talk to you later. Don't forget to give me a call when you hear something about the meeting."

"OK. And you better hurry up to see what your wife wants, or your head may need fixing when she hits it with one of your hammers."

After hanging up with Owen, Charles immediately called Ardon to let him know about Owen and Nellie joining the club.

"He sounded pretty excited," he told Ardon. "He wants me to let him know when we decide to have a meeting, so he and Nellie can attend. They are going to do some looking around for possible lawyers that we can suggest to the other members. I guess the more choices we have to choose from the better chance we have of hiring a good one."

"Good, good. I'm starting to see this club idea better and better everyday. Do you have any thoughts about where we should cut off the membership? I don't think we should have too many members. We don't want it to get out of hand, do you?" said Ardon.

"No, I think if we have too many, our chances of surviving will get less and less. Of course it would mean more money invested and interest paid, but look how hard it would be to outlive everyone else. I say keep it small, but that may be something we may want to bring up to the rest of the members at the first meeting," replied Charles.

"Good idea, Charles. Maybe we should be deciding where and when we want the meeting to take place, before people start getting restless and start changing their minds. I can start writing up an agenda for the meeting. If you think of anything that you think needs to be included let me know. Maybe the girls can come up with a place to hold the meeting."

"That sounds like a good plan," said Charles. The image of himself and Owen dressed in a tux and tie looking like a couple of penguins strolling across a dance floor and a thirty-piece orchestra playing romantic music in the background came to his mind. "I'll tell Hazel to start checking around for a few places."

After hanging up Ardon called Verina and told her the good news about Owen and Nellie.

"Do you think you and the other ladies could start checking out some place where we could hold our first meeting, dear?" he asked her. "I'll give you their phone numbers when I get home tonight...that is if you don't mind calling them."

"Sure. I don't mind at all calling them. As a matter of fact, I still haven't heard from Pearl. I need to call her anyway. Do you think it would be all right if I ask her to attend the first meeting even though she hasn't given us an answer yet? I thought if she was to meet some of the other members, it might convince her to join."

"I don't know why not. Maybe Bibi will have someone besides you to talk too."

"Oh, yeah, Bibi. I'm really looking forward to hearing Bibi's ideas. I just hope she doesn't scare everyone else away."

Verina put down the book she was reading and decided that she had better call Pearl, before she started preparing dinner. "I hope I haven't waited too long and Bibi hasn't caused her to refuse to commit to the club. I'll kick myself if I did. I should have called her as soon as I got home from the market the other day when I saw Bibi, but I had such a headache, that I couldn't even think straight. Pearl seems to tolerate Bibi, though, so maybe it will be ok, even if Bibi has told her that she is joining. I hope so anyway."

After several rings, Pearl finally picked up the phone.

"Thank goodness," thought Verina. "I thought I had missed her."

"Hello, Pearl? This is Verina. How are you? I haven't heard from you in a few days, so I thought I had better check to see if everything is OK."

"Hi! Verina. Yes, everything's fine. How are you? Are you calling to say we are going to get together to play bridge, since we didn't get to play the other day? I hope Thelma has all of her errands done by now!" she said jokingly. "I hope she knows she caused us to miss beating her and Bibi. I say, we gang up on the two of them next time."

"Good idea. I'm for that. But that's not really why I called. I called to see if you have considered joining the club yet. I think we are getting ready to organize our first meeting soon."

"Well, I did think about it. I have to be honest and say, I'm not real sure it's something I want to commit to right now. My mind is on Roy most of the time lately and that just about knocks all the energy out of me. I do wish they would pull out of that war and send all of our guys home. It's getting hard to sleep at night worrying about his safety. Bibi didn't help the other day with her comments about his infidelity either. Can I get back to you later on it? I'm just not thinking straight right now."

"Sure, Pearl. I don't think you have to worry about Roy being unfaithful to you. I've seen him around you when he's home on furloughs. He is more in love with you than any man could ever be in love with his wife. I wouldn't pay much attention to anything Bibi says. We both know what a twit she can be some times. She is always sticking her foot in her mouth about something. When she doesn't have her mouth full of food, that is. I swear, I don't know how that woman stays so skinny the way she puts food away. I pity the man who marries her…if one ever does marry her, that is. That's just Bibi's way. I'd just forget what she said."

"Thanks for the encouragement, Verina. I guess I was starting to take what Bibi said as a possibility. I guess with Roy not here I don't have much to do but think about stuff like that."

"That's OK. I'm here if you need some cheering up, you know. How about if you come with me to the first meeting for the club, you know, just to see what it's going to be like. It would be a nice evening out with some very nice people if nothing else. You wouldn't have to invest any money into it. We haven't even gotten that far anyway. It would just be a planning meeting to see what we need to do," "I'm not sure this is the right time or not to tell Pearl that Bibi would be there," Verina thought. "I don't want her to decline the offer because of Bibi."

"I don't know…?"

"Why don't you think about it and I'll call you later to see how you feel about it, alright? If you really want to play bridge, I can call the girls tomorrow to set up bridge for maybe Thursday of next week. Is that OK with you?"

"That sounds great. Maybe Thelma will be there and maybe Bibi won't get on my nerves by then. Call me when you get it set up. I'll bring some pretzels and celery and some carrot sticks. Let's see how many of those Bibi puts away."

"You are so funny, Pearl. And you don't have to bring anything. I'll furnish the pretzels, celery and carrot sticks, if you think you need to eat only that kind of stuff. Personally, I don't think you need to lose any more weight than you already have. If you keep losing, Roy will have to use a magnifying glass to find you when he gets home."

They both laughed and said their goodbyes. Verina was not going to give up on her friend not coming to the meeting, mainly because she didn't want to be stuck with Bibi
all evening. She knew her husband and his friends would be busy talking business and leave her to listen to that never-ending chatterbox.

Verina decided she still had a few minutes before she need to start the dinner preparations. Probably just enough time to call a couple of restaurants to see what kind of facilities they may have to accommodate the club meetings. "At least Ardon can't say I wasn't doing something to benefit the club today," she thought out loud. "Oh, I can hear Bibi's voice in my ears already."

Chapter Eleven: One Is Better Than None

Ardon wanted to talk to Landis as soon as possible, but he was trying to figure out a way to do it without Gladys present. He still didn't think it was such a good idea to go over to the school. He needed to talk to him in a more leisurely environment without a lot of interruptions. He knew that Landis ate his lunch in the school cafeteria after all the kids were on the playground. He definitely did not want to meet him there. "Who knows what kind of germs a person can pick up from those delinquents?" he said to himself. "It would be my luck that I would catch some disease that killed me and then there would go my money! Maybe I could wait for him in my car in the school parking lot. When he gets off of work, I can catch him as he comes out of the building. I just hope I don't get reported as a pedophile or predator by some concerned parent. Waiting in the car at the school seems to be the only solution," Ardon thought. "I guess I'll just have to take my chances."

He waited until it was almost time for the bell to ring before he found a spot just big enough for him to squeeze his fifty-two Chevy between a brand new Ford and a dented in Mercury. "I hope he comes out soon," he said as a group of noisy kids piled out of the building and down the steps, heading right toward him. "Oh, no! I hope none of those kids start harassing me." He suddenly remembered how he and his friends used to yell obscenities at the old people that came to pick up their kids from school. "Hey, look at the old…" The words came rushing back to his memory, as he felt a little ashamed of himself because he just realized that he is now the same age as those "old people" were then. "Hurry up, Landis, will you?" he said out loud, hoping none of the kids heard him as they ran to meet their parents or to climb on the school bus that was waiting for them at the end of the parking lot.

Landis didn't come out of the building until all the parking lot was empty and all the kids were probably already home. Ardon's stomach was beginning to growl. It was time for his dinner and here he was sitting in his car in a deserted school parking lot. The sight of Landis made him forget his discomfort and he quickly got out of the car practically running to catch up with Landis before he got in his car and pulled out of the parking lot.

"Hey, Landis! Wait up!" Ardon shouted. " Do you have a minute?"

"Oh, hello, Ardon. What are you doing here? You are a little old to be going to school aren't you?" Landis laughed. "Sure, I have a minute, but I need to get home soon. Gladys will probably have my dinner waiting on the table for me. I don't like to be too late. She gets to worrying if I'm too late getting home from work. She always thinks the worst. You know, I've been in an accident or something. I tell you that woman is such a worrywart, sometimes. But I love her, bless her little heart. What did you need?"

"I was just wondering if you and Gladys have made a decision about the club I was telling you about the other night. We are almost ready to finalize everything, so I thought I had better check with you, before we get too far along in the plans. We want to make sure we get your input along with everybody else's."

"Oh, that. Well, I'm afraid Gladys nixed that one right down the drainpipes. She said she had never heard of anything so crazy in her life. I sort of have to agree with her. It is something I've never heard of before."

"That's too bad, Landis. I was sure hoping you would be part of our group. Yes, it is different, but that's what makes it so interesting. Who wants to get involved with old hack stuff that's been around for decades?"

"I'm afraid Gladys likes old hack stuff," said Landis. "Sorry to disappoint you Ardon, but for now I guess I need to stick with my wife. After all, she is the one that controls the food at our house, you know," Landis chuckled. "Maybe later on down the road a piece we will reconsider, but for right now, Gladys is the boss."

"OK, Landis. You let me know when you're ready. I'll be waiting to hear from you. I guess you had better get going before Gladys comes looking for you. You have a good evening. Give Gladys my best."

"I will. And you have a good evening, too Ardon. And you tell your wife I send my best, too."

Ardon knew he was not going to have a good evening. Gladys has taken care of that. "I knew that woman would spoil everything. I think Landis has an invisible ring through his nose. I'm sure glad Verina isn't like that. Oh well, I guess I wasted a perfectly good afternoon sitting my rump in my car as a million germs probably flew in the window."

"I can't let Landis and Gladys Grey's refusal to become members steal all my enthusiasm about the club. After all, we do have nine members already. I think it's time to set the date for the first meeting. I had better work on that agenda I had promised Charles that I'd have ready for the first meeting." No matter how hard he tried to forget about Landis and Gladys, he found himself remembering "the look" that Gladys had given Landis a few nights ago.

Chapter Twelve: The First Meeting

Both Ardon and Verina were in a bad mood after three of their prospects for membership had disappointed them. There was nothing they could do but go forward with their plans to organize a meeting with the ones they did have. The longer they procrastinated, the bigger the chance of losing more members. No they just couldn't wait any longer to get the plans in order and to get to a lawyer as soon as possible. Arden decided he would work on the agenda for the meeting while Verina called all the women to confirm a place to have it. If they were lucky they would have their first meeting by Saturday night and hopefully be able to hire an attorney by the end of next week. The thought of actually having The Six Hundred Thousand Dollar Club as an official organization, with actual members, began to sink in to both Ardon and Verina. They hoped the others were getting as excited as they were beginning to be. Just saying the title of the club caused the both of them to get into a happier mood asthe evening progressed.

"I have made an outline for the agenda for the first meeting, Verina. Would you like to hear it? You can tell me if you see anything that I have left out or that may need changing. Here, take a look will you?" Ardon said as he handed the pencil written outline. "I'll type it up when we think everything is included and ready to go. If you don't mind, after I get it typed up, will you look at it again to make sure I haven't made any misspelled words or typing errors? I want this to be as professional looking as possible. I would have my secretary do it, but she would just be asking a lot of questions and start spreading gossip around about some secret club her boss is involved in. I really don't want to take the time to explain something that is not even her business or to stop her idle gossip. Marge is a good secretary, but sometimes I wish I could get rid of her and hire someone who would keep her nose out of everybody else's business and mine."

"I'll look at it right now, Ardon. Then I want to get on the phone to call Hazel, Doralene and Bibi. I told Pearl that she is invited to attend the first meeting, too, if she would like. I'm hoping she accepts the invitation and hopefully likes it so much that she decides to reconsider not joining. I know she would enjoy the social interaction if she would just give it a try. I think it would take her mind off of missing Roy so much."

"I do too, dear. I was hoping Landis would reconsider, also. Maybe after we see how it's going a while, I may approach him again, but not with Gladys around, that's for sure."

After reading through Ardon's draft of the agenda, Verina had a couple of things she felt should be added to the list.

"This looks pretty good, Ardon, however, I think maybe we need to elect a few officers, just to make it look more professional, as you said. I think we need to elect a chairperson to facilitate the meetings. We probably should have a vice chairperson, too just in case the chairperson is not able to attend a meeting. I also think we need a secretary to take minute notes and have a copy for each member to have in case something comes up later and someone says that he or she didn't know about it or that they had not voted on something. What do you think, dear?"

"I think that's a very good idea. And of course we probably need to bring up the point that theattorney that we hire should be part of the officers as an advisor, though he doesn't need to attend meetings or events. We would just want him to be available if an issue arises."

"I agree. We also should probably have a treasurer. Some one needs to collect and deposit the club fees and give a report about the interest and balance from the bank. Of course everyone will probably vote for you to take on that responsibility, since you do work in that area everyday."

"You are right again. I don't know about me being the treasurer, though. People maybe a little uncomfortable with me handling their money, since this whole thing was my idea in the first place. I wouldn't want anyone thinking I may take off with his or her money. But I do agree that we need someone dependable to do the job."

"Let's just hope no one suggests Bibi. By the time she gets done reading her report, we all may be dead."

"I'll add your suggestions to the agenda, and then you can read it again. Are you sure there is nothing else I need to add, dear?"

"I think you need to get one of those fancy, leather bound notebooks…what do they call them… portfolios?" suggested Verina. "That would really make everything more professional, don't you think?"

"Good idea. I'll pick on up after work tomorrow. Maybe I should pick up a steno notebook for whoever the secretary is. Oh, and one of those ledgers like we use at work for the treasurer to keep records and reports in. Thanks for the suggestions, love," he said.

Arden felt more encouraged that the club was going to be a success as he looked over his draft.

"Yes, this is going to be a very successful venture. When the members see how professional this looks and how well thought out the first meeting is going to be, they will definitely be glad they are the charter members of The Six Hundred Thousand Dollar Club...the only club of it's kind."

Verina handed back the final draft to Ardon. He had only made one mistake in spelling, but that may have been a typing error, she was thinking to herself. "Everyone knows how to spell mission statement." Ardon had left out one of the "S'es" in "mission".

She thought she had better call Pearl first so that Pearl wouldn't have something else to do the night of the meeting, when she realized Ardon had not told her the date and time of the meting. She thought they had said this Saturday, but she thought she had better ask Ardon. And on second thought, she might be better off waiting to call Pearl after she and the other ladies had decided where the meeting was going to be held.

"Ardon, dear, did you say the meeting was going to be this Saturday? And what time are you planning it for? I need to let the ladies know, so that we can get everything set up. And did you remember to put the date and time of the meeting on the top of the agenda? I guess I didn't notice when I looked at it for you. Sorry."

"Yes. It will be this Saturday evening at seven-thirty. That way everyone will home be from work and be ready for dinner at where ever you ladies decide. I thought we could order dinner and do the welcome and introductions while we wait for our food to come. And no, I didn't put the date and time on the agenda. Thanks for reminding me."

Verina called Hazel first. She thought she would call Bibi after she had called Doralene and Nellie. This way she wouldn't get caught up in one of Bibi's long stories. After they had decided on a possible location, she would call Pearl and tell her about the choices they came up with and see if she would like to suggest anywhere else or if she could recommend any one of the suggested ones the other women came up with.

"Maybe this will let Pearl know that we really want to include her," she said to herself. " I'm still not sure if I should mention Bibi, yet."

"Hello, Hazel, this is Verina. I'm calling to let you know we would like to have the first meeting of The Six Hundred Thousand Dollar Club this Saturday evening. We thought seven-thirty would be a good time. That way everyone has time to get home from work and have time to get to the meeting at dinnertime We need to come up with a place to have it though. The only one I can think of that could accommodate us would be the Red Carpet Cuisine. They have plenty of private meeting rooms. Their menus are great and their atmosphere is rather on the quiet, elegant style, even though their food is not too pricey. Do you have any other suggestions?"

"Well, the only other place I can think of is The Harbor down on Third Street and Lark Avenue. They serve only seafood, though. The accommodations are great, but everyone may not like seafood, so that may not be the best choice. I have never been to The Red Carpet Cuisine. It sounds like a nice place. I wouldn't mind trying it out once. If it's satisfactory for everyone else, it's fine with me," said Hazel.

"Good. I'll need to call a couple of other of the women to see if they have any other suggestions. I'll let you know as soon as I have talked to them."

"OK! Either way, I guess I'll see you on Saturday evening. I'll be waiting to hear from you. Bye- bye, Verina."

Verina called Nellie Wheeler next. She explained the plan for the first meeting to Nellie just as she had to Hazel. She told her about the two suggestions of restaurants and asked her if she could add to the suggestions or recommend either of them over the other.

"Well, my favorite restaurant is Phibies, but the last time Owen and I went there, it was so crowded that we had to wait two hours to get seated. Of course Owen didn't think it was necessary to call ahead for reservations as I had suggested. It is a bit noisy sometimes, too, especially when all those college kids come storming in at Happy Hour. You can hardly hear yourself think when that happens. Do you have any ideas of your own?" Nellie asked.

"Well I was thinking of The Red Carpet Cuisine. Hazel thought that The Harber might be nice. She said that they only serve seafood, though. She was thinking that everyone might not care for seafood. I tend to agree with her there. I'm thinking we should try to find someplace that we could continue to have all of our meetings. Of course, if we try one place and don't like it, we could always move the meeting to some place else. What do you think?"

"I agree. On second thought, I take back my suggestion of Phibies. I really don't see us getting much done there. It's just too noisy and crowded as I said before. Too many college kids!"

"Alright, then. I had better call the other ladies and get their opinions. So far it's The Red Carpet Cuisine. I'll call you later after I talk to the others and let you know where we are going to meet. Bye for now," Verina said as she hung up the phone.

"Hello, Doralene? This is Verina Steris, Ardon's wife. I called to let you know we are planning the first meeting of The Six Hundred Thousand Dollar Club for this Saturday evening at seven-thirty. We haven't decided where it is going to be yet, though. That's another reason I called. We are asking all the ladies in the club if they have any suggestions as to where we could have the first meeting. We can always change it later after the first meeting, but we would like to have a permanent place where we can meet each week. One of the other ladies suggested Phibies, but then she said it was too crowded and too noisy. Harbor was also suggested, but they only serve seafood and we were thinking everyone might not like seafood, especially if we decide to meet there every week. The Red Carpet Cuisine was also suggested, because of the atmosphere, the accommodations as far as rooms available and the food is great and is not too pricey. Do you have any suggestions?"

"Well, let's see. Fredrick mentioned a place he had lunch the other day. I think he called it Rose's Garden. He said they have delicious food but that it was pretty expensive. He said his friend bought his lunch or he would never have gone there. It would probably be too expensive for some people. I don't know what people are used to paying when they go out. You may know that. Fredrick and I go out, but we don't usually spend a lot, unless it's a special occasion, like our anniversary, then I can see Fredrick cringe when he get the check," she laughed. "Any place is fine with me. And like you said, we can always change to a different place later on."

Verina almost choked out a laugh, knowing exactly who that friend was. She could still see Ardon's face when he told her about how Fredrick had suckered him into buying that expensive lunch a few days ago. She could just imagine what he would say if he knew Fredrick's wife had just suggested Rose's Garden for their dinner meeting.

"Alright, then. I'll let you know what the final decision is as soon as I talk to one more person. Then I'll call to make sure we can get the reservations set up. I'll talk to you later. Goodbye, Doralene. See you on Saturday."

"OK. I'll be waiting to hear from you. I'm sure no matter where we meet, we will have a very interesting evening," said Doralene as she hung up the phone.

"Only one more to call," thought Verina. "The call I've been putting off. Well if it's got to be done, I may as well get it done and over with. I just hope I don't have to spend my whole evening on the phone with Bibi. Maybe I'll tell her I need to call a few more ladies. No, that won't do. She will want to know whom and after I tell her the other suggestions, she may figure out that there are no more ladies to call...again, knowing Bibi, she might not even think about that. Oh, well here goes," she said as she dialed Bibi's number.

"Hello, Bibi? This is Verina. How are you?" "Why did I ask that?" Verina thought that as she slapped the palm of her hand on her forehead. "That was stupid!" Thankfully, Bibi just replied with a single word.

"Fine."

"Are you alright?" "Dumb, again," thought Verina. "Just shut up and get to the point, before you get her started, Verina," she told herself.

"Yes, I'm fine. I was just watching this romantic love story on T.V. and I… well you know… What did you want? Are we having a bridge game? Remember, Thelma said she would bring the muffins…I mean the refreshments."

"No, that's not the reason I called. Well, yes we will be getting together for bridge soon, but the reason I'm calling right now is to let you know we are having our first meeting for The Six Hundred Thousand Dollar Club this Saturday evening at seven-thirty. We still need to come up with a place to meet. That's the other reason I called. I have called some of the other ladies that are in the club to get their opinion as to where we can have the meeting. Several places were mentioned. Let me tell you what they are and you can tell me what you think or if you have other suggestions, you can let me know. So far Phibies has been suggested, but the person who suggested it said she changed her mind, because it was too noisy and crowded." Verina almost said with college kids, but stopped herself. "That's all Bibi needs to hear…that there are single young men there and her mind would be made up," thought Verina. "Someone suggested Harbor, but they only serve seafood. The person that had suggested harbor said everyone might not like seafood, especially if we plan to have our weekly meetings in the same place. Rose's Garden was brought up, but I know for a fact that it is way too expensive for my taste, at least for a weekly meeting place. It might be nice to have a meeting or two there though. Maybe it would be the perfect place for one of our special events, later on. Oh, and the other place suggested was The Red Carpet Cuisine. I have eaten there and the food is outstanding and the atmosphere is perfect for a nice evening out. They have plenty of little private rooms where we can be served as we are holding our meetings. And that's all the suggestions we have so far. Do you have any place you particularly like, Bibi?"

"Well I do like the Cat and Mouse, but that's really just a bar. It is noisy and there aren't any private rooms…well not the kind of private rooms we would be interested in anyway. I don't even know if the serve anything besides sandwiches and fries. Other than that, I don't get out much, especially fancy places," Bibi said. "I'm with you on the seafood. One time I broke out in a rash after eating oysters on the half shell. I told myself that I would never touch seafood again. The Red…what did you call it?"

"The Red Carpet Cuisine," said Verina.

"Yes, The Red Carpet Cuisine sounds like a nice place. Is it very expensive? I have to save my money for the thousand dollar membership dues, remember? I have already saved a few dollars by not buying my TV dinners this week," said Bibi.

"It's pretty reasonable. And they have a variety of thing to choose from on their menu, so you can pretty much choose how much you want to spend, of course, don't forget, we will need to leave a decent tip, too," Verina told her.

"Oh, that sounds great, then. Is there anything else you want to tell me? If not, do you mind if I get back to my movie? I think the guy is just about to ask the girl to marry him. Some people have all the luck," she sighed.

"No, that's it. I'll call you when the final decision has been made, but it looks like it's going to be The Red Carpet Cuisine. I'll let you get back to your movie now. I wouldn't want you to miss the big proposal."

Verina was so glad she didn't have to tell her little fib to Bibi about needing to call other women about meeting places. "Thank The Lord for love stories on TV," she thought.

"I had better call everyone back to let them know that the Red Carpet Cuisine was going to be the official meeting place for the first meeting. I had better call Pearl back, too."

"I really think I'll decline your invitation this time, Verina," Pearl said. "Maybe I'll attend a later meeting, if the invitation is still on. I would like to meet your friends, but I'm just not in the mood right now. Thanks anyway."

Verina was disappointed but replied, "Sorry to hear that, Pearl. But you know you are welcome to attend any time you wish. The official roster has not been written up yet, so you have time."

After hanging up with Pearl and making the calls to the other ladies, Verina decided she should probably tell Ardon that the first official meeting of The Six Hundred Thousand Dollar Club was to be held at The Red Carpet Cuisine. She would wait until later to tell him of Doralene's suggestion of Rose's Garden.

Everyone waited excitedly to be escorted to the special dining area that had been reserved for them. There was even a card in the table that read "Reserved for The Six Hundred Thousand Dollar Club". Ardon was thrilled to see the name of the club in print. He looked around to make sure everyone was present. Shaking hands with each of the men and giving each of the women a kiss on the cheek and hug, he reached for his wife's hand. "This is such an exciting night," he thought. Smiling, he fidgeted on his right foot and then on his left. He gripped the new leather portfolio that held nine copies of the agenda in his left hand. Verina was in charge of holding onto the secretary's steno notebook and the treasurer's ledger. She didn't seem to have as tight of a grip on the items she held as Ardon had on his leather portfolio. When he had purchased it he had thought about having it engraved with his initials or the name of the club. He had second thoughts about putting his initials on it though. He was hoping he would be the one that the other members would choose to be the Chairman, but who was to say he would have to give up his beautiful leather bound portfolio to some one else. "It would be very embarrassing if I had to give it to some one else when it had my initials already on it. I guess I could have had The Six Hundred Thousand Dollar Club written on it. Oh well, maybe that can come later," he thought. "Or maybe we can just get another notebook if I'm not elected. After all, you would think that the founder of the club should have something nice to keep his notes in…maybe even something with his initials on it."

At last, after everyone had shaken everyone else's hand, they all sat down. Ardon cleared his throat and tapped the water glass that was sitting on the table in front of him.

"May I have everyone's attention?" he began. "We will have a time for introductions in a few minutes. If everyone will look over the menu and decide what they would like, we can order and then begin the meeting."

Everyone picked up the menu that was placed in front of them and the "oos" and "aahs" were heard around the table.

"Everything looks delicious," Someone said.

"I can't make up my mind," said another. "This may take all night to decide."

Ardon hoped whoever said that wasn't going to order something that took all evening to prepare. He knew he could cover a lot of territory while they were waiting for their food, but he would like to get down to the real business at hand without waiters interrupting or people asking for more drinks or replacements for dropped forks. He wanted to have everyone's attention when it came to electing officers and hiring an attorney. He would give them plenty of time to finish their meal and the table to be cleared before he would tap his glass to get their attention again, the signal indicating the official business would begin.

"Has everyone finished their meal?" he asked after the dessert had been devoured and coffee cups had been refilled. "If so, maybe we should start the meeting," he said as he stood up.

"Wait, dear. I think we ladies may want to use the powder room before we start," interrupted Verina.

All the women agreed and suddenly they all disappeared from the room.

"Not only the ladies need to visit the john," said Owen. "I think we men need to get rid of some of this coffee, too. Excuse me," he said as he pushed his chair away from the table and following the women out of the room, going in search of the men's room. All the other men followed him out. All except Ardon who sat gripping the leather portfolio even tighter than before.

"Will we never get this meeting underway, before we are all too old to remember why we're here?" he asked himself out loud. "Oh well, I guess I may as well visit the john like everyone else." He picked up his precious portfolio and took it with him to the men's room. "I'm definitely not leaving this here for someone to walk off with," he said.

When everyone finally returned to the table, Ardon tried once again to get everyone's attention. Just as he was about ready to speak, the waitress came by to ask if anyone needed anything and started pouring coffee into empty cups. Ardon couldn't stand it any longer.

"Will everyone please sit down and be quiet so we can get this meeting started some time tonight!" He took the copies of the agendas out of the portfolio and began passing them out around the table. "Here is a copy of the agenda for tonight's meeting. As you see there will be time allotted for questions and answers at the end. But first I would like to thank everyone for coming. We have a lot to cover, but I know we will all be patient, so all minds will be clear when we are through. Have you all been introduced to each other?" he asked, a little disappointed that they had not waited to be introduced according to his agenda. "If so, we can skip down to the third item on the agenda, the review of the purpose of the club and how it will work." Ardon gave a detailed review of the purpose and repeated the mission statement and the basic rules.

"Do we need to have any more discussion on the purpose, the mission statement or the rules? If not let's go on to the fourth item on the agenda." No one had anything further to add, so he proceeded to the next item.

"I think it is important that we conduct our meeting the same as any other club meeting. Therefore, I think we need to elect a few people as officers that will help us to keep things professional. First let me read off the offices I think are important and you can let me know if there should be any others, OK? Also, be thinking who would be the best person for each position and we will have a secret written vote for each office after nominations have been offered. Is that agreeable to everyone?"

Everyone seemed impressed with Ardon's thoughtfulness of coming up with such an idea. Ardon looked toward his wife and smiled. Verina just smiled back at him and didn't seem to mind that he had given her absolutely no credit for thinking up the idea of having officers.

After reading off each office, Ardon asked, "Now who do we think will be the best to lead our meeting as Chairman of the club? Does anyone have a nomination to make?" he asked, hoping someone would nominate him.

Everyone sat silently for a minute. Ardon thought it seemed like half an hour before anyone said anything. Finally, he heard someone say, "I think, since Ardon came up with this idea, I think he should be our Chairman." Ardon looked up to see Owen speaking. "I nominate Ardon," he said.

"I accept the nomination, thank you Owen. Is there anyone else who would like to make a nomination?" Ardon asked. Everyone thought a minute, before someone said, "No, I think you are it, Ardon."

"Fine, but I think if we still make this a secret written vote, it would be best, just in case someone is too shy to nominate who they really think would suit the position," said Ardon. All agreed and Verina handed everyone a piece of paper to write their vote on. After they were all collect, they were handed to Fredrick to count and report the results.

"Nine ballots counted and eight votes for Ardon to be the Chairman of The Six Hundred Thousand Dollar Club," said Fredrick. "I guess one person did not vote?" asked Fredrick.

"Yes, I did not vote," said Ardon. "I guess I felt a little funny voting for myself if there were no other nominations."

Everyone laughed and congratulated him his landslide victory.

"Thank you," said Ardon. "Now we need a Vice Chairman. Do we have any nominations for Vice Chairman or Chairwoman?"

No one said anything. Finally, Bibi raised her hand. "Can a person nominate himself or herself Mr. Chairman?" she asked.

"Oh, no," thought Verina. "Not Bibi!"

"I don't see why not, if no one has any objections," said Ardon

Everyone agreed that there should not be a problem.

When she didn't say anything else, Ardon asked Bibi, "Are you nominating yourself, Bibi?"

"No, I was just wondering if a person could do that if they wanted to," she replied.

After a few minutes with no one being nominated, Charles said, "I would like to nominate Owen Wheeler as Vice Chairman." There were no other nominations offered, so they voted silently again. This time when Fredrick counted the ballots, all nine were for Owen.

"I think we need a secretary to be elected next, Ardon," Verina said. This way we have someone to take this all down."

"Good idea. Do we have nominations for secretary?" ask the chairman.

Bibi nominated Verina and Verina nominated Hazel.

"It doesn't have to be a woman, does it?" asked Bibi. "I mean a man could be a secretary, too if he wanted?"

"I guess so," said Ardon. "But you just nominated Verina. Are you taking back your nomination?"

"No. I just thought I would ask, that's all."

"OK… are there any other women or *men* to be nominated?" asked Ardon, losing his patience rapidly.

"Now I see why Bibi runs Verina crazy," he thought.

With no other nominations the vote was taken. Fredrick counted and reported the results were Verina four and Hazel five. Ardon hoped his wife was not too disappointed that she was not going to be the secretary, since it was her idea to have one in the first place. He looked over toward her, but she didn't seem too upset as she congratulated Hazel.

"Now that we have a secretary, why don't we give her some time to write down all that we have covered so far?" He handed her the steno notebook he had bought. "Do we need to recap anything for you Hazel?" said Ardon.

"I think I can get it all down in a minute. But why don't I read everything back to you when I get caught up, just to be sure I haven't left out anything or made any mistakes?"

"That sounds like a good idea, Hazel. Just let us know when you're ready to go."

Hazel read everything she had and looked up to see if anyone had any comments. Since no one said anything, she took it that her notes were satisfactory.

"OK. Ready to continue when you are," she said to Ardon.

"Alright. The only office I can think of that needs to be filled is Treasurer," said Ardon. "We will need someone, *man* or *woman,* to collect and take the money to the bank for depositing. He or she should also be responsible for keeping track of the balance including the interest earned and give a report at each of our meetings.

"Do we have any nominations for Treasurer?"

Up went Bibi's hand again. "Oh, no," thought Verina. "Not Bibi for treasurer. The money would be moldy by the time she gets it to the bank. Besides, she's so scatter brained, I doubt she would even remember where she put the money once she collected it."

"I nominate Fredrick ...what's your last name, Fredrick?" Bibi said.

"Drake, Fredrick Drake," said Fredrick. "I would consider it an honor to be nominated Treasurer," he said as he smiled at Bibi.

"Anyone else?" asked Ardon. "Any ladies want to be considered?"

"Why doesn't he just take Bibi's nomination and shut up, before she gets any ideas?" said Verina.

"OK, then let's put it to a vote, ladies and gentlemen," said Ardon.

This time it was Charles who counted the votes. "All nine present cast their vote and all nine voted for Fredrick Drake as Treasurer," he said.

Everyone stood up and cheered that the election of officers had gone so well. They decided to take a break and coffee was ordered as each one took time to congratulate the new elected officers. All took advantage of the break to go visit the john once more before returning to the table to continue discussing the remaining issues on the agenda.

Calling the meeting back to order, Ardon announced that they still needed to decide what lawyer they were going to hire to represent the club.

"Do we have any suggestions?" he asked.

"Well, there is a young attorney that just graduated from the university of law down on Booker Street. I don't know his name, but I heard my barber talking about him the other day when I was there getting a haircut," said Owen. "I don't think he's had much experience though."

"I think we need someone with experience," said Charles.

"How about that lawyer that moved here two years ago from New Jersey. Remember, what's his name, Doralene? You remember when our neighbor had that lawsuit going on about his parents being caught up in that insurance scam?"

"Oh, yes. What was his name…George something?"

"Wasn't it George Imimes or something like that?"

"Yes. That's it, George Imimes, Attorney At Law, I think. I'm sure his phone number is in the phone book. He should be good since he is familiar with scams. I don't mean to refer to The Six Hundred Thousand Dollar Club as a scam, Ardon, but you know what I mean. He should be good at any kind of problems that might arise. And he is young. You did say we needed someone young, didn't you?" said Hazel.

"Well, we could check him out. Are there any other suggestions about whom we should hire? If not, how do we want to pay for this lawyer? Should we each contribute or should we take it out of the dues?" said Ardon.

After much thought it was decided to take the money out of the club fees and pay the lawyer as they were all at his office signing the contract and putting their money together. Fredrick would take the remainder to the bank right after they were done. He would record the balance in his ledger that Ardon had provided for him.

Everyone agreed that they would ask the lawyer to be an advisor to the club and to make periodical appearances at club meeting and that he would be invited to events as a guest.

The floor was opened for questions and discussion. At first everyone just sat without saying a word. It appeared everything was pretty much settled as far as business was concerned.

"I have a question," said Bibi.

"Of course she would," thought Verina.

"You said we would be having social events..." she almost said, "Where I can meet eligible men." "Don't you think we should have a social committee?"

"That's a very good suggestion, Bibi," said Doralene. "Of course we would need a chairperson to head up the committee."

"I nominate Verina to be the chairwoman of the Social Committee, then," said Bibi.

All were in agreement, that Verina would be a very fine choice for Chairwoman for the job. Verina chose to have all the ladies on her committee, even Bibi. She couldn't very well leave Bibi out, since she was responsible for her being the Social Committee Chairwoman.

Everyone was also in agreement that the very first meeting of The Six Hundred Thousand Dollar Club was a big success and that they were all looking forward to the next meeting and a were anxiously awaiting word from Ardon about the lawyer. He said he would call each one or send a letter to let them know what was happening as soon as he and Owen had talked to the suggested lawyer. If they thought he was satisfactory for their purpose they would go ahead and hire him if it was ok with everyone else. All agreed that would be fine and that they all respected Ardon's and Owen's judgment.

"One more thing before we officially end the meeting," said Ardon. "Secretary Hazel, do you think you could send everyone a copy of the minutes from this meeting? Maybe everyone should get a notebook to keep the minutes and other notes in for the club."

Everyone thought that was a good idea.

"Are all minds clear?" Ardon asked. "If so, the first meeting of The Six Hundred Thousand Dollar Club is adjourned."

Everyone began to applaud as they stood up and started to congratulate each other for taking part in the meeting. Someone suggested that they should make a toast to the occasion. Drinks were ordered and a hardy "Cheers to the Six Hundred Thousand Dollar Club! Long may we live!" was shouted by all.

Chapter Thirteen: Please Sign On The Dotted Line

Ardon called the office of George Imimes, Attorney Of Law the next morning after the meeting. He set up a meeting for the next day at three thirty in the afternoon. He hoped Owen would be able to get off of work a little early so he could accompany him to the lawyer's office as he had promised the club members. The receptionist had asked what it was about, but Ardon had told her it was a personal matter and that "George" would want to see him as soon as possible tomorrow anytime after three o'clock. Ardon was beginning to feel more and more like a liar every time he stretched the truth. He only hoped the rest of the club members had not noticed any of his little "stretches".

After picking up Owen from his job to save time, Ardon turned his car in the direction of the attorney's office when he realized he had forgotten to pick up his leather portfolio off of his desk on his way out this morning. He had a million things on his mind this morning and he was running late because he had over slept. He had had a hard time falling to sleep Saturday and

Sunday night because he couldn't get the club meeting out of his mind. He woke up several times during the night, once he did fall asleep, thinking about how he was going to explain the club to the lawyer once he got to his office. He hoped that Owen would step in when his words failed him.

"Maybe I should have met with Owen this weekend so we could go over what we were going to say. Maybe we should have even written some sort of script to follow. Not that we want it to sound like we had rehearsed or that we were reading a script, but at least have some notes that we could follow so that we don't leave anything out. Oh, well. Maybe we can go over everything now, on the way to the lawyer's office," he thought.

"Owen, I was thinking, maybe we need to go over what we are going to say to this lawyer when we get there. Could you make some notes that we can follow? We can think about it on the way, if you don't mind taking some notes. I need to run by my house to pick up my portfolio. I just realized that I forgot to pick it up when I left for work this morning."

"Sure, if you can pick up a pen and paper from your house. In the mean time we can get some ideas and I can write them down on the way to his office."

When they arrived at Ardon's house, they already had several items for Owen to write down. Ardon ran into the house, grabbed the portfolio, paper and pen and ran back out to the car. He looked at his watch. It was already three-fifteen.

"We better hurry. I don't want us to be late. Why don't you write down the things we already talked about and then we can think of other issues that we want to discuss with the lawyer?" said Ardon as he tried to catch his breath. "Why did I have to forget the portfolio this morning?" he scolded himself. "We would have already been at the lawyer's office by now."

When they arrived a few minutes later, the receptionist announced their arrival to her boss. Ardon hoped she wouldn't announce him as "Your friend" to see you, Mr. Imimes.

Shaking hands with Ardon and Owen, George said, "Good afternoon, gentlemen. What can I do for you?"

After explaining their reason for their visit, he sat back in his chair with his hands folded on his stomach.
"Well, I must say, this is a first for me. I've had all kinds of cases in my short time as a lawyer, but gentlemen this one takes the cake as the old saying goes. Let me think about this for a minute. I think I need a few minutes to just let all this sink in."

After a few minutes and after looking over his notes again, George said, "So, what is it exactly that you want me to do for you?"
"We would like for you to oversee the contract and be the executor of the club's finances. We have a treasurer that will collect and deposit the dues. He will also give the report to the members at our meetings, but we would like for you to attend once in a while to give us any report that you feel in necessary. Of course you are welcome to attend any of our events as a guest, also, if you like. But your most important duty would be to see that the rightful survivor gets the money in the end. Of course we would

like for you to help us write up a binding contract…and of course be a witness when all of the members sign the contract. We would appreciate it if you spot any loopholes or if you see anything that needs to be revised that you will take care of that, too."

"Well, I can see you gentlemen are pretty serious about this club of yours. How about I look it over for a couple of days, then I will call you and we can set up a time where you can bring in your other members to do the signing, if I don't find anything illegal about this, of course. As I see it right now, it looks perfectly legal, as long as all persons involved are in agreement, but as I said, I've never heard of anything like this before. How about I have my receptionist call you on Thursday to let you know how we stand."

"That sounds great!" said Ardon. He and Owen shook hands with George as they moved toward the door. On their way out they both said "Goodbye" and " Have a nice day" to the receptionist. They thought they heard the lawyer say to her, "You are never going to believe this one, Shirley."

On Thursday morning, Ardon's phone rang at nine thirty, shortly after he had arrived for work.

"Hello, Ardon Steris, speaking." he said. "How may I help you?"

"Mr. Steris, this is Shirley from Mr. Imimes's office. Mr. Imimes would like to know if you could come by his office this afternoon to look at the contract for your club. Shall I tell him you could be here around three forty-five? He said you needed an appointment some time after three o'clock."

"Yes, that would be fine. I'll be there. Thank you."

Ardon immediately called Owen to tell him that he should meet him at the lawyer's office by three forty-five.

"Try to be there a few minutes early, Owen, if you can. We don't want to be late. I wouldn't want the lawyer to have to wait on us." What he meant was he would need a few minutes to calm his nerves before facing the lawyer.

"I just hope he found everything in order. I would hate to tell the other members that the whole thing is off at this point."

"Hello, Mr. Steris, Mr. Wheeler. Come in. Have a seat."

Ardon could feel his palms sweating and the tension in his neck had gotten tighter by the time he met Owen in the lobby of the lawyer's office.

"Gentlemen, I have good news. I can't find any reason that you can't have your club. I have done some research and have spoken to several colleagues, and no one seems to be able to find anything illegal about such a club…assuming all parties are in agreement as I said before. So… if you want to look over what I have written for a contract and let me know if it is what you had in mind, we can proceed with getting your Six Hundred Thousand Dollar Club underway. I took the notes you gave me and made very few changes as you can see." He handed Ardon and Owen each a copy, keeping his copy on his desk in front of him.

After reading through the contract and then reading through it a second time, but more slowly this time, both Ardon and Owen were impressed.

"This sounds great to me," said Owen. "What do you think, Ardon?"

"I think we have a perfect contract. Thank you, Mr. Imimes. This looks just perfect. Now can we set up a time when we can have the other members sign?"

"First, I think we need to send every member a copy for approval. You will need to give them a few days to respond and then if we need to make changes, we will need a few days for that. Then I think we should be able to get this all done," said George.

"Oh, see, I didn't even think of that," said Ardon. "I guess that's why we need a lawyer…to keep us from making any mistakes."

"I'll have Shirley make copies and send them out to all your members. How many did you say there are?"

"Nine right now, but we may have a couple more in the future, if it's ok to add more members," said Owen.

"I don't see why you couldn't add as many as you please, as long as everyone agrees," said George. "The members will need to sign and send back the letter to me, so we know they have all received and agreed to the contract as it is written. You may want to contact them and let them know to watch for my letter and to let them know how important it is for them to get it back to me as soon as possible. Do you have any questions or concerns before you go?"

"I don't, do you Ardon?" asked Owen.

"No, not really. Everything looks good to me. Again we thank you, Mr. Imimes. We will be waiting to hear from you to set up the contract-signing meeting. I'll start calling everyone as soon as I get home tonight."

Ardon and Owen were so excited they forgot to say good-bye to Shirley as they left the office. They nearly knocked each other down as they collided going out of the door.

"I guess we have ourselves a lawyer," said Owen.

"And most importantly, we have ourselves a Six Hundred Thousand Dollar Club!" said Ardon as he rushed down the hall and out into the parking lot to get into his car. He could hardly wait to get home and tell Verina the good news and to start calling everyone else to tell them to watch for the letter from the lawyer and to get it signed so they could all meet with the lawyer to sign the official contract and put their first dues into the bank.

"I would take Verina out to dinner tonight to celebrate, but I need to spend time making all of those calls. Maybe I should stop by that jewelry store… what was its name …something like… More Gold Jewelry Store? I remember her saying something about a gold necklace and earrings that she liked…or was it pearls?"

When Ardon arrived home he thought he heard Verina in the bathroom throwing up.
"Verina, are you alright? Are you ill?"
"I'm alright. I just have a little upset stomach. I think I may have gotten some sort of bug. I'll be out in just a minute. There is fresh tea in the refrigerator if you would like some."
"Great. I think I will have a glass. Can I pour you one, too?"
"No, thanks. I had one earlier. That may have been what upset my stomach."
"So… you want me to drink something that may have made you sick?" Ardon teased.
"No. No. That wasn't what I meant. Anyway, I'll be out in a second."

When Verina came out of the bathroom and into the kitchen, she looked pale. Ardon could tell she had just washed her face, because her mascara was smudged.

"Are you sure you are alright? You look a little flushed. Here, sit down. Can I get you anything? Maybe something to eat or some water or something?"

"No, thank you. I just need a minute, that's all. I'll be fine in a minute. What would you like for dinner?" The thought of food mad her stomach queasy, but she knew Ardon would be hungry for his dinner soon.

"How about I just make myself a sandwich. I had a big lunch today, so I'm not that hungry. And you don't look like you feel like cooking tonight. I have some good news to share, when you feel like hearing it, dear."

"I'm fine now. What is your good news?"

"George Imimes called me this afternoon and had Owen and me come to his office to look over the contract he had written up for us. Everything looked pretty good. He really didn't make many changes; mostly just put everything in lawyer terms, so... Owen and I gave him the ok to send out letters to all the club members to be signed and returned to him as soon as possible. After everyone has sent back the signed letter, he is ready to set up an appointment for all of us to meet with him to sign the final contract and pay our club dues. Isn't that great?"

"Yes, dear, that's great," Verina replied. Her mind really was not on the club right now. She was almost sure she was about to throw up again when Ardon reached in his jacket pocket and drew out a little black box.

"What's that you have there, dear?" She thought she recognized the box as one from The More Gold Jewelry Store.

"Well, I was going to save this until after dinner, but I guess now is as good a time as any to give it to you. I thought I heard you mention something you liked from The More Gold Jewelry Store, so I stopped by there on my way home and picked this up for you. If you don't like it, I can exchange it for something else." He was sure she would be pleased. It cost him more than he had intended to pay, but he knew Verina was worth it. Besides, maybe it would make her forget her upset stomach.

"Oh! Ardon! It's beautiful. It's the gold necklace and earring set I was drooling over the other night. I didn't even know you heard me. I love them!" she said as she got up and gave Ardon a hug and a kiss. Her stomach was still tumbling, but she was determined to ignore it and put her full attention on her beautiful gift from Ardon.

"I was hoping this was the set you liked so well. I was afraid that I got mixed up. I know you said something about pearls, too, but I thought that you could exchange them if you really wanted the pearls."

"No way! I love these. I did like the pearls, but I will get more use out of these, because gold goes with everything. Thank you so much my wonderful husband."

"Here let's try them on. They do look nice on you, if I do say so myself. They would probably look even better if you didn't have mascara smeared all over your beautiful face. Are you sure you feel alright? How about I make a sandwich for you, too. And maybe some hot tea?"

"No thank you. I don't think my tummy could hold a sandwich right now. The tea does sound good though. I think I'll go repair my mascara while you pour the tea and then I think I'd like to lie down for a while if you don't mind."

"No problem. As soon as I finish my dinner, I need to start calling the other members of the club to let them know about the forthcoming letters from the lawyer. You just drink your tea and go take a rest. You might want to take off your necklace and earrings though. I'll pour our tea in a couple of minutes."

After Ardon had finished his sandwich and tea, he moved to his office and began making the calls to the club members. As he told each about his and Owens' visit to the lawyer's office today, he could feel himself getting more excited. He was concerned about Verina, but he knew he needed to get the calls done and then he would look in on her.

"I hope nothing serious is wrong with her," he said.

Everyone had received their letters from George Imimes and had returned them signed within the week. Ardon had called everyone a second time just to remind them of the importance of returning them promptly. He was glad that Verina was feeling better. He had heard her in the bathroom throwing up only twice in the last couple of days. He insisted that she make an appointment to see the doctor, just in case the bug wasn't completely out of her system. She had reluctantly made an appointment, but said she would postpone it if it interfered with the time and date that the group would need to be at the lawyers' office for the contract signing. Ardon finally agreed and said he would call her from work as soon as he heard when George wanted them to come in. He wanted to give her plenty of time to change her appointment. She definitely needed to be at the signing, but she also needed to see the doctor.

"She may not be throwing up, but she still looks pale," he thought.

"Hello, Mr. Steris, this is Shirley from George Imimess' office again. He wanted me to call you to tell you he has received everyone's signed letters back and he wants to know if you all could come to his office this Friday at four o'clock. He normally goes home early on Fridays, but he said to tell you he will stay late because he knows this is important to you and the other people involved. He said if everyone is on time he could still avoid the late Friday evening traffic. I don't think he intended for me to say that part, though," she said as she gave a little snicker.

"Great! Great! I'll call everyone right away and let them know. I'll remind them that it is very important to be on time. Thank you, Miss …Shirley. You have a very nice day!"

Ardon called Verina first. He was glad she sounded much better on the phone than she had when he left this morning. She told him that her doctor's appointment was later in the afternoon today, so he was relieved that he didn't have to ask her to change it.

As soon as Ardon got off the phone with Verina, he began calling each club member to let them know about the meeting on Friday. Everyone was excited to hear and said they would try to be at the lawyer's office at least fifteen or twenty minutes early.

Ardon was surprised to see Verina making dinner when he got home. He had been living on cold sandwiches all week. He could smell the noodle casserole when he stepped through the door.

"Mmm, something smells delicious," he said. "You must be feeling better. What did the doctor say?"

"Yes, I am feeling better. We are having a noodle casserole. I found the recipe in a magazine in the waiting room at the doctor's office. I hope you like it."

"I'm sure I will. I have to admit; I was getting a little bit tired of sandwiches. So, what did the doctor say?"

"Oh, he gave me some pills to settle my stomach and told me to get some rest."

"That's it? He didn't tell you what the bug was that you had?"

"Well, yes. He said the bug should be gone in about nine months."

"Nine months? What kind of bug is that?"

"Oh, one that will be around for a while."

"Be around for a while? What is that supposed to mean?"

"It means, that in nine months we will be having a little bug that we can push around in a bug-gy."

Ardon had to think for a few minutes before it dawned on him what exactly it was that Verina was trying to tell him.

"Verina, are you trying to tell me that you are pregnant...that we are going to have a baby?"

"That is exactly what I am trying to tell you, Ardon. What do you think? Do you think you can handle being a daddy and be the chairman of The Six Hundred Thousand Dollar Club, too?"

"I...I...I think... I think I can handle it very well," Ardon said as he went over to his wife and gave her an extra tight bear hug.

"Good, that settles that," said Verina. "Now are you ready to try my new noodle casserole?"

Ardon couldn't decide if he was more excited about the club or about the fact that in nine months he was going to be a father. He felt like he was giving birth to not one baby, but two.

"Shouldn't we be calling someone to share the news?" he asked over dinner.

"Why don't we wait a while...just to make sure everything is all right."

"Why? Is something wrong? You and the baby are going to be all right aren't you?"

"Yes. Everything is fine. But I have heard of women having miscarriages, not that we have to worry, but ..."

"Don't even think like that, Verina."

"OK, but wouldn't it be fun to make the announcement at our next meeting after the lawyer business is over?"

"It sure would be starting off our club with a big bang. You're right. Let's wait and surprise everyone. You may have to make a toast with milk, instead of champagne, though."

"That's not funny, Ardon. Is this how you are going to be treating the mother of your first child?"

Everyone was on time for the meeting with George Imimes, Attorney Of Law. They were all trying to talk at once...no one could hear what the other was saying. Finally, everyone was asked to take a seat around the large round conference table in one of the outer offices. Everyone was handed a copy of the contract and asked if they had had time to think about what they were about to commit to by signing the contract. The all mumbled "yes" or nodded their heads.

"Good," said George. "Now we will proceed with the actual signing of the contract. Everyone will get a copy with everyone else's signature. The signatures will not be copies, so it will take some time for each of you to sign everyone's copy of the contract...and of course I will keep one for my records, also. Are there any questions or comments before we begin?" He hoped there would be none. He thought about the traffic he was going to have to fight to get home tonight.

No one had any questions or comments, so they each began to carefully put their signature on the contract copies. When all had been signed, George collected them and reviewed each one to make sure they had all been properly signed.

"All seem to be in order," he announced as he handed each person a copy. "I advise you to put you contracts in a safe place. Someplace that is safe from fire or theft. A safety deposit box at your bank would be one place I would suggest. If there are no questions or comments, then I here by declare the Six Hundred Thousand Dollar Club as official. Congratulations to you all."

Everyone began cheering and congratulating each other.

"I do have one question," said Bibi.

"Oh, no! Now what?" thought Verina and Ardon at the same time.

Everyone stopped and starred at Bibi.

"Yes, what is it Miss Mercille?" asked George. He couldn't believe she was asking a question now. Not after everything was signed and agreed to. "I may never get to go home tonight," he thought.

"I noticed you are not wearing a wedding ring. Are you single, Mr. Imimes?"

"Well, yes I am."

"Well in that case, I hope you will be attending some of our meetings and special events."

No one could believe what they had just heard Bibi say. Verina and Ardon just shook their heads.

"I can't believe this," said Verina. "Bibi never gives up."

Chapter Fourteen: And Baby Makes Three...

For the next nine months, everything was going smoothly for the club. Weekly meetings were held at the Red Carpet Cuisine. George Imimes had even attended a few, to the delight of Bibi. Verina and the social committee had planed two events and both had been a success. One had been a bar-b-que at the Drakes and the other had been a dinner dance at the Latin Club. Both had left Verina frazzled, but she and the committee had had fun planning them. The men even seemed to enjoy the events, even when it meant that Charles and Owen had to drag out their old penguin outfits. Verina's and Ardon's new addition was due in a week or so. She was glad that the events were over.

"I was afraid that I may have to give birth out on the dance floor," she told Doralene.

"Well, that could have been our third major event," laughed Doralene. "I would have liked to have seen the look on those men, all dressed up in their tuxes and standing around wondering what to do next. You think they looked uncomfortable in those things, can you imagine how they would feel trying to figure out a way to escape that!"

"Well, I'm just glad I wasn't the main attraction, that's all."

Little seven pound two ounce Beth Marie Steris was born on Easter Sunday morning. Everyone from the club showed up throughout the day, bearing gifts. Large Easter baskets filled with jellybeans and chocolate bunnies filled Verina's hospital room. Congratulation cards filled with well wishes took most of the space on the table along the wall. Ardon received so many slaps on the back that he thought for sure his back had bruises. "The hugs from the ladies made up for it," he thought.

The women from the club had given Verina a baby shower last month, so Beth Marie would be going home to a beautifully stocked nursery of little newborn outfits and enough diapers to make a sail for a schooner ship if they were all sewn together.

"Look at all of these diapers, Verina," said Hazel at the baby shower. "Who are you going to get to change these? As I remember, someone said she didn't think she could stand changing dirty diapers… remember that, Verina?"

"Maybe we should make Beth Marie our club mascot," suggested Owen.

"I don't think I want my first born growing up with the reputation of being a mascot," laughed Verina. "Let's just let her be a little girl, OK? We may have to bring her with us to the weekly meetings for a while though, if no one minds. I don't really want to leave her with anyone until she gets a little bit older. But if you all think it would be an inconvenience, I could skip the meetings for a few months. We don't have any events planned for a while, and even if we did, the rest of the social committee is very capable of taking care of it or… we could have the social planning meeting at my house."

"I don't see a problem with bringing Beth Marie to the meetings. Do any of you?" said Charles. " If it becomes a burden for you, Vernia, I think you should decide that for yourself."

"Sounds good to me," said Hazel. "I don't see a problem."

Everyone else agreed with Charles and Hazel.

As everyone gave Verina a good-bye hug and one last slap on the back to Ardon, they slowly walked out of the hospital room, leaving the two new happy parents alone.

"Can you believe we are actually Mommy and Daddy?" asked Ardon. "We really are parents of a beautiful baby girl. Congratulations, Mommy," he said

"Congratulations to you, too, Daddy," Verina replied.

Chapter Fifteen: One War Ends…Another Begins

"I am so glad Roy gets to come home from Korea," Pearl told Verina. "Here it is nineteen fifty-three. When he went over there three years ago, he thought he would be back on American soil in a few months. He's been away most of our married life. I don't begrudge you and Ardon of getting started on your family, but I sometimes think I am doomed to never having any children at all. All Roy writes in his letters is stuff relating to the war. I keep bringing up the subject of starting a family when he gets home, but he never mentions it when he writes back. I told him you and Ardon were expecting your first baby soon, but he seemed to just ignore it."

"Well, maybe things will change when he does get home. He probably just wants to get this war over first. Keep your chin up, Pearl. Things will change soon. This war can't go on forever."

"Maybe you're right, Verina. I guess when I see my friends all having babies, I sort of feel like I'm missing out. I guess I just have to be patient."

Pearl waited by the dock. She could feel the tears burning her eyes as she watched for Roy to come down the plank and onto "American soil", as he had put it in his last letter. She stood on her tiptoes so she could see over the other people's heads. Mothers, wives, girlfriends, sisters and of course dads and younger boys all crowding together to see their soldier coming home. Many of the young women held babies in their arms or small children by the hand, all waiting impatiently to see their dads, some of them, for the first time and some too young to remember a dad at all. Loud cheers went up as the men began appearing, carrying dusty or dirty duffel bags. They seemed to be just as anxious as the families that were waiting for them. They too, searched the crowed for recognizable faces. They began to run forward as each one spotted the long missed loved one. Squeals of laughter and cries of joy were all around Pearl.

"Where is Roy?" she said to herself as she felt herself getting more anxious as more and more soldiers united with their families. Finally she thought she spotted him. She moved closer, pushing her way through the crowed.

"Yes! Yes! It is him!" she heard herself shouting. "Roy! Roy! Over here! I'm over here!"

Spotting her, Roy dropped his duffel bag and ran toward her, catching her into his arms. He swung her around until she was so dizzy that she almost fell down when he let her go. Neither one said a word for a few seconds. They both just stood there, with tears in their eyes, holding each other among the crowd.

"I have missed you so much," Roy said at last. "I don't remember leaving such a beautiful wife. Remind me. Why did I leave?" he said as he kissed her again.

"I have missed you even more. And I think you left to fight a war if I'm not mistaken, Sergeant," she teased.

Pearl and Roy decided that they would spend their first night of Roy's leave at home. It seemed strange to Roy to be able to just sit and do absolutely nothing just as they chosen to do all evening. He felt like he was being catered to too much as his wife fluttered around bringing him snacks and drinks while he just sat with his feet up on the ottoman, relaxing.

"Come sit down," he had told her several times, but the next thing he knew, she was asking him what she could get for him as she jumped up and headed toward the kitchen.

"I don't want anything but to sit with my wife in my arms and look upon her beautiful face this evening."

Roy and Pearl spent the remainder of his furlough visiting with friends and spending time rejuvenating their marriage. Most of their evenings were spent at home just cuddling and talking about anything but the war... "And babies," thought Pearl. Every time she brought up the subject, Roy would change the talk to something entirely different. "Maybe he just needs more time to get used to not hearing bombs going off above his head," she thought with a sigh. "Yes, I do just need to be patient, I guess."

"It seemed like it was just yesterday when I was standing at the dock waiting for you to come home, and now you are leaving again," Pearl said with trembling lips and tears running down her cheeks. "It just doesn't seem fair that you have to leave already. I'm starting to miss you and you haven't even gotten on that ship to leave yet. Where are they taking you guys on a ship? I thought Army men walked or were transported by plane or train or bus or something," she sobbed.

"Well, normally they do, but I'm being sent back to the Pacific again for a few months for a special training. I should be back in no time. In the mean time, just remember that I love you and will think of you every minute that I'm gone." He kissed her and held her tight, lifting her head, said, "Now don't cry my beautiful wife. I'll be home soon."

Watching him board the ship, Pearl felt more alone than she ever had before. "It seems like each time he comes home and then leaves again it gets harder and harder," she cried as she turned to go to her car and drive the long lonely road home.

When she stepped into the house, she could feel the loneliness even more. The silence seemed to over take every thing around her. She dropped to the couch and let the dam of tears burst from her heart. "I want him home NOW! Here at home with me and our non-conceived baby!" she shouted as she punched the decorative throw pillow and threw it across the room.

The subject of starting a family was never brought up again after the third week of Roy's furlough. "I just have to be patient," Pearl reminded herself. "I just have to be patient," she said again for the hundredth time, picking up the tossed pillow and hugging it to her breast.

Trying to get back into a regular routine after Roy's departure, Pearl had mopped and waxed the kitchen floor twice and cleaned out the refrigerator, getting rid of the leftovers from the meals she and Roy had shared while he was home. With each leftover tossed into the garbage, she felt part of her heart went right out along with it. Sitting down to take a few minutes to have a cup of tea, before tackling the closet and cleaning the bathroom again for the fourth time this week, she began to think of her friend, Verina.

"Maybe I should give her a call and see what she's up too. She is probably getting pretty big by now with the baby due soon. No, seeing her will just cause me to get more depressed. Maybe I'll call Bibi instead. How can I get depressed with her around? She's not going to get pregnant very soon. She doesn't even have a boyfriend. Yes, that's what I'll do. I'll call Bibi and see if she wants to do something tonight.... not a movie, though. They may still be showing those war clips that they used to show before the movie starts. I am definitely not in the mood for that."

The next four years dragged by slowly for Pearl. Roy had come home several times on furlough, but each time he left he took a little piece of Pearl's heart and the hope that she had of starting a family with him. Pearl was about to give up when she received a letter from him telling her he was coming home and that he had made a very important decision that would affect their future, and that he wanted to share it with her in person.

"Oh, I can hardly wait!" she told Bibi on the phone. "Of course, I'm excited to have him home, but I'm pretty sure now is the time he has decided he is ready to start our family."
"How exciting for you," said Bibi. "I just wish I could get a date!"

The next two weeks passed slowly. Pearl found herself more than once walking by The Baby Shop, just to get a glimpse of the latest baby outfits and baby furniture.

Finally the morning that she was to meet Roy at the train station had arrived. She woke up extra early, so she could have plenty of time to give the house one last dusting. She went to the florist shop and picked up fresh flowers for the dinning room table where she planned to serve Roy's favorite dinner, lamb chops and roasted potatoes.
"If I don't dally, I'll have time to freshen up before meeting Roy at eleven-thirty at the station. I want to leave early enough that I have plenty of time to find decent parking," she told herself.

Roy's train was just pulling into the station when Pearl got out of her car and started to walk toward the waiting area in front of the train. She could feel her heart pounding loudly as she watched for him to appear when the doors of the train opened. Several soldiers got off. Then a young woman with two small children was next.

"Where is he?" she said to herself. "I hope he didn't miss his train." Just then she saw his handsome face smiling, as he walked toward her.

"Hi, sweetheart," he said as he kissed her. "Your soldier boy is home again. And by train this time."

"And for good, this time, I hope," she replied.

Roy just smiled and gave her another kiss. This time he took a little longer before he let her go.

"What do you mean, you have reenlisted!" Pearl shouted at Roy. "How could you do such a thing without discussing it with me first? I thought you were coming home to stay. I thought that you were coming home so we could at last start our family! How could you do this to me, Roy? How?"

"I thought you would be pleased. Reenlisting means a better retirement for the future."

"Retirement? You are planning on this being your career? You prefer to spend your life in the Army over spending it with me…your wife? Does that mean that you have decided that we are not going to have a family… no children? Just you and your Army buddies? Is that what you're telling me?"

"You know I want to spend my life with you, but we just need to put things on hold for a while, that's all. It won't be forever, just a few more years… then we can think about starting that family of yours."

"Of mine? So, it's my family...not yours, is it? Well, we can just forget it. I don't want to be here raising our children while you are overseas someplace playing soldier boy, Roy! Excuse me, but I have dishes to wash and then I'm going to bed...alone! I suddenly have a headache and want to get some sleep!" She knew she would not be sleeping very well tonight. Her mind was spinning until she began to feel dizzy and her heart was aching so badly, that she doubted it would ever mend... "At least not for a long, long time," she told herself. "This was not what I expected to hear from Roy," she said as she sobbed into her pillow. "I don't know if I can face Ardon or Verina and their little girl again... not when I know my dream of a family will never be."

Roy left to go back to his army base a few days after his announcement to Pearl. He didn't realize that starting a family was that important to her. "I guess it was pretty stupid of me to reenlist before talking to her about it. It's too late now, though. I can't just walk in and tell my superiors that I changed my mind. My wife wants to have a baby instead."

He thought he would send he a letter to apologize for his stupidity as soon as he got back to the base. She didn't seem too much in the mood to listening to him when he was home. "Home?" "Were is my home really?" he asked himself. "Pearl is right. I have spent more of our married life in the service than I have with her. How can I make it up to her? I'm stuck here for another four years. I just hope she still wants to start that family by then," he said.

On September twenty-sixth, nineteen fifty-nine, Pearl's hopes were dashed to the floor even harder when the news reported that a new cold war was about to begin.

She had heard "cold war" before. This time terms like "military conflict" were being tossed around like footballs.

The Second Indo China War was on the agenda. Before long everyone in the United States Service would know it as the Vietnam War. A cold war that was to last sixteen years and take many lives.

Pearl prayed everyday that Roy would be sent home. "Why did he have to reenlist again? Why did he not just serve his time and come home, get a job in some office or factory and be tossing a football around with his son in the front yard by now?" she asked herself. "Surely they have plenty of other guys that can take his place. Why does he think he needs to be right in the middle of all the action all the time?"

She decided sitting around worrying was not doing any good and it appeared that Roy would not be getting to come home on furlough for some time. "Maybe if I get involved in some kind of activity, time will pass faster for me. I wonder if the offer to join The Six Hundred Thousand Dollar Club is still on? Maybe I'll give Verina a call to find out. I don't really care about getting any money if I'm still alive after everyone else bites the dust, but the social life is something I am interested in. I can't just let my life pass me by while soldier boy plays war games. Yes, I think I will call Verina right now, before I change my mind."

"Hello, Verina, this is Pearl. I was just wondering if the offer still stands to join your club? It appears that Roy won't be coming home in the near future, and I would like to get out of this house once in a while. I know I would be way behind in the dues, but if I can make arrangements to make payments to catch up, I could do that…if the offer still stands, that is."

"Oh, Pearl. That would be wonderful. Everyone will be so excited to have you join us. I'm sure we can work something out about the dues. The other members are pretty understanding people. We could talk to them and see what you need to do to catch up. Have you heard from Roy lately? Do you know where he is exactly?"

"I haven't heard from him in a couple of weeks. His letters don't come as often as they used to before this conflict thing started. I don't think he is allowed to say exactly where they are. Now that he is a lieutenant, he probable has to spend more time doing secret stuff. I'm afraid that this cold war is going to be just like the last one...a full fledged war."

"Let's hope not. Anyway, I'll let the members of the club know that you have decided that you want to join us and we can set up a special meeting to get you in. How about I give you a call back as soon as I get everything arranged."

"Great. I appreciate it, Verina. By the way how is your little girl, Beth Marie? How old is she now? ...Five or six?"

"She's fine. She will be six pretty soon. It seems like it was yesterday when I was at the hospital giving birth to her, now she's getting ready to start school in a few days. I didn't think I would ever want to have more than one child, but now that she going off to school, I sort of wished Ardon and I had had a little sister or brother for her...or maybe I'm just going to miss having a little one around the house to keep me company while she's at school."

Pearl didn't make any comment. She could still feel the ache in her heart when she thought about what she had missed because of Roy's decision to make a carrier of the Army.

A month had gone by and Pearl had not heard from Roy. The activities of the club had helped her take her mind off of Roy and the war for a while anyway. She had decided to participate in as much of the events as she could, volunteering when something need to be done. She was beginning to really enjoy the friendships she was forming with the other members and found herself laughing and even humming to herself at times. Her sleeping habits were improved, too. She woke in the mornings and felt as if she had had the most restful nights than she had had in years. "Yes, I think I have definitely made a good decision by joining this crazy, fun loving and lovable group of friends," she thought.

All was going well in Pearl's life, except for the fact that she received fewer and fewer letters from Roy as the months dragged on, but that was to be expected since in the last letter from Roy, he had told her that he was about to be sent farther into the front lines of Vietnam. He couldn't tell her any specifics, he had written, but it would probably be a long while before she would be getting any more mail from him. She tried not to let it bother her and spent as much time with the others at the club meeting as possible. All the members tried to cheer her up when she found herself almost in tears with worry and depression.

"How did I get along without these supportive people?" she asked herself more than once in the last few months. "I guess they have become my only family right now... at least until Roy gets home."

The sun was shining brightly, reflecting off the kitchen window over the sink as Pearl looked out over the lawn where two squirrels were playing tug of war over an acorn they had found under the tree in her back yard.

"Now you two, stop that fighting, there's enough war going on in this world," she said out loud.

Just as she was about to put her coffee cup in the sink to be washed later, she heard the doorbell ring.

"Now who could that be at this time of the morning?" she said as she walked through the living and toward the front door. Looking out of the window, she saw an official Army vehicle parked on the street in front of her house. Her heart leaped into her throat and her legs began to give way. There could only be one reason why a military personal would be at her door so early in the morning ... "or any other time," she thought. She heard some one say, "No! No!" and realized it was her own voice she had heard. With trembling hands she was barley able to open the door.

"Mrs. Preston? I'm Captain Mc Graw. I am sorry I have to deliver this bad news. May I come in, Ma'am? I think it is best if you sit down."

Pearl could feel the floor swirling out from under her feet. She felt as if she was going to faint any minute. Her throat so tight that she had a difficult time letting her breath escape from her lungs.

"Mrs. Preston I'm sorry to inform you that your husband, Lieutenant Roy..."

Pearl never heard the last words that the captain had said. She could only remember feeling herself drifting into darkness. When she came to, Captain McGraw was on the telephone calling an ambulance for her.

Chapter Sixteen: Ten Plus One Equals A Full House?

It had been six years since Gladys; Landis's wife had passed away. Her opinion of the club had never wavered, even during her illness of cancer. Landis had brought it up several times over the years, but her stern look always caused him to drop the subject as soon as he brought it up. He loved his wife and cared for her during her illness, but there were times when he wished he could get away for a little while and just spend time with his friends, especially Ardon. He often wondered what was going on at the meetings and sometimes, when he was out of hearing range of Gladys, he would ask Ardon about their latest event. He would laugh and say, "You people sure know how to throw a party alright." All the time wishing he was there having fun too.

Landis was sitting reading his morning paper as he did every morning since Gladys's death. The headlines and reports of yet another war did not cheer him up in the least bit.

"I have to do something besides sit here day after day, all by myself reading this stupid paper and reading about more depressing news than one man should have to read," he told himself. "There is nothing I can do about it anyway, so why do I care if those people want to do themselves in with all that fighting? I'm too old to go help them fight, so I just sit here getting more and more depressed by the day. I need to find something to occupy my time. Maybe I'll just call Ardon and see how that club of his is going. I don't want to anger Gladys, rest her poor soul, but I just might consider joining that bunch of nuts. I know I'm a few years behind in the dues, but I have a little money stashed away. I can probably afford to let go of some of it, I guess," he said as he put his newspaper down on the floor. Reaching for the telephone, he dialed Ardon's number. "Forgive me Gladys, but a man has to do something with his days," he said looking up toward the ceiling.

"Ardon Steris, here."
"Hello, Ardon, this is Landis. I have a question. Is it too late to join that club of yours?"
"Why, no, Landis. Why, are you considering joining us?"
"Well, if it's not too late and if I can get caught up with the dues. I wouldn't want to miss out on getting all of the inheritance because some guy joined late and owed back dues," he laughed.
"Well, in that case, I see no reason you can't join. Are you sure Gladys isn't going to come back and give you the what for?" Ardon teased.
"I thought about that. I'll just have to tell her that it's time I made my own decisions, that's all," Landis teased back.

Landis went to the bank and got enough money out of his savings account to pay his dues and enough to pay for a round of drinks for everyone at the first meeting he attended in his honor of being the eleventh and last member to join The Six Hundred Thousand Dollar Club.

He had had so much fun at the first meeting that he had forgotten all about his deceased wife and her opinion of the club. When he got home that night, he sat down on the edge of his bed and took off his shoes and socks. He glanced across the room to where the gold-framed photo of Gladys sat on the dresser.

"Sorry, Gladys. I think you were wrong. This is the most entertaining club a fellow could ever join. I am an official member of The Six Hundred Thousand Dollar Club, with or without your blessing."

Chapter Seventeen: Nineteen Seventy-One... The Accident

Beth Marie had talked her dad into buying her a horse for her sixteenth birthday. She and her mother both had become very good riders after many riding lessons over the past year. They both took turns riding Misty everyday. Usually Beth Marie would ride when she came home from school and Verina would ride Misty in the morning before she would meet with her bridge club or some of the women of the Six Hundred Thousand Dollar Club to go over the next club event. At first, Verina thought it was a bad idea to give Beth Marie a horse, since she would be going off to college in a couple of years. But today, Verina was glad she had something to do that was both fun and good exercise. She had come to appreciate the fact that she had become such an expert rider and felt proud to show off for her friends when they came by to visit during her riding time. Sometimes she would even extend her time riding Misty, knowing the bridge club girls would be arriving any minute and see in her riding outfit, prancing around in the corral atop Misty. "Oh, hello girls. I guess I didn't realize it was this late," she would say as she waved her gloved hand at the women. "I'll just be a minute. I need to unsaddle and brush down Misty. I'll be right in. You girls can go ahead and set up the table, if you want. The refreshments are on the kitchen table." The women always waved and went into the house. They knew the routine well enough by now.

"She thinks we don't know that she is just showing off," said Bibi. "She does the same thing almost every week. I say, let's change the time of the bridge game to the afternoon. Then we will see if she's still on her high horse when we get here."

Every one laughed at Bibi's unintended pun.

"That is a good one, Bibi," said Pearl. "You always seem to come up with something that makes me laugh. Now, let's see what kind of goodies Verina has prepared for our snack today. I hope it's something with chocolate." After Roy's death, Pearl had given up on her diet. She didn't care if she gained a few extra pounds now. "What does it matter, if I don't have anyone to impress? I may as well enjoy life. Bring on the chocolate! I say."

On Monday, Verina was about to finish up her morning ride when she noticed that she must have left the corral gate open. She rode Misty toward the gate. "I may as well ride you through the gate toward the barn," she whispered in Misty's ear. Just as she cleared the gate, she thought she heard the telephone ringing in the kitchen. She gave Misty a little kick in the side with the heel of her riding boot. Misty gave a jump and started to rush through the gate. Verina could feel the stirrup catch on the latch of the gatepost, pulling her leg backwards, twisting it as the horse continued to rush out of the corral. Verina was holding onto the reins as tight as she could, but the searing pain in her leg caused her to let go. As she fell to the ground she could feel the snapping of vertebrae in her back. Suddenly, she couldn't feel any pain in her leg or her back. She reached out to touch her leg, but felt nothing. She touched her other leg with both of her trembling hands…nothing. She could hear the phone still ringing through the kitchen window. She wished she could crawl to it, but her legs would not move. Terror had begun to take over where the pain had left her body. She began to shiver. "I feel so cold," she said, "I need to get to the phone." She could feel tears running down her face.

"Please, someone help me," she heard herself yell, but she knew there was no one to hear her cries for help.

Verina lay on the ground for hours, hoping someone would stop by to visit. "It will be four o'clock before Beth Marie even gets out of school. Please, someone. Please come find me." She was amazed that she had not gone into shock. She wished she could feel some of the pain that she knew she should be experiencing. "If only I could feel something," she whimpered. "I would rather feel the pain than lie here paralyzed with no one to help me."

It was almost getting dark when she heard Ardon's car in the driveway. Beth Marie had apparently had after school French Club and then probably had gone over to a friend's house to do homework after the club ended. "At last someone's home," she heard herself say. She began to scream for Ardon to come find her.

"Ardon! Help! Ardon! I'm here in the corral! Help! Help!" she shouted through her tears. "Please! Ardon! Help me!"

Ardon thought he had heard shouting as he got out of his car. "What could that be? Did I just hear someone shouting for help? It almost sounded like Verina, only … there, I heard it again," he said. "Verina, is that you?" he said as he ran toward the direction that he thought he had heard the shouts. "Oh, my God! What happened, Verina, are you alright?" he asked as he reached her. Kneeling down beside her he could see that she was crying.

"I can't move. I can't feel my legs, Ardon. Please help me," she begged.

"Ok, just don't try to move," he replied. "I'll get help." He ran to the house to call an ambulance. On his way out the door he remembered to grab a blanket from the linen closet and rushed back to the corral to do what ever he could to help Verina. He was afraid to try to move her. He didn't want to injure her any more than she was already.

"No, it was best to wait for the professionals to take care of moving her. I just hope they get here soon," he said to himself. "How long have you been out here on the ground?"

"I was riding Misty this morning and I noticed the gate was opened and since I was done ridding anyway, I started to ride her through the open gate when my foot got caught on the latch as I went by. For some reason, Misty spooked and started to run. I couldn't get my foot loose and I was pulled to the ground. I felt something snap when I hit the ground. I couldn't get up. Ardon, I can't even feel my legs. I should be in a lot of pain, but I can't feel anything. I'm so scared." She began to sob again. "I'm so scared."

"You mean you've been lying out here on the ground since this morning?"

"Yes. I don't know where Misty ran too. I think I heard her near the barn."

"Don't even think about that right now. I'll go round her up after the ambulance gets here. Here, let me cover you up with this. Just don't try to move. Can I get you some water? You must be thirsty."

Verina nodded as Ardon ran to the house to get a glass of water for her. When he returned, he could hear sirens coming down the street.

Everyone from the club was waiting with Ardon in the waiting room of the hospital. Verina was still in surgery. Ardon walked the floor nervously while everyone else sat with hands in their laps and eyes looking toward the floor.

"I shouldn't have made that remark about her showing off," said Bibi. "I wish I could take it back." Tears started to push their way over the rims of her eyes.

Pearl reached over and patted her on the hand. "It's OK, Bibi. We all say things that we wished we could take back at some time in our lives."

When the surgeon appeared at the doorway of the waiting room, everyone jumped up and ran toward him hoping he had good news.

"Mr. Steris, may I speak to you alone for a minute, please?" he said as he guided Ardon toward a small room to the left of the waiting room.

"The surgery took a little longer than expected. I'm afraid that we did all we could, but it appears that it didn't do a lot of good. Two of the vertebrae were damaged beyond repair. Unless we receive a miracle, your wife is going to be confined to a wheelchair for the rest of her life. I'm sorry."

Ardon was stunned. He couldn't speak. "How could this happen to us? How am I going to tell Verina that she is never going to walk again?"

Chapter Eighteen: The Mystery Begins

Verina had spent so many years in her wheelchair, that she was able to manipulate it even on the dance floor at the yearly spring dinner dance. "Being confined to this contraption is not going to slow me down one bit," she told the ladies at the review meeting after the spring event. It was customary now to meet after of each major event to go over the results.

"This way we can plan to do better next time and either add or subtract things that just don't work well," Doralene had said after one of their events was not as successful as they had hoped. "I think the Santa Claus was a little too much for folks our age. I did not enjoy being forced to sit on some fat stranger's lap," she had remarked. "And that red suit was so dirty, I could smell the body odor on it, not to mention the stale cigarette smoke smell."

Verina had not returned to be the Social Chairman after her riding accident. Nellie was elected to take her place, even though she had been to a heart specialist that told her she needed to take it easy and not get too tired or excited. He had given her medication that he said would relieve any stress to her heart. The medicine seemed to help and she had experienced only a couple of incidents that she could actually feel when her heart began beating a little fast.

Verina was beginning to miss being in charge of the events and was hoping she would be elected again at the next meeting.

"And all in favor of Nellie Wheeler to continue to be the Social Committee Chairwoman, please signify by raising your hand," said Hazel. "OK, then, it looks like Nellie you have the position for at least another year. Congratulations."

From not even being nominated, Verina could feel the hurt, but she smiled and gave Nellie a congratulatory hug. She decided to invite Nellie over for lunch one afternoon, just to let her know that she was supportive of her and the great job she was doing for the club. She planned to have a light lunch.

"I think a salad and little tuna and egg salad sandwiches would be nice. That won't take much effort and it would still be elegant if I put them on one of my fancy little crystal platters. Maybe I'll make my Rhubarb pie for dessert."

"Everything was just delicious, Verina. Thank you for inviting me. I was thinking that maybe I should have nominated you to be the Social Chairwoman again. Are you missing it?"

"Well, I did enjoy doing the job, but don't worry, I'll get my chance again. We never know what may happen by this time next year, do we?"

Two days later, Nellie was doing her weekly grocery shopping at the new market near her house. She suddenly felt dizzy and she could feel heaviness in her chest. She could feel herself sliding to the floor. She tried to grab the shopping cart, but it moved forward with her weight.

"Help, help me. Please, someone help me," she heard herself whispering.

By the time the ambulance arrived, Nellie was already turning gray and her flesh was as cold as ice. The medical assistant shook his head and pronounced her dead on arrival. The doctor at the hospital confirmed what the medical assistant had suggested...her heart had given out. Nellie Wheeler had had a heart attack right in the middle of the new grocery market.

"So...they think Miss Nellie had a respiratory problem, did they? Well they are right...she did, thanks to my little bit of help. If that stupid, incompetent medical assistant had checked her condition better or if that just as stupid doctor at the hospital had done his job, they would have known what caused her wee little heart to give out. Oh, well, one less person to have to worry about getting that six hundred thousand dollars in the end, thanks to me. Only nine more to go...permanently, that is."

Chapter Nineteen: The Break Up

Things were beginning to get back to normal after Nellie's heart attack. It took Owen some time before he could even attend the weekly meetings. After much encouragement and prodding, he finally agreed it was time to get his life back in order. His dream of Nellie and himself being the lucky couple to wind up with the six hundred thousand dollars was not to be. Nellie was gone and he was alone…except for his friends at the club, he had no one left to spend the rest of his life with. "I guess that's better than nothing," he told himself. "At least I have my club friends left…for now anyway."

Things were not going so well for other members of the club either. Verina was beginning to get grouchy and demanding. Ardon was beginning to lose patience with her demands. Bibi was beginning to get on everyone's nerves because of her constant chatter and her continuous questioning about when the club was ever going to get eligible men as she had been promised. She was reminded that there were two illegible men already in the club with both Landis' and Owens's wives deceased. Both men objected to the suggestion that was implied.

Fredrick's real estate business was taking a drop in profits. He was not selling as many homes as he had hoped. He and Doralene were having financial difficulties because of it. He seemed to spend more and more time at his office, saying that it was necessary to be there just in case a prospective client came in.

"OK. I'll meet you tonight at say, seven thirty? OK. See you then," he said as he hung up the telephone.

"Who were you talking to, Fredrick?" asked Doralene as she walked into the living room. "Did I hear you say you are going out again tonight? Don't any of your clients look at houses during the day any more? This is the fourth time in the last week that you have met clients after your normal office hours."

"Well, if I want to make sales, I have to do what the client wants...even if it means meeting them after hours. I may be late, so don't wait up for me."

After three more weeks of Fredrick's after hour meetings, Doralene was beginning to get suspicious. "I can't believe he is meeting this many clients in the evening and not getting home until the wee hours of the morning and not selling a single house," she said. "I'm beginning to wonder if he is even meeting clients. I have never heard of any other real estate broker spending this much time with clients." She wanted to believe that her husband was faithful, but her doubts were taking over. The more she thought about it, the more she became convinced that Fredrick was having an affair. She wanted to be fair and give him a chance to explain himself, but she was not willing to sit home every night while her husband had his *little sweetie*, whoever she was.

The Six Hundred Thousand Dollar Club 133

"I *will* get to the bottom of this when he gets home tonight," she said. "He had better have positive proof that he was working or his butt is out the door."

When Fredrick came home, he went directly to the bathroom to take a shower. Doralene followed him into the bathroom, as he was getting ready to get undressed.

"You are taking a shower before dinner?" she asked.

"Yes. Oh, and I won't have time for dinner. I have to meet a client in half an hour. Would you mind setting out my gray suit and light blue tie?"

"No! I will not set out you gray suit or your green suit or your any other color suit! I want to know where you are going and who it is that you need to meet at this hour? I don't want any of your bull about meeting clients. I know it's a lie and I want you to tell me the truth, now!" She could feel her throat tightening and tears burning her eyes. She wanted to hear the truth, but she was afraid of what she knew she was about to be told.

"I...I...what are you talking about, Doralene? You know I have to work to keep my job. I can't just drop clients because my wife wants me to be home for dinner, can I?"

"You know you are not meeting clients...and I know you are meeting some young thing for dinner and an evening of ...who knows what...of course you know. You planned it. I want answers and I want them now, Fredrick!" she screamed.

"Ok! OK! I am meeting someone tonight. I'm sorry, Doralene. I guess I've been under so much stress, that I've let my emotions get in the way of my thinking."

"And just how long has this been going on? Quite some time apparently, seeing how you have been leaving and not coming home at night for, let's see...at least a month now? I'll tell you what Fredrick, you get your shower, take your... what ever color suit you decide on and get your butt out of this house. You might want to take any of your other valuable items with you too, because you won't be coming back here. The next time you see me it will be in divorce court. Good-bye, Fredrick. Have a wonderful evening with your *Client!*"

Six months later Doralene was sitting in the courtroom. She saw Fredrick walk in with his new fling on his arm.
"He probably only brought her to aggravate me," thought Doralene. "How low can a person go?" She had truly loved Fredrick and thought about their many years as husband and wife. "How could he do this to me?"
"The divorce was official in just ten minutes. All those years and it only took ten minutes to end it all," Doralene cried as she drove home to her empty house.

Fredrick dropped his membership from the club a month after his divorce was final. He was having a hard time just keeping up with the alimony payments that the judge said he had to send to Doralene on the first of every month.
"All that money going down the toilet," he said. "All those years of paying dues, just so someone else reaps the benefits. What a mistake that was," he said. "I knew I should never have joined that stupid club." He never once mentioned the fact that his biggest mistake was cheating on Doralene.

"Way to go Fredrick. You just made things a bit easier for me. One less person to have to figure out how to escort out of this world, leaving that six hundred thousand dollars behind. I hope you and your new girlfriend have a very happy life together. Thank you for making my retirement a little better. Only eight more to go."

Chapter Twenty: Affair Number Two?

Meeno Max had been hired by Ardon as a driver to chauffeur Vernia to do her shopping or any place she wished to go during the day when he was not available. He had been out of work and needed a job that would pay for his cigarettes and his occasional beer. Ardon had told him that he could use the guesthouse, which had been the barn before Ardon sold Misty because of Verina's accident and because Beth Marie had gone off to college and found some young "prince charming" to marry. The apartment, as Meeno referred to it, was going to be part of his pay. Ardon had told him it would be good for both of them because he would have a place to live and he would be close so that Verina could call him when she needed to go somewhere at the last minute. Meeno thought it would be an easy job and he would be getting paid for just sitting around most of the time.

"Will I have a television in the guesthouse?" Meeno asked. "And will I get days off and vacation pay?" He figured he might as well get as many perks as he could. "How hard can it be to drive an old lady around?"

He soon discovered that Verina would keep him busier than he had expected. Besides her regular weekly shopping trips, she demanded that he take her to the hairdresser's once a week, to the library every two weeks and to the movies every time a new movie came out. He had to wait in the car until she was ready to return home or go somewhere else on her way home. He didn't mind dragging her wheelchair in and out of the trunk of the car, but he was beginning to hate the long waits and her constant complaining about his driving or the smell of the cigarette smoke on his cloths. He decided it was best if he only smoked when he was in his apartment or if she was going to be extra long on one of her trips, so that he had time for the smell to get out of his clothes before she got into the car.

With Meeno driving Verina, Ardon found he had more time to himself. He was glad that he wasn't the one to have to wait for her on her trips.

"Yes, hiring Meeno was a good idea," he told himself. "A very good idea indeed."

Meeno had been working for the Strerises for over three years. The novelty of the job was beginning to wear off. Verina was beginning to get on his nerves and Ardon had become as demanding as Verina. It seem as though he had become a babysitter rather than just a driver for Verina. When Verina needed company, he was beckoned to come sit with her and listen to endless lists of complaints about the club members or the downfalls of her husband. He tried to let it go in one ear and out the other as the saying goes.

"I do not want to get involved in the gossip about a bunch of crazy old coots from some club or come between Verina and her husband. I just want to drive their fancy car and get my pay on Fridays," he told himself. "This was not part of the deal when I was hired," he said to himself. "I am a chauffeur, not a nanny."

Verina had come down with a bad cold and had decided to stay in bed. She missed two of the weekly meetings. Ardon told her to call Meeno if she needed anything.

"I may be late tonight. I want to go over the plans for next month's activities with Doralene, Hazel, Pearl and Bibi after the main meeting. You get some rest and I will see you in the morning," he told Verina.

She heard Ardon come in at one-thirty in the morning. He thought she was asleep, so he didn't say anything, but quietly got into bed.

"Where were you last night? I heard you come in at one-thirty. Why did your meeting last that long?"

"Well, a couple of us went out for coffee after we met about the activities for next month."

"Why didn't you just have coffee at the Red Carpet Cuisine after your meeting?"

"We felt we needed to get away from our meeting place and relax at a different location, that's all. Do you have a problem with that?"

"No, I guess not. It just seems strange, that's all…to leave one restaurant to go to another, I mean. So what did you all decide about the plans? Anything I should get involved in?"

"We didn't get everything settled yet. We might have to meet again to go over a few things. No, I don't think you need to do anything. You just need to get some rest and get rid of your cold."

Later that day, after Ardon had gone out, Verina couldn't stand not knowing what went on at the meeting. It was bad enough to not be able to go, but to not be included in the plans was more than she could take.

Ardon didn't seem to want to share information with her, so she planned to find out on her own. "I'll call Bibi. She will fill me in on the plans, I'm sure."

"Hello, Bibi, this is Verina. How are you? I bet you are pretty tired after being out so late with the meeting last night aren't you?"

"Hello, Verina. Are you feeling better? Yes, I am a bit tired, but I usually don't get to bed until around nine o'clock anyway. After the meeting last night, I did come home and watch some television until nine-thirty, though."

"You got home by nine-thirty? Then you didn't go for coffee after the regular meeting with Ardon and the other girls?"

"No, did he go out for coffee with the others? I didn't know that. Hmm... I thought everyone left to go home when I did. Who went with him?"

"I don't know. I thought you all did. I guess that was an assumption on my part. Sorry you weren't invited Bibi. Was there anything discussed at the meeting that I should be aware of? Do I need to do anything?"

"No, not particularly. I think we have everything all set up. We planned to have a spaghetti dinner in about two months. We have the menu and everything all planed out. We didn't assign anything to you, because we weren't sure how you would feel. Ardon said you weren't feeling too well and he didn't know when you would be feeling better. We know you will always be willing to step in and help if need be, anyway."

"So... you already have everything all taken care of, you say?"

"Yes, pretty much."

When Ardon came home, Verina had a few questions for him. "I talked to Bibi this morning. She said she didn't go to with you to have coffee after the meeting last night."

"No, I guess she didn't. I guess I forgot that she said she was going home."

"She also said that everything was all planned out for the spaghetti dinner you plan to have in a couple of months. I thought you said that there was still planning to do."

"You know Bibi, she never gets things right. She was probably talking while we were discussing it and so she thought because she was through listening, that everyone else was through, too," he said with a snicker. "What else did she say?"

"Nothing else. Just that if you all needed anything else to be done that I would be included, that's all." Verina could feel she was becoming less and less important to the club. "After all I've done for the club, too," she thought. "Now they want to leave me out of everything. It's probably because I'm confined to this stupid wheelchair. They think I can't handle being in charge of anything any more. Well, I'll show them. I refuse to be treated like a helpless invalid."

Ardon had scheduled after meeting meetings with the women to do more planning.

Verina didn't seem to be able to get rid of the bug she had. She was getting out of bed, but didn't go out of the house at all. She declined when Ardon's suggestion that she ask Meeno to take her for a ride just to get out of the house. "No, I think I will just sit here and read today," she had replied. "Maybe I'll ask him to take me down to the library tomorrow. I do need to pick up some new books to read. I've finished all the ones I had borrowed."

"I'll be late again tonight. I want to meet with the women about finishing up the final details for the spaghetti dinner."

"Can't you do that at the regular meeting? We always completed all of our business at the meetings. I don't see why you need a special meeting with only the social committee."

"I just don't want to hold everyone else up, when it's the social committee that is involved."

"I suppose you plan to go out for coffee again after that?"

"Well, I might. Do you mind? I'll tell Meeno to keep an eye on you in case you need anything."

"I don't need anyone to keep an eye on me! I am perfectly capable of taking care of myself, thank you!"

"OK! OK! I didn't mean to upset you. I just want to be sure you are comfortable and have everything you need while I'm out."

Ardon didn't get in until after midnight again. "I think it's time that I do a little checking up on these after meeting meetings that Ardon seems to think he needs to have all of a sudden," thought Verina as she turned over to let Ardon have more room in the bed.

Verina decided to call Pearl this time.

"So... Pearl did you go to have coffee with Ardon and the rest of the women last night after your planning meeting?"

"What meeting? Did I mess a meeting? I didn't know we had one planned for last night. Sorry if I missed it," said Pearl.

"You didn't go to the meeting? Hmm…. Ardon implied that you all were there. Maybe he meant just Bibi, Doralene and Hazel. I wonder why he didn't tell you about it."

"I don't know. But…Bibi didn't go to a meeting either. She and I went to a movie last night. Maybe she didn't hear about it either."

After hanging up with Pearl, Verina decided to call Hazel, just to see what she had to say about the meeting with Ardon and Doralene and herself.

"No… I didn't know we had a meeting. Did everyone else go?" said Hazel

"Apparently not," said Verina. "It seems as though it may have been a private meeting. I'll talk to you later. Oh, do you mind not saying anything to Ardon or the rest of the group about what I called about? I think I need to have a little talk with Mr. Steris when he gets home."

Verina decided not to say anything to Ardon, but to do a little snooping into these private meetings. Maybe she would need to ask Meeno to take her for a little ride after all.

Ardon continued to have his meetings. Sometimes he would call a meeting between the regular meetings. Verina gave up checking with the other women about what had happened and who had attended. She was beginning to feel more ill by the day. Not from the bug she had, but because she had a feeling down deep in the pit of her stomach that these meetings were attended by invitation only…and the other club members were not invited. She missed so many meetings that she began to feel as if she was no longer part of the club. But she had paid her annual dues, so she was still a member, whether she was able to attend or not. She began missing the meetings on purpose, just so she could question Ardon about them. Finally she had an idea that she thought would give her more answers to the puzzle. It seemed that all of the women were going directly home after the regular meeting and knew nothing about any extra meetings between...all except Doralene.

After checking with the others about the meeting that Ardon had had last night and finding out that no one seemed to know about that meeting either, she decided to make one more call.

"Hello, Doralene, this is Verina. I was just wondering how the meeting was last night? Did everything get settled about the dinner dance coming up?"

"Oh, yes. It...it...did. We worked till the wee hours of the morning, because we wanted to get everything settled so we could... start working on the next event after that one."

"OK, then. I was just wondering if there is anything I can do to help."

"Well, I think everything is under way, but you might ask Ardon when he comes home from work tonight."

"Oh, I'll ask him ...alright," thought Verina. "Since she is the only one who attended this little meeting, I'm sure she and Ardon got a lot done...a lot done indeed."

"Meeno, do you know where Mr. Steris has been holding his meetings lately?"

"No Mrs. Steris. All I know is that he told me to make sure you have everything you need here at the house and that I shouldn't drive you anywhere after eight o'clock. I guess he doesn't want you to have a relapse in health," he lied. He knew Ardon was doing something other than going to club meetings. He remembered that Ardon had slipped by saying not to drive Verina anywhere by...and then he didn't finish his sentence.

"I know something is going on. Maybe if I play my cards right, I can get a little extra bonus from Mr. Steris by keeping my mouth shut," he thought. "If not, I can probably get a little extra from Mrs. Steris for opening my mouth. Either way, I think I have a nice little bonus in my future."

Verina kept her suspitions to herself. She would deal with Ardon and Doralene later, in her own way. For now she intended to start going to the regular meetings and she was going to be sure that she was back on the social committee from now on. Any extra meetings were to be had, she would be the first in line to attend.

Chapter Twenty-one: And Then There Were Eight

Verina gave up her quest to catch Ardon in his extra meeting rendezvous. He began doing more of the business of the club during the regular weekly meetings. He only went out a few times a week, saying that he needed some fresh air and maybe a little conversation with his buddies at the neighborhood bar. He had not spent much time at the bar until lately. Though Meeno had taken some of the burden of caring for Verina, she was still a demanding woman that seemed to be more moody than usual lately.

Verina wasn't sure she could believe Ardon when he said he was going to the bar, but she was not going to follow him around like a jealous wife. She had other things on her mind right now. The club was her main concern.

"If Ardon wants to have his little fling, let him," she said to herself. "It is getting harder and harder to sit quietly by at the meetings while I know my husband and Doralene are having their own little meetings, but I'm not going to make myself sick worrying about it now. After all, if I don't stay healthy, what chance do I have of out living the other members and getting all that I have invested?" she asked herself.

Meeno had witnessed Ardon and Doralene coming out of The Silver Slipper Nightclub several times in the past few weeks. Once he thought Ardon had spotted him watching them as they walked to Ardon's car. "If so, it might make it easier for me to squeeze a little cash out of him, since he knows I have information that his wife might be interested in. I'll just wait and see if he brings it up. If not, then I'll keep an eye out for anything else that I might be able to add to the fire," said, Meeno to himself. "The more I have, the more profitable it could become."

Ardon said nothing about being seen with Doralene, so Meeno decided to drop a few hints. When he was waiting for Ardon to write out his paycheck for the week's work, Meeno thought this might be a good time to mention the Silver Slipper.

"Thank you, Mr. Steris," he said as Ardon handed him the check. "I've heard that they have good food at the Silver Slipper Nightclub. Have you ever eaten dinner there?"

"No...I haven't. Why do you ask?" Ardon said slowly.

"Well, I just thought I might take a lady friend there one of these nights. I've heard they have a good band and dance floor. You know how women seem to like good bands and good dance floors," he said grinning. He could tell Ardon was becoming nervous by the way he began to fidget and look away. Apparently Ardon had not seen him watching as they exited the nightclub. "This is not only going to be profitable but I think it is going to be enjoyable as well." He decided he was entitled to a little enjoyment for all the humiliating things he had had to do for the Sterises over the past few years. Sitting for hours waiting for Verina. Sitting with her when Ardon wasn't home. Even toting that wheelchair in and out of the car was beginning to get aggravating, especially when Verina shouted at him to not scratch her Lincoln Town Car or to be sure he wiped the wheels of the wheelchair before putting it in the trunk so the carpet would not get dirty. He was getting tired of both of these rich old biddies anyway. "Maybe I should just stuff her in the trunk of her precious Lincoln Town Car. Let her lick the dirt off of her own wheelchair wheels," he said.

Meeno sat in his car in the shadows near the Silver Slipper Nightclub several nights when Ardon went out in the evening without Verina. "Hmm… Ardon must have decided it was safer to find a new rendezvous location for himself and his mistress. I guess I'll have to do a little snooping to find out where this new place is. At least he took the hint that I knew something that he definitely did not want me to know. I can't believe that he would think that it was just a coincidence that I was asking about the Silver Slipper Nightclub."

It didn't take long for Meeno to find Ardon's new date location. He was about to enter Ardon's home office to empty out the wastebasket, another one of his new duties assigned to him by Verina, when he heard Ardon on the telephone. "OK, then I'll pick you up at eight o'clock down by the groves. We can go to the Purple Orchid for dinner and then we can see what happens after that, ok? I love you, too. See you at eight." he heard Ardon say.
"Wow! This is going to be good," said Meeno as he slipped back away from the door. "I'll see you at eight, Mr. Steris," he said. "Yes sir, at eight it is."

After making sure Verina was all set for the evening, Meeno told her that he would like to go out for a while if he wasn't needed. Verina said she would be fine and to go ahead and enjoy his evening. "Thank you, Mrs. Steris. I will. I definitely will enjoy my evening, that's for sure."

Just as he had expected, Meeno watched Ardon and Doralene going into the Purple Orchid arm in arm. They were too busy laughing to notice him in the shadows near by. He waited until ten thirty when at last they emerged from the club. They got into Ardon's car and drove to a nearby motel. "Oh, this is getting better and better," thought Meeno. "I'm sure I can take advantage of tonight's little rendezvous. I need to find a subtle way to work this into a conversation so that Ardon knows I know. If nothing else, I can just come right out with it and see what his reaction is. The worst thing that can happen is he will fire me, but then who will he get to babysit his wife while he is out entertaining his lady friend?" Meeno said to himself. "Meeno, ol' buddy, this could be your lucky night."

The next opportunity that Meeno had to talk with Ardon, he was sure he was going to find a way to bring up the Purple Orchid and maybe even if he really got brave, to bring up the name of the motel that hehad followed Ardon and Doralene to. "If I don't get any reaction from Ardon… them maybe it is time to see what Verina can do for my finances. I'm almost certain she will be willing to pay for some juicy information about where her dear husband has been spending his evenings. I just have to figure out a way to bring it up so that I get a little something for my effort," he said.

Meeno was out in the circular driveway, polishing the Lincoln, when Ardon stopped to ask him if he would take Mrs. Steris for her weekly hair appointment and then bring her home and keep her company until it was her bedtime.

"I have an appointment this evening and will be home late. Please see that Mrs. Steris gets her evening tea and make sure she is in bed by nine-thirty. If she doesn't get her full nights' sleep she will be a real bear in the morning. Don't forget to lock the door before you leave," Ardon told Meeno.

"Yes sir, Mr. Steris. Oh, Mr. Steris, do you mind if I take the Lincoln out tonight after Mrs. Steris goes to bed. I have a date and my old beat up Ford is not the kind of transportation my girl would like to be seen in at the Purple Orchid." He hoped Ardon would take the bait.

"The Purple Orchid? You are going to the Purple Orchid? It seems like…" Ardon stopped himself from saying, "you are going to the same places that I go a lot lately", but stopped himself before he incriminated himself. "…like you have a lot of dates lately, Meeno," he said instead.

"Yes sir. I have been seeing this lady on a regular basis lately. Nothing serious. We just like to go out and have some fun, that's all. By fun I don't mean going to some sleazy motel or anything. We usually go have something to eat, a few drinks and do a lot of talking." He tried again to get some reaction from Ardon. So far, it was not working.

"I know Meeno knows something," thought Ardon. There is no way he just happens to be interested in the exact same places to take his so called date that Doralene and I go. He thinks I don't know that he is dropping hints. I don't know how he found out about us, but I am sure he knows. I just hope he doesn't plan to tell Verina everything. I'm afraid she would not take too kindly of having her husband and her friend being secret lovers. If Meeno keeps asking questions, I may have to do something to keep his mouth shut. Firing him will never do because he could still blab everything to Verina. I will probably have to pay him off. And I imagine he won't accept any small change. No, he is going to take me for as big of a blackmail pay off as possible. For now, though, I don't plan to do anything. I think I will just wait and see what he says next before I bring up the subject. I can play this cat and mouse game too. Yes, I'll just wait until the mouse gets a little closer before the cat jumps on its tail. Mr. Meeno Max, you are not as smart as you think you are."

Ardon and Doralene had another date that evening. Ardon planned to pick her up at eight. They decided they would go to a new restaurant just outside the city limits, just in case Meeno decided he wanted to follow them. Ardon planned to check the odometer before he left to pick up Doralene and then he would check it again the next morning, so he would be able to tell how far Meeno had driven the Lincoln. If it showed the same mileage as he and Doralene had driven, he would know for certain that Meeno had been following them.

Verina was having an early dinner alone since Ardon had announced that he had a meeting and would not be having dinner with her tonight. Verina was sure that he was having dinner with someone other than the regular club members, since she had called all of them to find out if there were any meetings scheduled for the next few days. All had said that only the regular meeting was on the schedule and they thought she already knew about that one...every one except Doralene that is. She said that Aardon had called a special meeting, but he had told her that he thought that Verina would rather stay home and retire early since she had not been feeling too well and that he didn't want her to have a relapse of her previous illness.

"So… He has called a little private meeting has he? He must believe that old saying about the wife is always the last to know. Well, this wife already knows and I don't care who else knows before me. It's the fact that I know that counts."

"Where are you going, dear?" asked Verina.

"I called a special meeting with some of the club members to discuss the plans for a bar-b-q we would like to have in a couple of weeks. I didn't say anything to you, because it is mostly the men that are planning it this time. And besides, I thought you needed your rest. We wouldn't want you to have a relapse. I'll pick up something on the way to eat, probably something from a fast food joint. Don't wait up. You know how these meetings are some times. You never know how long they will last."

"OK, dear. Oh, but before you go will you taste this salad for me and tell me if you think it has enough dressing on it? If you are not going to be here for dinner, I thought I might ask Meeno to join me. I know he likes salad, but the last time I put too much oil and vinegar and my salad tasted terrible. Since I had that bug, I don't seem to be able to smell or taste anything. I would be very embarrassed if I fed Meeno a salad that tasted like an oil slick or was floating in vinegar." She held out a fork full of salad for Ardon to taste. "Well? she said. "What do you think…more oil? More vinegar?"

"Um, I guess it's alright."

"No, don't guess. Here taste it again," she said as she offered him another fork full.

"Yes. It's just right. Not too much oil or too much vinegar. You make a lovely salad dear," he said.

"Thank you, dear. You have a good meeting. Drive carefully."

"OK. I will. Try to get to bed early. You need your sleep."

Ardon picked up Doralene as planned. They were headed south toward the edge of town. Ardon kept his eyes on the road but also glancing into the rear view mirror just in case they were being followed. He didn't see anything that looked like his Lincoln Town Car. "Of course, Meeno is probably sitting in the dinning room feasting on Verina's salad and listening to her constant complaining right now, so he probably won't be following too closely," thought Ardon. He seemed to feel a little nervous tonight for some reason. Was it the fact that he knew Meeno knew about his secret rendezvous with Doralene or was it because he knew he was going to have to confront him about what he was going to have to pay him as hush money? Either way, it was not going to be a pleasant situation as far as Ardon was concerned.

Ardon began to feel his pulse quickening and he began to feel weak. "I have to stop worrying about this," he told himself. "There is nothing I can do about it right now anyway. I just need to relax and enjoy my evening."

"Are you all right, Ardon?" Doralene asked. "You look as though you don't feel well."

"I'm ok. I guess I'm a little nervous tonight. It seems as though my driver has an idea that we are seeing each other. I'm not sure how he found out, but I'm pretty sure he knows."

"Oh, no! What are we going to do, Ardon? What if he tells Verina?" Doralene said as she turned in her seat to look at Ardon. Her hand automatically flew up to her heart.

"At this moment, I'm not sure. I think I may be able to offer Meeno enough money that he will keep his mouth shut. But first I want to be sure he knows. I wouldn't want to open a can of worms that didn't need to be opened."

"Um," groaned Ardon. " I feel a little strange. My muscles are aching but yet my feet are sort of numb."

"Maybe we should forget tonight. If you aren't feeling well, you should go back home and go to bed."

"No, I'll be all right. And besides the only bed I want to go to is one that we will be sharing."

After a few minutes Ardon said, "My legs seem to be falling to sleep. I just hope I can drive the rest of the way."

"Do you want me to drive?"

"No, I'll manage. You just sit back and enjoy the view of that beautiful moon and those beautiful twinkling stars."

Soon Ardon could feel the intense pain in his muscles. He began to get weaker and weaker. He could hardly hold onto the steering wheel. His eyes were becoming blurry as he tried to focus on the road ahead. He rubbed his fist against his eyes to try to clear his vision but it didn't seen to help. It was becoming more and more difficult for him to breath.

"I...I...I...can't...seem...to..." Ardon's mouth seemed to have difficulty moving as he tried to speak. The car began to swerve across the road. His hands lost all feeling as he lost total control of the wheel. He couldn't speak and felt like his body had left him in a dream. His whole body had become paralyzed. He could feel his lungs ache and then he couldn't feel them at all. He fell against the steering wheel as the car sped across the road headed toward a tree. He could hear Doralene scream as the car slammed into the tree. Then blackness. He couldn't see or feel anything as his mind told him he would not be the lucky sole survivor of the six hundred thousand dollars.

Doralene shook him but she knew there was no use to try to wake him. His body was stiff and he had quit breathing. In her panic she drug herself out of the crumpled car and started to stumble toward the dark empty road. She had to get back to town. She couldn't be caught out here with Ardon's body. She couldn't even call for help without everyone knowing about their secret.

"How could you have a heart attack or whatever you had now, Ardon? How could you and leave me stranded on this deserted road alone?" she cried.

Doralene could feel the stones from the dirt road cutting into her toes as they kept getting into her opened toed heels. She was sure she had blood running through her stockings. She shivered as the cold breeze lifted the hem of her skirt. She had not thought to bring a sweater or shawl to put around her shoulders before she left home. She was too anxious to get into the car and head to the restaurant with Ardon. The sound of a wild animal scurrying into a bush along the road made her jump. She moved closer to the edge of the road. "I hope that was just a squirrel," she said to herself. She started to imagine other animals like snakes and mice running along beside her as her walk turned into more of a run. "I hope I didn't leave anything in the car with Ardon's body. That's all I need to have whoever finds him find something that could incriminate me. How would I ever explain how something that belonged to me could possibly end up in Ardon's car next to his body? Ouch!" she said as she stumbled on a large rock and almost lost her balance. "Now I know my toe is bleeding."

She saw the headlights of an oncoming car as it neared the curve of the road just ahead of her. "Should I try to get the attention of the driver? No! No! That would be stupid. If I do that, then how would I explain my being out here on this deserted road at this time of the night? I can't say I was in an accident, because how would I explain why I was in the car with Ardon? No, I'll just try to hide in these bushes until the car passes and hope there are no creeping things already there," she said as she jumped over the embankment, nearly falling as her feet slid on the mud and loose rocks. Catching herself she darted behind a bush and hunkered down low just as the car passed. She waited until she thought the car had plenty of time to get out of sight before she climbed back upon to the road's edge. Rubbing her arms where the bush had scratched her, she tried to shake some of the mud out of the toes of her shoe. The mud on the soles of the heels weighted her feet down and made it difficult to walk. Stopping to rub the bottoms of her shoe along the pavement of the road, she tried to scrape as much of the brown mucky stuff off as she could. She didn't know which was heavier, the mud stuck on her shoes or the secret she held in her heart about leaving Ardon's cold lifeless body back there alone in the dark. If only she could go back and do something, anything to ease the pain she began to feel as she thought about the plans they had talked about for their future. How Ardon had said that Verina would probably be out of the picture soon and then they could begin their future together. "None of that would ever be now. I can't even tell anyone that Ardon is lying back there in a car wrapped around a tree," she thought. "I am so sorry Ardon. I don't know what else to do. I just need to get home."

It was one thirty in the morning when Doralene finally reached her front porch. She held onto the railing as she pulled off her muddy shoes and rubbed her bloody, battered feet. Her stockings were only shreds by now. She would throw them in the fireplace and burn them when she got inside, she thought. She clapped the shoes together to remove any mud that may have survived the long trek.

"Maybe I should just burn them, too. No, I think I better just clean the mud off and make sure there are no stones embedded in them. If I put them in the fireplace, they may leave unburned pieces that someone may question. It would be more logical to have a little mud or stones in a shoe than to explain why I would be burning a perfectly good pair of shoes in my fireplace."

Stripping her stockings off, she went to the fireplace and lit a roaring fire. She tossed the muddy shredded stockings in. She could smell the pungent burning nylon as it melted into tiny black ashes. She watched as each ash drifted upward into a smoky dark cloud. Quickly removing her dusty evening dress, she headed toward the shower. Running the steamy hot water over her body, she could feel the chill from the night all the way to her bones.

"If only I could wash away the horror of this night as easily as I'm washing away this bitter chill," she thought. "I just can't believe that Ardon's body is lying back there when only a few hours ago we were laughing and looking forward to a wonderful evening of romance," she said as her body gave an unexpected shiver.

The warmth of the shower only lasted for a few minutes. Now she was shivering uncontrollably. After drying herself off, she put on a flannel nightgown, hoping it would take away some of the cold. "I hope I don't come down with pneumonia," she said as she climbed into bed, covering herself with a heavy quilt.

"This is going to be a long night, I'm sure," she said as she turned out the lamp on the nightstand.

Every time she closed her eyes, visions of Ardon lying there in the dark made her cry. She got up and went to the bathroom medicine cabinet to see if she could find something to make her go to sleep. Finding a bottle of outdated sleeping pills, she took two as she looked at herself in the mirror. "You have got to pull yourself together, Doralene," she told herself. "There is nothing you can do to help Ardon now. You need to get some sleep so you have a clear head tomorrow in case there are any questions you need to have good answers for. You have to be able to think. Think!" she said as she slowly walked back toward her bed. Pulling the covers over her head she tried to block out all the thoughts of the events of worst night of her life.

Ardon's body was not discovered until nine o'clock the next morning. The sheriff was relieved that he had identification on him, so it was easy to trace his home. "It appears this poor sucker has either had a heart attack and ran off the road and wrapped himself around this tree, or he's had a little too much of the vino tonight and did himself in by the side of the road," said the sheriff to his deputy. "I don't really smell any liquor, so he probably had the big one."

"NO! NO! NO!" screamed Verina when the sheriff told her of Ardon's death. "It can't be. Not my husband! How can I live without him? He's my life!" she shouted. She started to sway forward in her wheelchair as if she was about to faint. The sheriff caught her and held her into the wheelchair until she had recovered from the shock. He went to get her a glass of water. When he returned he asked her if he should call someone to let them know about the tragedy.

"Yes, yes," she said in a whisper. "There is some one you can call for me, thank you sheriff. Would you mind calling Doralene Drake. Her number is right here in this book. She will call the rest of our friends for me."

Just then, Meeno walked into the room. "What's going on, Mrs. Steris? Why is the sheriff here? Has something happened?"

"Oh, yes, Meeno. There has been a terrible accident and Ardon... Ardon has been killed," she wailed and began to sob. "My poor, poor husband. If only he had stayed here with me and had dinner with me last night instead of going to that club meeting...he...he would have been alive," she cried louder. "Oh, Meeno, what am I going to do?"

"I am so sorry, Mrs. Steris. I don't know what to say. I can't believe this happened. Are you sure it was Mr. Steris in the accident?"

"Sorry to say, but yes it was Mr. Steris all right. He had his identification on him. Mrs. Steris, you may want to go down to identify his body, though."

"Oh, how can I? I don't know if I can handle seeing my dear husband lying there on one of those cold tables covered in a white sheet, his poor body all cold and ..." she began to cry again."

"I'll go for you if you want me too, Mrs. Steris. It's the least I can do for you and Mr. Steris. You are like my family," he lied. "If that is all right with the sherrif, that is. Is there any reason I couldn't ID. his body, sheriff?"

"No, I don't see any reason you can't do it if Mrs. Steris says it's all right."

"Oh, Meeno, you are such a dear. I would appreciate it if you would go for me. Just be sure it is Mr. Steris." She began to wail louder than she had before. "I want my Ardon back. I just want my Ardon back," she cried as she rocked back and forth in her wheelchair.

"I'll go to the morgue right now, Mrs. Steris, while the sheriff is here with you. I'll be right back. Do I need anything to show that I am allowed to identify Mr. Steris, sheriff?" he said as he stood to leave.

"No, but if anyone questions you, have them call me here and I will get everything straightened out for you. Thanks for doing this for Mrs. Steris. I'll wait here until you return."

"No problem. I'm glad to do it." As he walked out the door he said to himself, "Thank you, *Mr. Steris*, for ruining my plans to expose your little secret and loosing that little cash I was so hoping to gain from it. Thanks a lot!"

"If you will be all right for a few minutes, Mrs. Steris, I'll make that call to your friend Doralene now," the sheriff said.

"Yes, yes, you do that, sheriff. She will be very upset to hear of Ardon's death, I'm sure."

Doralene was just drifting off to sleep when the phone rang at ten o'clock. "Oh, no. It's beginning already," she thought. "I wish those sleeping pulls had worked last night. I am so tired now that I can hardly remember my name. How am I going to answer questions if I have too? They must have found Ardon's body. I don't really want to answer this. I don't even know if I can speak, much less lie," she said." She reached for the phone next to her bed, thinking it was better to get this over with.

"Hello," she said as she brought the sheets up around her shoulders. The chill from the night before still settled in her body.

"Hello, Mrs. Drake? This is Sheriff Klarner. I'm afraid I have some bad news. A friend of yours was killed in an automobile accident. His wife asked me to call you and let you know. She said that you would call the rest of their friends and let them know, if you don't mind. It was Mr. Ardon Steris that we found along side of the road. Mrs. Steris is taking it pretty hard. She said she doesn't think she would be able to let other people know about her husband, so I asked her who I could call and she named you."

Doralene tried to sound shocked. She had no trouble faking her cries. Real tears flooded from her eyes, as she relived the night before.

"I...I...I...will certainly call everyone," she stammered. "I... I... just can't believe Ardon is gone. Are you sure it was him, sheriff?"

"Yes, pretty sure. It was his I.D. that we found on the body. Mrs. Sterises' driver is going down town to make a positive I.D., but I'm pretty sure it was him. Sorry to put you through all of this, Mrs. Drake, but you are the one that Mrs. Steris said to call."

"It's OK. Sheriff. I don't mind making the calls. Is there anything else I can do for Verina?" she said. "Why did Verina choose me to be the one to make her calls? Of all the people she could have chosen, she just had to choose me. If she only knew I was the last person that should be doing this is me," she thought as she hung up the phone. Dragging herself out of the bed, she went to take another shower. "As if another shower would wash away all of my troubles," she said to herself.

After a quick shower, she dressed and went into the kitchen to make a cup of coffee. She could still feel the cold. "Will this freezing never stop?" she asked herself. Opening the drawer next to the sink, she took out the address book that listed all of the club member's addresses and phone numbers. She looked at each one, trying to decide which one she should call first. She finally decided to just start with the first one in the book. Reaching for a coffee cup, she went over to the coffee pot and poured herself a strong cup of the hot brew. "I think I am definitely going to need this today. I just hope I can get through this without tripping up and giving anything away."

"Hello, Bibi? This is Doralene. I am afraid I have some very bad news. There has been an accident and Ardon was killed," she said as the tears gushed from her eyes. She could feel her chest crushing into her lungs as she tried to choke the words from her throat. "I...I...I'm trying to make the calls to the club members for Verina. The sheriff said she was not able to do it. She is taking this pretty hard. Maybe someone should go over to be with her." "Maybe I should not have said that to Bibi," she thought after it was too late. "I doubt that Bibi will be of any help. With her constant jabbering, Verina will probably be a nervous wreck, as if she isn't already."

The phone was silent for a few minutes before Bibi finally said, " Did you just say Ardon is dead? Please tell me that I heard you wrong."

"Yes, Bibi. They found Ardon in the car. I just can't believe it myself," Doralene said as she began to sob loudly. "I don't know how I can possibly call all of the members and let them know. I can hardly control my emotions as it is," hoping Bibi would volunteer to make the calls for her. She didn't want to the make calls, but she also did not want to be the one to go comfort Verina either. "How am I even supposed to face Verina?"

"How about I call Pearl and Owen and Hazel and maybe one of them can call Landis. Of course Hazel will tell Charles. Do you want to call Fredrick or would you rather someone else call him? I know he would want to know even if he is not part of the club any more."

"Oh, Fredrick," thought Doralene. "I sure do not want to be the one to call him." "Do you mind calling him or having one of the other members call for me, Bibi? I just don't think I can call him, though we get along OK, we still have our differences, especially over the alimony that Fredrick has to pay me. He can sometimes be very sarcastic and today is not the day that I can handle any of his sarcasm."

"Sure, I can call him or I'll ask one of the other members to call him. Maybe it might be better if one of the men call him anyway. By the time I've made all of these calls, I may not be in shape to talk to him either," Bibi said. "I guess that leaves us with one less member to worry about getting all of our money. Too bad it had to be the founder of the club that had to go so soon, though, don't you think?"

"Yes, too bad indeed," replied Doralene.

"Only seven to go. Sorry, Ardon. What a pity. Especially since you were the founder of the Six Hundred Thousand Dollar Club. Now you will never get to see how it all ends. But, I can tell you how it is going to end...I am going to be the final victor, that's how. Thanks to your ingenious idea, I will be a very wealthy person in a little while. The only sad part is that your lovely mistress, Doralene, didn't bang her beautiful head into that tree and die with you. Now

I'll have seven, instead of six, friends to say good- bye to before I get to claim my money."

Chapter Twenty-Two: My Dear Granddaughter

The funeral was a beautiful gathering of friends. Verina was the only relative of Ardon's at the funeral. All of the club members and Fredrick attended as well as neighbors and previous coworkers. Doralene and Verina seemed to be the most affected by the open casket as they walked past and looked down at Ardon's body.

Verina and Meeno were just finishing up breakfast when the telephone rang.

"Shall I get it for you Mrs. Steris?" he asked. By her request, he had started to join Verina for her meals since Ardon's death. Once he was tempted to tell her about what he had witnessed with Ardon and Doralene, but decided it would not help matters and he definitely did not want to upset Verina any more than she was already. The hope of gaining any financial benefits from his knowledge was out of the question now anyway.

"Yes, would you please, Meeno? If it is one of the club members, tell them I'll call them back later. I just don't feel like talking to any of them right now."

"Yes, ma'am. Hello Steris residence," he said.

"Hello. My name is Shana Willow. I am trying to find my grandmother, Verina Steris. I don't know if this is the correct Steris residence that I am calling, but I was hoping that it is. I have just arrived here this morning from San

Diego and was hoping to make contact with her. My mother had said that she lived in this vicinity. Since my mother and father have both passed away, I thought it would be wise to look up my only living relative, or at least I believe she is my only living relative, she and my grandfather Ardon."

"Just a moment, please," said Meeno, covering the receiver with his hand, he turned to face Verina. "Mrs. Steris, it is a woman who says she is trying to find her grandparents. She seems to think you may be her grandmother. What should I say?"

"What? Who is she? What is her name?"

"She said her name is Shana Willow," he said still covering the receiver.

"Oh, my God! I can't believe this!" Verina said as she clutched her hand to her heart. "My granddaughter has suddenly appeared out of nowhere? How can it be? Yes! Yes! Give me the phone, Meeno. Give me the phone!" she said as she reached for the receiver, nearly knocking over her coffee cup and tipping over a chair with her wheelchair.

"Hello, hello! Is this really Shana? Oh, my word! Where are you, dear?"

"Yes, this is Shana. Are you my grandmother Steris, I hope? I've been trying to find you since Mom and Dad died last year. I am so glad I could find you and Grandfather Steris."

"Oh, dear, I have terrible news. Your grandfather was killed in an automobile accident a few weeks ago. I thought I was the only family member left on this earth."

"I am sorry Grandmother. Maybe this was not a good time to try to have contacted you. You must be grieving so. Is there anything I can do? I hope I haven't made things worse for you."

"No, no, dear. If anything you probably have made things better. I miss Ardon so much and Meeno, my driver tries to help, but he gets frustrated with me sometimes I can tell. Where are you? You need to come here right a way. I want to see my only granddaughter as soon as possible," she said with a little chuckle.

"Well, right now I am at a pay phone outside of a little café. I just drove here from San Diego this morning and stopped here to get a bite to eat before looking for a decent motel to spend the night. I thought I would look through the phone book to see if I could find you first, though. Mom had told me that if anything ever happened to her or Dad, that I should look up my grandparents so that I would have at least someone in the family that could share family history with me. She didn't remember too much about too many of our relatives. I guess it was because she and Dad had moved away when she was young and never kept in contact with you and Grandfather. I am really sorry about that too, Grandmother. I know it must have been hard on the both of you not being able to be around your only daughter and grandchild. Did you even know about me… that you had a grandchild?" Shana asked.

"I had heard about you right after your mother had you, but after that I never heard from her again. I was notified when she died of that overdose, but I never heard from your dad at all. I didn't even know he had died."

"Dad died of the same thing Mom died of…drugs. I guess neither one of them ever grew up. My neighbor practically raised me. I only spent a few days at a time with Mom and Dad. Most of the time my neighbor kept me hidden from them and the police when Mom and Dad were on their high."

"Well, you just come straight over here to my house right now. We can discuss all of that when you get here.

We have a lot of catching up to do. I can hardly wait to meet you, Granddaughter."

"And I'm anxious to meet you too, Grandmother," said Shana.

"Shall I send Meeno, my driver, to bring you?" asked Verina.

"No, that won't be necessary. If you just give me your address or directions to your home, I think I'll be all right. I've driven this far, so I shouldn't have any trouble finding your place."

After giving Shana the address and directions and after having her repeat it back to her, Verina told Meeno to keep a look out for her newly found granddaughter. She put their breakfast dishes in the sink to be washed and asked Meeno if he could please go out to the flower garden and cut a nice bouquet of fresh flowers for the dinning room table and a few more for the various tables throughout the house. She asked him to check to see if the guest room was ready for her visitor and to put a bouquet in there as well. Verina could feel the excitement rising in her chest as she sped around straightening up magazines and making sure everything was in its proper place awaiting her granddaughter's arrival. She found herself humming as she went through each room of her house and looking on the back patio to be sure that there was nothing that needed to be done out there before Shana got home. "Home," she said to herself. "My granddaughter is coming home."

An hour later, Meeno said, "I do believe your granddaughter has arrived, Mrs. Steris. Does she drive a small, light blue Civic?"

"I don't know. I guess I forgot to ask her what she was driving. But it must be her. Who else would be coming to visit me at this time of the day? Go, Meeno and help her bring in her bags. You can put them in the guest room up stairs. If she has other things that need to be brought in, bring those, too, please."

"Yes, Mrs. Steris, right away," he said as he headed down the steps to meet Shana.

Verina was right behind him, wheeling her wheelchair as fast as she could to the edge of the step. With outstretched arms, she was ready to meet her granddaughter for the first time.

"Welcome, welcome," Verina said as she reached up wrapping her arms around Shana. Tears slid down her cheeks as she gave Shana a hug and kissed her on the forehead when Shana bent down to hug her. Verina bumping her wheelchair into things, nearly dragged Shana into the house.

"Oh, dear, you are so beautiful. You look so much like your mother when she was young. Come, come. Sit down. Would you like something to eat or maybe a nice cold glass of tea? Meeno will get it for you as soon as he returns from getting your things from your car."

"No, thank you. I just had a bite to eat as I said on the phone. A glass of water would be nice, but I can get it myself. Would you like something though? I can get it for you, if you will tell me where the kitchen is."

"No thank, you dear. But the kitchen is that way to the left," Verina said as she pointed toward the kitchen. "The glasses are in the cabinet above the sink. Water is in the refrigerator. If you do see anything that you would like, just help yourself. Meeno will help me make lunch in a little while. Is there anything special you would like for lunch, dear?"

"No, Grandmother. I would just like to sit here and get acquainted with my grandmother. I am so excited that I can hardly stand it. I can't believe I'm really here in your home, sitting across from you, about to hear all about my family. As I said, my mom didn't tell me much about our family. I hope you have photo albums filled with lots of pictures and stories that you can share with me."

"Oh, I do child. I do. But I think we need to just sit here and get acquainted with each other first. We will have plenty of time to look through old photos and hear old stories about our crazy family," she chuckled. "You are planning on staying aren't you my dear? Your room is all ready for you. I want you to make my home your home, Granddaughter."

"Well, it would be nice to spend a few days getting to know my grandmother, but I don't want to impose or cause extra work for anyone."

"Good. Good. And I can assure you that you will not cause anyone any extra work or be imposing on anyone. It will be such fun to spend time with my dear granddaughter. I can hardly wait to tell the club members about you. They are just going to love meeting you my dear."

"What club is that Grandmother?"

"Oh, wait until you hear, dear. You are not going to believe the club your grandfather and I started a long time ago. It's called The Six Hundred Thousand Dollar Club. I'll tell you all about it in a little while, after we have had time to relax and get caught up on what has been happening in your life and mine," said Verina as she sat back in her wheelchair.

"Now, you go get that water and I'll tell Meeno to see what we can have for lunch."

Meeno returned to the living room after putting Shana's bags in the guest room.

"Is there anything else you would like for me to do, Mrs. Steris?" he asked.

"Yes, Meeno, there is. Would you please help me to put together a little lunch later? What do you suppose a young girl would enjoy having for lunch? I really have no idea. Probably something with chocolate for dessert, I'm sure."

"Yes, Ma'am. I'll see what we have in the way of salad. Maybe cheese and ham sandwiches? I think I saw one of those boxed brownie mixes in the cupboard. I can manage that if you like. Shall I go out to the vegetable garden and bring in fresh tomatoes and maybe a few radishes for the salad, Ma'am?"

"Oh, that would be splendid, Meeno. I do love the fresh tomatoes from my garden. But, make sure you get the ones from the garden in front of the barn. That garden on that side never produces good vegetables or flowers. I think the drainage is so poor around there that nothing will ever grow properly other than weeds, I'm afraid."

"What time shall I serve lunch, Mrs. Steris?"

"Probably not until around one o'clock today, since Shana said she has just eaten. But feel free to have your lunch whenever you like, Meeno. Maybe you could bring in a pitcher of tea and glasses for us before you go prepare lunch. If you have other plans for yourself today, please resume as planned, except for preparing the lunch. I'm sure my granddaughter and I will have plenty to keep us entertained today. Oh, Meeno, I am so pleased to finally have my granddaughter in my life. I never thought I would ever meet her and now here she is soon to share lunch with me."

"Yes, Ma'am. It really is too bad that Mr. Steris isn't here to share that pleasure too."

"Yes, it is. He would have been pleased as well, bless his soul."

"If you will excuse me, I'll go get the tea for you then go out to the garden to gather the vegetables for the salad and see about those brownies, Mrs. Steris."

"Of course, of course, Meeno. And remember to only get the good vegetables from the front garden. Only the best for my Granddaughter," Verina chuckled.

It was five until one when Meeno returned to ask if he should serve lunch in the living room, the dining room, kitchen or would it be more enjoyable on the patio.

"Oh, my goodness, Shana. I didn't realize it was so late. You are probably starved. I can't believe we have been sitting here all these hours chatting. I don't think I have had such a wonderful time in years."

"The lunch, Mrs. Steris. Where would you like to have your lunch?"

"Oh, sorry Meeno. I think it would be nice to have it on the patio. It is such a beautiful day. We may wish to have our dessert back in here so that Shana and I can continue getting to know each other. Is that alright with you, dear?"

"Sounds great to me, Grandmother. I am having a wonderful time getting to know you, too. I hope we will have time to look at those photo albums. I really don't know much about any of my relatives."

"Well, dear, you may be better off not knowing about some of your relatives," Verina laughed. "We've got some pretty odd ones in our family as you'll soon find out."

"Great! I can hardly wait."

After lunch, Verina and Shana settled back into the living room.

"I brought more tea and those brownies, Mrs. Steris," Meeno said as he placed the refreshments on the coffee table next to the two women.

"Will there be anything else, Ma'am?" he said. "I don't know how I became her servant and house maid," he thought to himself. "I just hope having her Granddaughter here isn't going to mean more work for me. I think she's forgotten I was hired as a chauffer, not a maid."

"Just one more thing, Meeno if you don't mind. Will you please bring the photo albums from the library?"

"Yes, Ma'am," he said as he left to go get the albums.

"Will there be anything else?" he asked as he placed them on the table next to the brownies and the tea.

"No thank you Meeno. Why don't you take the rest of the day off? I think I would like to just spend the rest of the day sharing old family secretes with my Granddaughter."

"I have a few *old family secrets* I could share with *you and your Granddaughter* too, Mrs. Steris," he thought.

Verina and Shana spent the rest of the day looking through the stacks of albums. Verina told stories about each person in the photos as Shana pointed and repeated names or asked questions about people she had never had the privilege to meet.

"We did have some pretty interesting people in our family, didn't we, Grandmother?" she said. "I wish I had been around to meet some of them like...what was Great Aunt's name that carried her money and her wristwatch in her pantaloon pocket?" she asked as she pointed to the photo of her Great Aunt.

"Aunt Mabel. Her name is Aunt Mabel. Yes, she was a strange duck all right. As I said, she was so afraid that people were going to steal from her that she would take her watch off and put it in a pocket that she had sewn on her underpants. She would take the bus downtown, and then she would go into the ladies room in the J.C. Penney, go into the stall, lift her skirt and remove her watch to see what time it was and then put it back and continue her shopping. If she had more than two dollars with her she would put her money in her pantaloon pocket, too. I think she spent more time in the J.C. Penney's bathroom counting her money and checking the time than she did shopping," laughed Verina. "She was just plain loony, I say. But not as loony as Uncle Jake. Now he was loony!"

"This is Uncle Jake", Venina said as she pointed to the yellowed photo of a toothless old man in coveralls. Uncle Jake raised chickens and pigs. He would go out to the pig pin every morning and feed his pigs. Then he would go get a bucked of soapy water and a scrub brush and begin giving his pigs a bath, yelling at them all the while, telling them how bad they were for wallowing in the mud and getting all dirty. He would tell them that he would not stand for dirty pigs and that they would be an embarrassment to him if his neighbors ever saw them looking like that. Then he would go feed his chickens and start in on them about one thing or the other."

"I would have loved to seen that," giggled Shana. "I guess they just don't make relatives like they used too, thank goodness."

"No I guess not. I guess with all the loonies in our family tree, I wasn't surprised about anything your grandfather came up with. When he came up with The Six Hundred Thousand Dollar Club, it just seemed natural to me."

"Oh, yeah. What is that all about anyway, Grandmother? You were going to tell me remember?"

"Well it's a long story. Here have another one of those brownies and sit back and I'll tell you all about your grandfather's most wonderful idea."

It was nearly nine o'clock by the time Vernia had finished explaining the club. All the photo albums had been looked at twice and discussed thoroughly. Both Shana and Verina began yawning more than they were talking.

"Well, dear I think we had better have a bite to eat and then get our beauty sleep. We can continue our get acquainted party tomorrow. I would like to introduce you to the club members tomorrow, if that is all right with you. They are an interesting group, too. But please don't share all of this family information with them. They may think we are all from the loony farm. I do have an image to uphold, if you know what I mean, dear," Verina chuckled sleepily.

Shana found herself chuckling as she thought about her crazy, but most interesting, family.

"Yes, Grandmother we do have some funny monkeys in our family tree."

She fell asleep nearly the moment her head touched the pillow. She dreamed of her family members jumping from trees. Some looked like themselves, some looked like monkeys. Uncle Jake was washing down his pigs and scolding his chickens while Great Aunt Mabel scurried off the city bus pulling up her skirt as she ran into the J.C. Penney's restroom to retrieve her watch and her cash. She dreamed of her mother and her father smoking pot and of Grandmother Steris with giant photo albums on her lap as she held her finger up to her mouth and made shushing sounds and told her "not to tell about the loonies".

Though her dreams were busy and strange, Shana awoke rested and feeling a joy she had not felt …ever. "At least I know I had a family," she told herself. "And I have a grandmother who loves me."

Chapter Twenty-Three: Shana Meets The Club

Verina had eggs, bacon and toast ready when Shana came down for breakfast. She had gotten up early and had called Meeno to make sure he would be available to take Shana and herself to a specially called meeting with the club members later today. After breakfast she would call the members and ask them to meet her for lunch at the Golden Goose. She did not plan to tell them about her newly found granddaughter, instead she planned to surprise them as she introduced Shana. None of the club members had met Shana and Verina could not remember if she had ever mentioned having a granddaughter. After Verina's riding accident, Beth Marie had gone off to college and never made contact with Verina. Verina figured it was because Beth Marie believed it was her fault that her mother was confined to a wheelchair. Beth Marie was the one who talked her father into buying her the horse in the first place against Verina's wishes. The truth was that once she learned to ride, Verina enjoy the horse as much as Beth Marie did.

"Something smells delicious," Shana said as she entered the kitchen. "What time did you get up, Grandmother?"
"Oh, about two hours ago. Did you sleep well, dear?"

"Oh, yes, very well." Shana had to smile as she thought about her dreams. "If only Grandmother knew," she thought to herself.

"Good. Now sit down and have some breakfast, dear. I hope you don't mind, but I thought you and I could meet the club members for lunch today. I know you will like them and I'm sure they are going to love you."

"Oh, Ok" Shana thought to herself, "I wonder if they are going to be as interesting as our family. I can just imagine what my dreams will be like tonight."

"Good. I thought we could meet them at The Golden Goose. They don't know about you, so it will be a nice surprise for them when I introduce you as my long lost Granddaughter. I can hardly wait to see the look on their faces," Verina chuckled. "It is going to be such fun. Now, sit, sit dear. Eat before everything gets cold."

After Verina and Shana had finished breakfast, Shana picked up the breakfast dishes and loaded them into the dishwasher while Verina went directly into her office and began to call the members of the club to arrange the lunch meeting.

"I have a surprise for all of you," she told each member. "Please try not to be late. I'll see you at twelve o'clock sharp at The Golden Goose."

Verina could feel the excitement mounting with each call. "Yes, this is going to be such fun. I can hardly wait for twelve o'clock to arrive. Now what should I wear? Hmm… Maybe that new green dress I bought last week at The Fashion Finery. Too bad Ardon is not here to see me in my new green dress and to meet his granddaughter. Sometimes I do miss you so, Ardon. I really truly do miss you."

Verina and Shana spent the rest of the morning talking about the club Ardon and Verina had founded and about each club member. Verina explained how it started and how each member had been added to the membership. Verina also shared how the deceased members had died and how Fredric and Doralene had divorced and how Fredric had to resign from the club. She caught herself before she blurted out her feelings toward Doralene after her secret affair with Ardon. "Not the time to think about the dark past now," thought Verina. "I want this to be a happy day."

"Meeno, will you please bring the car around front. It is nearly 11:30 and I don't want to be late for lunch. Shana, dear, will you get me my wrap? It is supposed to be a little cool today. Oh my, I am just so excited. Listen to me giving orders to everyone. I'm usually not like this dear. Come, come everyone. Are we ready?"

"No, she's usually more demanding," thought Meeno as he left to get the car.

When the car appeared in front of the house, Verina and Shana were waiting on the sidewalk.

Meeno went to the back of the car, opened the trunk, and then went to help Verina into the front seat. Shana started to roll the wheelchair to the rear of the car when Meeno reappeared and took it from her and lifted it into the trunk.

"Got it," he said. He went to the side of the car, opened the door for Shana to get in and then got in behind the steering wheel and started up the car.

"Are you going to take all day, Meeno?" Verina said as she gave him a sideways look.

"Sorry, ma'am," he said as he put the car in gear and stepped harder on the gas peddle than he intended.

"At last!" sighed Verina as they pulled up in front of The Golden Goose. "I hope everyone gets here by twelve. I don't intend to sit around and wait on people. It's ten to twelve already and I don't see everyone's cars here yet. Meeno, will you help me out of this car? Where is my wheelchair? Shana, dear, do I look all right? Don't you think the green of my dress makes my eyes look greener? Ardon always liked the way green made my eyes sparkle."

"Yes, Grandmother. You look beautiful and you do have a sparkle in your eyes. I think if you relax, though you will look even more lovely," Shana said as she took her Grandmother's arm to help her into the wheelchair that Meeno had so carefully place for Verina to get into.

"I am sorry, dear. Please forgive me. I guess I just get so excited. Meeno will you push my chair? Please? I want Shana to walk beside me as we go into the restaurant. Come dear, come walk beside me. Here take my hand," she said as she straightened the green wrap across her lap.

All the members except Bibi were sitting at their usual table in the back of the restaurant. When they met at the Golden Goose they always requested the same table next to the window that overlooked the beautiful rose garden below. The other members had called each other and made arrangements to carpool to the restaurant. It had been several weeks since they had last met and they decided it would be a good time to catch up and then they planned to take a ride down to the beach for an evening of leisurely talk and a few drinks after the lunch. It had been months since they had spent a casual afternoon together. Bibi said she would meet them at the restaurant because she had an appointment with her doctor at ten thirty and may be a little late. They had planned to ask Verina if she wanted to go along when they met at noon, but they knew she probably would decline because of her wheelchair.

"She can still enjoy the visit and the drinks on the beach front," Pearl had said. "She really needs to get out more. Living out in the country and so far from the beach must be lonely for her. She seems to only get out when we have our meetings. I guess she still misses Ardon."

"Where is Bibi?" asked Verina as she drew her wheelchair up to the end of the table. "I told everyone to be on time."

"Bibi had a doctor's appointment so she maybe a few minutes late. The rest of us came together. We plan to go to the beach after. Would you like to come along, Verina?" asked Pearl. "We thought we could spend the rest of the day just enjoying each other's company and maybe have a few drinks along the beach front...maybe at one of the little outside patio places. It's been a while since we have just wasted a day doing nothing in particular. We don't have to go down to the sand."

"No, I don't think I want to go to the beach...unless you want to go, Shana. Oh, everyone...this is my surprise. I wanted everyone to be here for the introduction, but since Bibi is going to be late...this is my granddaughter, Shana. Shana this is the Six Hundred Thousand Dollar Club."

"Your granddaughter?" gasped Doralene. "I didn't know you had a granddaughter!"

"Neither did I!" said Hazel.

Everyone began to talk at once, introducing themselves as they grabbed her hand and began hugging Shana.

Shana hugged each one back and repeated each of their names hoping she could remember who was who.

They all sat back down after they had given Verina a congratulatory hug. Verina sat up straighter in her wheelchair and folded her hands across her lap. "I was surprised myself," she said, "when I got the call from Shana yesterday. I could hardly wait to share my good news with you. Isn't she the most beautiful little thing you have ever seen?"

"Oh, Grandmother! You are embarrassing me. I am so glad I got to meet all of you. Grandmother has been telling me about the club. I must say it is a very interesting concept. I have never heard of such a club in my life," she chuckled.

"Shall we order?" said Verina. "Bibi can order for herself when she gets here." Verina still felt a little miffed that Bibi was late. "Everything is on me today. You may all order what ever you would like...my treat," she said.

"Wow! That is kind of you, Verina" said Doralene.

"Well, it's not everyday that a long lost granddaughter shows up on my doorstep."

"In that case, I'll have the lobster and steak," said Landis.

"I think I'll try the shrimp," said Doralene.

"That sounds good to me. What about you, dear?"

"I guess I'll have the cheese burger with fries," Shana said as she looked over the menu. "I'm not into seafood too much. Do you mind terribly, Grandmother?"

Verina slowly placed her menu on the table. "Of course not, dear. If that's what you want. Are you sure you wouldn't like a steak or the prime rib? They make them both very tasty here," she tried to hide the disappointment from her voice. "I hope my granddaughter doesn't plan on living on that greasy garbage while she is here. I guess I will have to teach her the ways of the more upper class life. Poor thing has probably never been in anything other than those awful greasy spoon joints," thought Verina.

"No, thank you Grandmother. A burger and fries will be fine...oh, and a coke, if that's OK."

Just as they were about to order, Bibi came rushing toward them.

"Sorry I'm late. I met the nicest man at the doctor's office. He is single and said he visits Dr. Watson often for his arthritis. He made an appointment next week for a follow up so, I made my appointment at the same time. I think I'll arrive a little early...just in case he gets there early, too. Oh, hello everyone. So sorry I'm late."

"We were about to order," said Verina. "You missed my announcement, Bibi.."

"What announcement? Is someone dropping out of the club?"

"No. If you weren't so preoccupied with finding a husband, you would have been on time to hear me introduce my granddaughter, Shana. Shana, this is Bibi."

"Your granddaughter? Did you say your granddaughter?"

"Yes, Bibi. It's so good to meet you," Shana said. "I hope you don't have any serious illness."

"Oh, no. I just went to have my regular check up. You know...the woman kind of check up."

"Bibi, you are so old, why do you need to go have a woman's check up? It's not like you are going to get pregnant soon or something," chuckled Doralene.

"One can never be too careful with one's health when we reach our golden years, DORALENE!" Bibi shouted. "Besides, Dr. Watson says that all women should have a regular good check up no matter what their age."

"OK! OK! Can we just order and have a meal without bickering about women's issues and old age?" said Owen.

"I agree," said Charles. "Especially since Verina is so kind as to pay for our meal. I say, let's start the celebration!"

"Here! Here!" said Landis as he lifted his water glass for a toast. All the others did the same.

"What are we toasting?" asked Bibi as she raised her glass.

"Shana, Verina's newly found granddaughter, Bibi!" shouted Doralene. "Have you forgotten already?"

"Oh, sorry," replied Bibi. "I guess I'm still thinking of that gentleman at Dr. Watson's office. Did I mention that we have the same date for our next appointment?"

"YES!" everyone shouted at once. Shana just dropped her head to her chest and smiled. "Yep, this is definitely an interesting club."

Chapter Twenty-Four: Rules Are Rules

After lunch, Meeno drove Verina and Shana back home. The rest of the club went to the beach as they had planned.

"I wonder where Verina's granddaughter came from all of a sudden?" said Bibi as she and Pearl were walking along the boardwalk. "I wonder why she showed up now after all these years. Seems to me that Verina would have known she had a granddaughter."

"Well, I don't know," said Pearl. "I know she has not heard a word from Beth Marie in years. I heard she and her husband were heavy into drugs and both died from overdoses. I don't know when exactly, but I think it was a couple of years ago."

"But, wouldn't you think that they would have let Verina know she was a grandmother?"

"I don't think she really got over Verina's accident. I think she always felt that it was her fault that her mother is in a wheelchair and never wanted to face her mother again after she went off to college. I think she went out of state to college so that she would not have to face her mother everyday. I know Verina doesn't blame Beth Marie, but she couldn't convince Beth Marie of that."

"Well it still seems strange to me ...Shana's showing up after all these years."

"I've heard it happens all the time...long lost relatives showing up out of the blue...or relatives you never knew you had. I'm just glad Verina found out and met her granddaughter before it was too late."

"Too late? What do you mean...too late?"

"You know, before Verina passed away. At least they will have a few good years to spend together...you know before it's too late."

"Oh. Well, yes, I guess it is a good thing...before it's too late. I have to wonder though, why now?"

"What do you mean? Why does it matter when Shana showed up as long as she did?"

"Oh, I was just thinking...I hope she doesn't plan to take advantage of Verina, that's all."

"What makes you think she would take advantage of Verina? She seems like she really loves her grandmother, though they just met. I can't see where she could be taking advantage of Verina, Bibi. After all, Verina invited her to stay at her home so they could get acquainted before Shana has to go where ever it is she's going."

"I was thinking that maybe Shana might have alternative motives is all."

"Like what, Bibi? What do you mean, *alternative motives*?"

"Well, it seems mighty strange that she shows up when Verina is in her golden years...and so are the rest of us. I was thinking she may have found out about the club some how and decided to come check it out...you know just in case her grandmother out lived us all and then who would be the heir of all that money? None other than Verina's long lost granddaughter herself."

"Oh, Bibi, that's crazy! I swear, you come up with the craziest ides sometimes. Wherever did you get such an idea as that?"

"Well, I don't think it's such a crazy idea. You can never trust these young people nowadays. Why would a young thing like her all of a sudden decide to find an old woman like Verina?"

"Maybe because she is her only known living relative and she wants to reconnect with her family? Did you ever think of that, Bibi? Some younger folks do love their grandparents, you know."

"Well, I'm not so sure. I was thinking that she may even hope to join the club and of course she would out live all of us...getting her hands on the lot."

"Bibi, I think you have a very strange imagination. I'm thinking you are losing it."

"If she ever had it in the first place," thought Pearl. "Relax, Bibi and enjoy the day. It's so beautiful here along the beach. How can anyone have such dreadful thoughts while walking along this beach? I do enjoy watching the seagulls as they swoop down among the waves to gather food. Aren't they beautiful, Bibi?"

"Yes, I guess they are," Bibi said as she barely glanced in the direction of the ocean. "You know what I think, Pearl? I think we should meet with the club and discuss the rules. I think we should stipulate in the rules that no new people should be allowed to join. After all, it is our years of dues that are at stake. Why should some young thing come along and "steal" our money. I, for one, would be infuriated if that happened."

"I think you are being silly, Bibi. For one thing, no one said anyone was going to come along and "steal" our money. And we have not even taken in any new members in years...not since Landis joined us after his wife Gladys died. Besides, all of us will die someday and where will the money go? I can't see it all being spent by any one person of our age. What could we possibly spend it on? The rest of us don't have family left to pass it on to. I think you are worrying about something that you don't even need to think about right now. Just enjoy the day, Bibi, please?"

"If I outlive everyone else, I plan to pass it on to my husband."

"But you don't even have a husband, Bibi."

"Well, who's to say I won't have one someday? And even if I don't get married, I may want to give the rest of the money to my favorite charity."

"Which is?" asked Pearl.

"I don't know yet. I have plenty of time to decide that before I die," replied Bibi.

"For goodness sakes, Bibi. Just enjoy the day, OK?"

The next morning Bibi decided to call Verina to suggest the club have another lunch meeting. Bibi had not slept well thinking of the possibility of Shana joining the club. She just had to get the rules set down so that it would be clear to everyone that there would be no way that their money could be stolen from them by a much younger person who just happened to show up and want to join the club. "I am not going to let that happen to my money," she said to herself as she waited for Verina to answer her phone.

"She's probably busy getting "acquainted" with her granddaughter. And Shana is probably getting "acquainted" with Verina's bank account," she said as she tapped her foot impatiently.

"Where is she? Why is she not answering her phone?"

Just as she was about to hang up she heard Verina's voice. "Hello?"

"Oh, there you are. Hello Verina. This is Bibi. How are you?"

"I'm fine. What do you need, Bibi?"

"Well, I don't actually need anything. I just wanted to ask you something."

"What is it Bibi? What do you want to ask?" she said, getting more impatient with Bibi by the minute.

"Does it have anything to do with the club?"

"Actually, it does. I was wondering if we could all meet to discuss the rules."

"The rules? Don't we already have a copy of the rules from when we first started the club?"

"Yes, but I can't find anything it them about new people joining *now*."

"Why would we need a meeting to discuss that? Is there someone you want to join at this late date? That would mean someone would have to come up with a whole lot of money to make up for the years since nineteen fifty-three when we started the club. Do you know anyone with that kind of money to invest? I sure don't."

"No, but I do have a few questions that I think the club members might want to consider, that's all. Anyway, I was thinking that maybe we could meet for lunch tomorrow to talk about a few things."

"Alright, Bibi. Why don't you call everyone and set it up. Give me a call back when you're done that and let me know the details. I'll see if Shana wants to come along. She so enjoyed everyone's company yesterday. Isn't she just the sweetest thing you ever met?"

"Oh, she will be coming, too? I thought only the club members would be attending meetings."

"Well, we have had visitors before. I don't see where there would be a problem. It's not like she is going to vote on anything that is club business. She would just be enjoying everyone's company. She really has not had much of a social life in a while. I'm hoping she will make friends here and maybe consider this her permanent home. I'll ask her if she would like to join us for lunch after you get back with me. Why don't you go ahead and call the others? I'll be waiting for your return call, Bibi."

"Oh, alright. I'll call them and I'll see you and *Shana* at lunch. Have a good day, Verina. Goodbye."

After calling all of the members of the club, Bibi called Verina to let her know that lunch would be at noon at the Golden Goose.

"I was hoping no one would want Shana to be there, but I guess everybody but me seems to think she is just *the cutest little thing*," said Bibi to herself. She went to the bathroom and began putting on fresh makeup. After choosing her favorite pink dress from the closet she dressed and touched up her makeup for the second time. "I'll show them who's *the cutest little thing*," she grumbled.

"So, what is this meeting about?" asked Charles. "Are you paying since you called this meeting, Bibi?"
"No, I am not! Since when does the person who calls a meeting required to pay for the meal?"
"I am only kidding, Bibi," he said as the others tried to hide their snickers behind their menus. "I think I will have the trout with rice…since I'm paying for my own."

After everyone had given their orders, Bibi cleared her throat. "Um, I hope I don't sound mean, Shana, but I am concerned about your purpose for coming to our meeting."
"What? My grandmother invited me. Is there a problem? If there is, I don't need to be here. Grandmother would Meeno be able to take me home…I mean back to your house?"
"Bibi! How could ask such a thing. You know I invited Shana. What is the problem?"
Everyone began to talk at once. "We don't understand, Bibi. Why would you ask such a ridiculous thing? How

could you be so rude?" said Pearl. "I am so sorry, Shana. I don't know what has gotten into Bibi."

"Bibi, you need to apologize to Shane and Verina," said Owen.

"I'm sorry, Shana and Verina. I was just concerned about Shana trying to join the club now and getting all of our money. It's obvious that she, being so young, would out live all of us."

"Bibi, I have no intention of joining The Six Hundred Thousand Dollar Club. Why would I do that? And where would I ever get enough money to make up for the lost years of dues anyway? You have nothing to worry about. I just like all of you and enjoyed your company yesterday. I guess that's why Grandmother asked me to join you today for lunch. I'm sorry if this has caused a problem."

"No problem at all, dear. Bibi just isn't thinking straight today, that's all. Right, Bibi?" Verina said.

"I guess so. Sorry everyone. I just let my imagination get the best of me. Please feel free to join us for lunch anytime, Shana," she said as she smiled over at Shana.

"No problem, Bibi. You were only thinking of the club's welfare," Shana said as she reached over and gave Bibi a hug.

The rest of the meal was enjoyed in conversation about dropped and deceased members and stories about some of the more interesting events and meeting of the past.

"I'm still not sure I believe Shana," thought Bibi as she undressed for bed. "We will see. They better not blame Bibi when what I said comes true. It would serve them right if all of their money gets stolen by the *cutest little thing*," she said as she yawnd and turned off the lamp. "Sweet dreams Six Hundred Thousand Dollar Club. Sweet dreams."

Chapter Twenty-Five: Don't Drink The ...

"Well," thought Verina as she and Shana sat at the breakfast table. "After Bibi's remarks yesterday, I think we need to have a more pleasant get together soon. What we need is a celebration. I think we need to have a dinner dance. We haven't had one in several years. I think the last one we had was several weeks before Ardon ... Ardon passed away. It's time we started having real social events again. And we should have it someplace where you can meet some people your own age and make new friends, Shana. Some place like The Swinging Gate."

"The Swinging Gate? What kind of place is that, Grandmother?"

"It's really classier than it sounds. It's a very nice place with a live band and delicious food. It has a large dance floor. The band plays music from the forties through the nineties, so people from all age groups can enjoy showing off their moves. Ardon and I went there once. Your grandfather could really cut a rug in his younger days," she laughed.

"It sounds like a fun place, Grandmother, but I'm not so sure I would be welcomed to another one of your club events. I know Bibi apologized, but I'm not so sure she truly meant it."

"What makes you say that, dear?"

"I could see it in her eyes. She said the words, but her eyes said, "I still don't like it", if you know what I mean. I don't want to come between you and your club, Grandmother. I enjoyed all of the members, but I don't want them to feel that I am a threat. I've never been a threat to anyone."

"Don't worry, dear. Bibi is just a strange little bird. Some of the things she comes up with we all just laugh off and consider that it's just Bibi talking. All of the club members love having you. They all know that you have no intention of taking over the club or their money. Please don't feel that you are not welcome. They will be delighted when I suggest we have a dinner dance at The Swinging Gate. They may even have friends that they will want to invite to meet you. They always get overly enthusiastic when it comes to dances and matchmaking."

"Matchmaking? Grandmother, I thought this was going to be a dinner dance to meet new friends. I didn't know match making was in the plan. I'm definitely not ready for any matchmaking."

"Don't worry, dear. I promise that any match making to be done will be for Bibi. She's determined to marry before she kicks the bucket. She is always in favor of having social events in a location that is crawling with men her age or younger… just in case some unsuspecting bachelor happens to be caught off guard and winds up in her web."

"Well, OK, I guess. But you better clear it with the club before I say I'll go."

"Of course you'll go, my dear. It will be in your honor… so you can meet new friends, remember? I'll call the club and set it all up and make the reservations at The Swinging Gate. You just worry about something pretty to wear. Maybe we can have Meeno take us to town to do some shopping later. Oh, it's going to be such fun, Shana. I can't wait. I haven't felt this happy in a very long time. Too bad Ardon is not here to share the joy. He so loved the dinner dances."

"You must miss him a lot, Grandmother. I wish I had met him. I bet you two were the happiest couple of all the club members. I can just imagine the two of you swirling around on the dance floor."

"Yes, we were the envy of everyone until...until... well until his tragic accident. But enough of this talk. You go get ready for our shopping trip and I'll make my calls."

After making the calls to the club members and making reservations for the club dance at The Swinging Gate, Verina met Shana and Meeno in the driveway.

"Are you ready to hit the best dress shops in town, Shana? I'll introduce you to my favorite boutiques and after we can have lunch at my favorite little lunch spot. The Silly Dilly has the most delicious desserts. I hope you like chocolate, because they have every kind of chocolate dessert that you have ever tasted."

"Maybe we should eat first. If the Silly Dilly's desserts are a scrumptious as you say, we may not fit into our new outfits," laughed Shana as she climbed into the back seat of the car.

Everyone sounded excited about the idea of a "meet the new girl in town" dinner dance. Shana seemed to be the only one not so thrilled about the event.

"I just hope a bunch of "nice young men" don't show up expecting me to be their next catch," said Shana at breakfast.

"Don't worry, dear. I'm sure Bibi will take care of any 'nice young men' that you don't want. That woman can never remember, that she is not a young chick anymore... not that she ever was a "chick". She just never gives up on snagging herself a husband. I swear she will be looking for eligible men at her own funeral."

"Well, you can't blame her for trying, Grandmother. You never know what may happen. Older people than Bibi have gotten married ...and for the first time, too. Maybe that's what makes her life worth while...just waiting for Mr. Right to show up."

"I guess you're right. It's just that seems to be all she talks about. Always asking if there will be any eligible men at every event we have. Sometimes I wish I could buy her a husband just to shut her up."

"That may work if she lived in one of those overseas countries that trade camels for wives," Shana laughed.

"Well, enough about Bibi, dear. Let's start making plans for the dinner dance. Are you sure you are satisfied with the gown we bought for you? Do you like the color? Do you need any other accessories? Shoes, jewelry?"

"No, Grandmother, I think we got everything yesterday. I really do like the gown we picked out. Teal is supposed to be the universal color, meaning it looks great on everyone."

"I just hope you are satisfied, dear. I know you would look beautiful in anything you wear, teal or any other color. After all, you are my granddaughter."

"Thank you, Grandmother, but I think you may be just a wee bit partial. I've never owned a formal gown before. I mostly wear jeans or skirts, as you may have noticed. I'm sure I'll feel beautiful, even if I know I'm not as beautiful as you say. Besides, we wouldn't want Bibi to think I was trying to grab all the men," she chuckled.

"No, Heaven forbid. We wouldn't want poor Bibi to feel like the ugly duckling at the dance, would we?" Verina teased.

Shana helped Verina gather the breakfast dishes and load the dishwasher.

Do you mind if I take a walk, Grandmother? I haven't had a chance to see the countryside or even look around the grounds here. You seem to own a pretty big piece of property. It must have been fun for Mom growing up here and ri...," she started to say "riding her horse", but stop when she realized mentioning her mother's horse riding may cause her grandmother pain.

"It's OK, dear. My accident is long in the past. Nothing can be changed now, so why hold painful memories in your heart? You are right. Your mother and I both had wonderful times riding around on the property. Those are the things I try to remember...the good times, before the accident and before your mother went away. But now I have my beautiful granddaughter here, so I'm happy again."

"I'm glad for you Grandmother. I love you."

"Yes, you go for your walk, dear. Just be careful. You aren't used to this area. Be sure to wear comfortable shoes and watch out for traffic if you go on the road. It may be country, but drivers seem to think this is a drag strip sometimes. We don't get a lot of traffic, but sometimes...well, just be careful. Oh, and don't go near the area behind the barn. Ardon said he saw snakes and mice out there not too long ago. The weeds are high and any kind of creature may be living in there...even spiders. I wouldn't want you to get bitten by something."

"Ok, thanks, Grandmother. I'll be careful. What are your plans for today? Would you like for me to push you for a walk? You could tell me about the area."

"No, no, dear. I think I had better pass on that this time. I have some mending to catch up on. Meeno lost a button off of his shirt the other day, and he asked me to sew it back on for him. I promised that I would do it as

soon as I had a chance. Today would be the perfect time, since you are going for a walk. You go ahead and enjoy your walk, dear. And don't forget what I said about staying away from the barn."
"OK, Grandmother. I'll see you in a little while. I promise I'll be careful and I won't be long. Bye-bye."
"Bye, dear," Verina said as she rolled her wheelchair into her sewing room.

"I can't believe I haven't used my sewing machine in years. I hope I can remember how to use it. Now where is that button can? And I forgot all about all of this beautiful material I had bought years ago. I remember buying this pretty pink taffeta to make Beth Marie an Easter dress," she said as she rubbed it gently against her face. "I really should make use of this material or else give it to some charity. I wonder if Shana knows how to sew? I'll have to ask her before I get rid of it."

After finishing her sewing project and looking over some of her stored fabric, Verina left her sewing room and headed toward the patio. She decided it was such a beautiful day, that she would spend some time outside while Shana was taking her walk.

"I really do need to get outdoors more," she thought. "I haven't been out here since...since before Ardon's accident." Now, don't start thinking about that now, Verina," she scolded herself. "I have a dinner dance to look forward to. I know I won't be doing much dancing but it will give me such pleasure to see Shana enjoying the evening. She so looks like her mother. Ardon, it's a shame you aren't here to share in the joy it gives me to have her here. Too bad indeed. Ardon, it's also too bad you can't see how beautiful our oleanders are this year. I don't think I've ever seen the red ones so red. I always liked the pink ones, too. But my favorite was always the white ones. They look so pure and innocent, there between the reds and the pinks, don't you think? Verina, what has gotten into you?" she asked herself. " Here I am sitting here talking to my dead husband about oleanders when I could be using my time to work on the plans for the dinner dance." She spun her wheelchair around and went back into the house where she grabbed her notebook, containing The Six Hundred Thousand Dollar Club notes from 1953 through the last meeting last week. "We have sure collected a lot of history over the years," she said as she wheeled into the living room where she sat looking through the notebook and reminiscing the afternoon away. "A lot of history, indeed."

The evening of the dinner dance had finally arrived. Everyone was excited and expected the extra guests that were not really members, but were invited to serve as dance partners for Bibi and Shana. The Swinging Gate was usually pretty crowded on Saturday nights, but Verina had reserved a room for the club, so that they could have their dinner and still be near the dance floor, just in case someone would want to venture out on the dance floor, they could still be viewed by those left at the dinning table. She was hoping Shana would have every opportunity to meet and dance with some young people her own age. She was surprised when all of the men of the club bickered about which one of them would have the pleasure of escorting Shana onto the dance floor first. She could tell this did not set well with Bibi.

"Bibi has a look on her face that could turn a lemon sour," she thought. "I hope one of these men ask her to dance soon or who knows what she might do."

"Isn't it wonderful that Shana is having such a good time?" said Hazel. "I do hope she makes a few friends while she is here. The other guests seem to enjoy her company on the dance floor."

"Yah, she seems to keep everybody entertained, alright," said Bibi. "I hope she leaves them with enough energy, that someone will ask me to dance sometime tonight! "

"I'm sure you will get to dance tonight, Bibi. If you're not asked, why don't you ask someone to dance with you? It's OK for women to ask men to dance nowadays, you know," said Pearl. "That's what I'm going to do if no one asks me."

"I just may do that!" said Bibi. "After all, life is too short to sit on the sidelines while someone else had all the fun."

The evening was one of the best that the club had had in years. Everyone except Verina had spent time on the dance floor. Bibi had finally been asked to dance by Landis. Later she asked Owen if he would like to dance. Both men seem to enjoy Bibi's moves, though Owen suggested they stick to the slower dances, saying he didn't want to be the next club member to have a heart attack, especially not tonight. Not after he had drug out his old tux and had it cleaned for the occasion.

After a few minutes of "time out", everyone decided the next dance was a good time for everyone to join in the Bunny Hop. They were hoping it would not be too taxing on their hearts and other body parts.

Verina decided it would be the perfect time to make a visit to the lady's room.

"Are you sure you don't want me to push you in line in your wheelchair, Grandmother? It will be so much fun."

"No, thank you, dear. You just go ahead and join the others. Have a good time. That's what you're here for, remember? I really need to use the restroom anyway. I'll try to get back in time to get a picture or two of you all for our club album. Now, scoot, scoot! On to the dance floor! Or should I have said, Hop, Hop?"

"Ok, Grandmother. I love you," Shana said as she kissed Verina on the cheek and then hopped toward the others on the dance floor.

"Boy, that was definitely a workout," said Charles. "I haven't done that in years. I didn't even know people still did the Bunny Hop. Hazel, you better not try to drag me out on that dance floor for a while, no matter how slow it is. My heart is pumping a mile a minute." He reached for his glass and gulped down the martini in one swallow. He almost choked on the olive that slipped into his mouth.

"You better take it easy, ol' pal," said Landis. "If your heart doesn't get you, that olive might."

"He's right sweetie. You don't want to kill yourself now. Remember, we have a large investment in that six hundred thousand dollars," said Hazel.

"Don't worry. I won't. I do think I need to order another round of drinks, though. How about it everybody? More drinks?"

"Are you buying?" asked Owen.

"Sure, it's my turn, I think. Someone else can buy the next round."

"In that case, I'm in," said Owen.

" Me, too," said Landis.

"Ladies?" ask Charles. "More drinks?"

"Sure. Let's all have another round," said Verina. "And I'll buy the next."

More drinks were ordered, drank and Bibi and Landis were headed toward the dance floor again, followed by Doralene, and Owen. A few minutes later, Pearl and Shana found partners and were waving for Hazel and Charles to join them.

"I don't feel so good," said Charles as he and Hazel returned to the table. "I feel like my heart is going to burst. Look how sweaty I'm getting."

"Are you alright, Charles? Should we get you to a doctor? Maybe you shouldn't have had that last martini or danced that last dance. Charles, I asked you if you are alright!" shouted Hazel.

"Should I get someone to call 911, Charles?" asked Verina? "You really don't look good."

"No, no. I'll be fine. I do feel like I need to throw up. Maybe that will relieve some of the too much alcohol feeling. Excuse me, but I need to head to the men's room before I barf right here."

He nearly ran toward the men's. He could feel himself getting weaker and weaker by the minute. He threw up and slid to the floor.

"I need to get some help," he said to himself. "Help, someone, help," he could hear himself whispering. "I...I ...need a doc...tor. Someone please help me..."

A few minutes later, Landis opened the bathroom door.

"Charles, are you in here? Hazel said you weren't feeling well. Are you OK? Charles? Charles, are you in here?" he said louder.

"Charles, ol' buddy, are you in here? It's just us guys, if you are embarrassed. Remember, we have all had our nights kissin' the porcelain. Charles? He began banging on each stall as he called out Charles name louder and louder. He looked under one of the stalls to see Charles leaning against the commode with his head nearly in the water.

He reached under and pulled Charles' lifeless body from under the door. Checking for a pulse, he was sure it was too late for Charles. He looked down into hazy gray eyes that stared back at him. He left Charles' body on the floor and ran to get help. He could feel the cold on his hands from Charles' body. He could smell the vomit that still floated in the toilet and the bits of it still remaining on the sides of Charles' mouth and face.

"Help! Someone help! Charles is …," and he remembers that Hazel will probably be in shock when she hears that her husband's body lay on the bathroom floor.

"What? What is it? Landis? Where is Charles? Is he alright?" said Hazel.

"Some one better call 911. Charles is not breathing. I found him on the floor. Please someone, call 911, now!" he repeated.

"What? Charles is not …" Hazel ran toward the men's room shouting his name.

Everyone rushed toward the men's room. Everyone shouting out his name.

When the paramedics arrived, all the club members and other patrons of the Swinging Gate were standing by the bathroom door or next to Hazel in the dinning room. Hazel had fainted and was shaking and pale. Someone had placed a shawl around her shoulders to keep her from going into shock.

A few minutes later, Charles' body was being lifted into an ambulance without the sound of a siren. The dinner dance was ended and all of the club members and Shana
followed behind the slow moving vehicle transporting their friend...the fourth member of The Six Hundred Thousand Dollar Club that would never be spending the gold at the end of the rainbow.

"Too bad, Charles. You were such a nice guy, too. Buying all of those drinks for everyone. What a way to get out of paying the bar bill. Did you enjoy that martini? Was it worth it? Oh, well. You gain some and you lose some. I'll pay for my own drinks. As long as you say good-by to our money...my money, I mean. This little get together for Shana was a very good idea. It made it so easy to eliminate one more of my old friends. Only six more to go and I'll be a happy, happy, prosperous old person."

Chapter Twenty-Six: Who Do You Trust?

The following week was spent consoling Hazel and helping her get through the funeral arrangements. The funeral would be held on Thursday afternoon. It would be a graveside funeral, since Hazel didn't feel right about having it in a church. Because Charles had died right after buying everyone a round of drinks, and because her Baptist background that frowned upon the use of alcohol, she said she did not feel comfortable having him lying there facing up toward Heaven with martinis on his breath.   Everyone told her he wouldn't still have martinis on his breath, but she was not convinced that his services should be in the church, just in case God had a good sense of smell.

On Wednesday, Hazel thought she heard her doorbell ring. She walked slowly toward the window and looked out to see a man in brown suit at her door.
"Mrs. Ron, I am Detective White," he said as he showed her his ID. " I am sorry about your loss. I hate to bother you at this time, but I need to ask you a few questions concerning you husband's death. May I come in and sit down, so we can talk?"
"Questions? What kind of questions? Charles died in the men's room at the Swinging Gate. We had been

The Six Hundred Thousand Dollar Club

dancing and he had a few martinis and he died. What other questions could there be?"

"Sorry, ma'am. I know this is hard for you, but it is important that I get answers to a few questions. I'll try to be brief. If you'll just answer as truthfully as you can...and as detailed as you can remember..."

"What do you mean truthfully? Why would I not tell the truth? Is something wrong? Is there something you aren't telling me, Detective ..."

"White, Detective White. Well, it seems that your husband had some odd substances in his system."

"I told you he had a few martinis. He had prime rib, a baked potato, some vegetables and a chocolate cheesecake for dessert. What other substances could he possibly have in his system? He did have eggs and toast and a cup of coffee for breakfast. He skipped lunch because he wanted to get the car washed before going to the dinner dance and he said he was running late and could eat later, but...he never did...eat, I mean." She began to sob thinking about their last day together.

"The substance I'm speaking of was not the usual food type. It's more of a poison. I'm not positively sure yet, Mrs. Rom, but it looks like your husband was poisoned."

"Poisoned! Poisoned! How could he have been poisoned? Who would have poisoned him? Everyone loved Charles," she wailed. "No one would have poisoned him. Please tell me it's a mistake...your tests made a mistake!" she yelled as tears rolled down her face. She jumped up from the couch and began pacing the floor, wringing her hands as she shook her head in disbelief. "This can't be true. It just can't be true."

"I'm sorry Mrs. Rom. We are still checking everything out, but ...well, we'll make sure we find out how your husband died. If it was foul play, we'll find out the "who","what" and the "why" your husband died. Now if you will tell me who was at the dinner dance with you and Charles. I'll need names and contact information... addresses, phone numbers...relationship to the two of you...anything you can give me ...any disagreements, enemies...anything at all, no matter how insignificant it might seem." He took out his note pad and began writing as Hazel gave him all the information for the club members as well as Shana's name and information. When he asked her to go over the whole day's events from the time she and Charles woke up through the time that his body was removed from the men's room floor, Hazel tried to give detailed information without crying. She was not very successful and had to stop to control her tears several times before she was through.

"Thank you, Mrs. Rom. I'll do everything I can to see that we find out who or what killed...poisoned your husband. I'll be speaking to all the folks on the list that you gave me, so I can get everyone's version. Again, my condolences," he said as he walked toward the door to leave.

Hazel watched as his car drove around the corner and out of sight. "I still can't believe this," she began to weep out loud again. " Who would want to poison my sweet, sweet Charles?"

Everyone was shocked to hear the report that Detective White repeated to each as he made his enquiries. Shock and disbelief. "How could anyone poison Charles?" was the question on everyone's mind.

"I don't understand, Grandmother. Why would anyone want to poison Mr. Rom.? He seemed like such a nice guy. And how could anyone have poisoned him when we were all together the whole night?" asked Shana after Detective White left.

"I don't know dear. Maybe he ate something by accident."

"I don't see how. I didn't see him eating anything other than what he had ordered."

"I don't know why the detective would be questioning me. I really wasn't even at the Swinging Gate except to see that you and Shana got in all right," said Meeno. "I went back to the barn...apartment and waited for you to call me to come pick you up. Why would he think I had anything to do with someone's death? I'm just the hired baby... chauffer. I don't even know these people except to say "hello" when I drive you to the meetings and to your outings. Why would I want to poison anyone of them?"

"I don't think he is accusing you of anything, Meeno. I think he was just trying to get everyone's whereabouts and version as to what happened that night," said Shana.

"Shana's right, Meeno. He said he was asking everyone the same questions so he could get his facts straight. The important thing is to get this whole thing settled. I'm sure none of us would have poisoned Charles. I think it was some sort of accidental poisoning."

"Let's hope so, Grandmother. I would hate to think that one of the club members or you or I or Meeno, poisoned poor Mr. Rom. I know I didn't."

"And I know I didn't either." said Meeno as he huffed out of the room.

The club members decided it was best to call off their regular weekly meetings until Charles' death mystery was solved. Tension ran high and everyone avoided everyone else when possible. No one spoke the words out loud, but it was on everyone's minds that if Charles had indeed been poisoned...possibly by one of the club members, no one wanted to take a chance on being the next victim.

After three weeks and no further answer to the mystery, Verina decided enough was enough. She was not going to let this alleged poisoning destroy The Six Hundred Dollar Club. Not after all the years and money she and Ardon had invested into it.

"People just have to move on. Accidents happen and life goes on with or without our friends," she said to herself. "When Ardon had his accident, I didn't stop living. I didn't stop having our club meetings. It's time to start meeting as usual. I think I'll call the group and see if we can set up a meeting next week. It may be a little early for Hazel, but the rest of us should be more than ready to get on with business."

"I'm not sure I can make it," said Bibi. "I may have to do something that day. I'll have to let you know."
Verina knew Bibi was only making excuses for not attending the meeting. She thought about telling Bibi that there would be eligible men at the meeting, but though even Bibi would not fall for her lie.

After calling all the other members and getting similar excuses, Verina decided she would wait one more week and try again.

"It's time we get the club functioning again," she told each one. "We need to think of the future of our investments. We can't just let everything drop. Remember what you have put into The Six Hundred Dollar Club. Think about what it meant to Charles *and* Ardon. They would not want us to just drop the club now, would they?"

Everyone agreed that the club had come too far to not continue. A meeting was planned for the following Friday.

It was decided that a lunch meeting would be best. An evening meeting would only bring back the memory of the last evening event. The last event when their friend, Charles, had met his maker.

All but Hazel attended the meeting at The Hungry Tiger. Hazel was still grieving Charles' death. She told Verina that she was thinking about dropping out of the club.

Pearl called her and convinced her that she shouldn't do anything about dropping until some time had passed and she could think more clearly.

"OK, I'll give it time. Charles really did enjoy the club. He probably would be disappointed if he knew I dropped out. It's just going to be hard to sit through meetings and not have Charles next to me," said Hazel.

"I understand, Hazel. Don't worry about missing a few meetings. Come back when you feel you are ready. I'll make sure you know when the meetings are, just in case you decide to attend. Remember, we are all here for you," said Pearl.

"I hope so. I hope there isn't someone who is not so "here" for me."

"I do too, Hazel. I do too."

The meeting was quiet and short. Everyone tried to keep the conversation going, but a cloud of darkness seemed to hang above each of their heads. Even Bibi had very little to say.

"I think we should make more effort to comfort Hazel," said Pearl. "She is really having trouble without

Charles. I'm sure she wants to join us, but she's not sure how to handle not having Charles here with her."

"I know how she feels," said Verina. "It was hard for me the first time I came without Ardon."

"I...think I understand, too," said Doralene. "I mean, after Fredrick and I divorced...well, it's just hard, that's all. It's just hard," she said as she glanced over at Verina.

"Yes, very hard," said Verina as she glared at Doralene.

"I agree that we should do more for Hazel. Maybe we could send her more flowers from the club or maybe we could go visit her. Not the whole club at once, but one or two at a time...just until she feels like rejoining us. After all, Charles and Hazel were the first to join after Ardon and I started it," said Verina.

"I don't think we should do things just because they were the first to join. We should be doing it because they are our friends," said Landis.

"Of course not. But you know what I mean. Hazel is a friend, of course," said Verina. " I only meant she has been a long time member, that's all."

It was decided that each member would try to visit Hazel in the following weeks and flowers would be sent with well wishes from the club. It was also decided that the regular meeting would resume, but any special event would best be put off for a few months, or at least until the mystery of Charles' death was solved.

Three months have passed and the investigation into Charles' death is still in process. The police have arrested no one. They still have not come up with any clues or evidence as to how Charles came to have poison in his system. No suspects, no motives, though the possibility that The Six Hundred Thousand Dollar Club may have something to do with his early demise had crossed

Detective White's mind, though he had not a speck of evidence to back up his thoughts. He had to agree that he found nothing irregular about the club other than the club itself.

"It's probably just a bunch of crazy old nuts having a little fun hoping for a little money in the end," he told himself. "I can't find anything they have done against the law. And they do have that lawyer. He verified everything is on the up and up. Everybody getting along, having dinner and drinks together all the time. Can't see any murderers among them."

Hazel was finally starting to attend the meetings after much prodding from the club members. It had been six month since Charles' funeral and her days were beginning to seem normal again. She had days that she wept uncontrollably. She also had days that she missed her friends and longed to spend time with them doing the things that they did before the "poisoning accident"…or whatever it was that took her husband from her. She still couldn't figure out how Charles could have accidentally gotten poison down his throat and not known it. "Accident" was suggested by the police and by the club members. She was not convinced. Detective White had told her that they would keep working on the case. She hoped they would.

The fall was always a special time for the club because every year they had a Fall Festival Dinner Dance. It was always planned weeks ahead and everyone was expected to help with the preparation. This year was no exception. Hazel was not expected to do a lot, but she wanted to do her part. She thought it might help take her mind off of Charles, but instead it brought back memories that made her depressed. She was determined to fight the sadness in her heart and took on more of the planning than she had in previous years.

"I can get through this," she told herself as she looked over the list of her duties. "I will and I will enjoy it," she lied.

"You know, I think instead of a dance we should just have a dinner," said Owen as he was lifting his tux off of the hanger. "I probably will need to take this monkey suit to the cleaners. I don't know why we have to have a dance every year. It's always the same only less partners to dance with. I think I'll see if I can convince the others to just drop the dance and stick with nice dinner instead. I'm almost positive Hazel would agree, since it was a dinner dance where her husband was poisoned," he said as he laid his tux on the bed and went to the phone to call Landis, Hazel, Pearl, Doralene and Verina. He asked Pearl if she would call Bibi. He knew if he got Bibi one the phone, he would be in for a long night of constant chatter. He was in no mood for that tonight.

"Well, I agree that we have less choice for partners," said Verina, "but I don't see that it matters. I guess if the others want to have a dinner, we can discuss it. Why don't we meet tomorrow and decide?"

"I agree with Owen," said Pearl as she took out a notebook to take the minuets. Or maybe we could have a potluck instead. We could have it at a park or at someone's house."

"AH... I'm not so sure I want to eat food that someone cooks at home...no offence, ladies, but ...you understand... after what happened to our friend, Charles. Sorry, Hazel. I hope I didn't upset you, but..." said Landis.

"Landis is right. Not that I fear that one of us is a murderer, but no sense taking chances," said Doralene.

"Well, then how about a bar-b-que?" said Bibi.

"No, a bar-b-que would be the same as a potluck. Still food cooked at someone's house. Not a good idea," said Landis.

"I say, let's just go as we had planned. The plans have all been made and everyone has been working hard on the preparations. The room had been reserved so we can put up our decorations and everything already. If we want to eliminate the dance part, then fine, but let's stick with the dinner anyway...at the Jade Turtle. If someone feels like dancing, they can...if not we can just have our dinner and enjoy each other's company," said Verina.

Since no one could come up with a better idea, all the members agreed to stick with the original plan. The Annual Six Hundred Thousand Dollar Club Dinner Dance would be held in two weeks at the Jade Turtle. "Dance if you wish...just eat if you don't" was the theme this year.

Chapter Twenty-Seven: The Revenge Begins

"Shana, dear, I hope you will be thinking about what you plan to wear to the fall dinner dance. I don't think you will want to wear the same gown that we bought for the last one. We wouldn't want people to think that's the only gown you own."

"But it is the only gown I own, Grandmother. Remember, I'm a jeans and sweatshirt girl. Besides, I'm not sure I will be going. I feel like I have a little touch of the flu coming on. The dinner dance is only two days away and I wouldn't want to spread germs. Will you be terribly disappointed if I don't go?"

"Well, no, not if you aren't feeling well, dear. But if you feel better tomorrow, I think we should go do a little shopping…just in case you decide to go."

"OK. In the mean time, do you have any aspirin? I feel like my head is about to explode. I think I have a fever, too."

"Come let me feel your forehead, dear. Yes, yes, I think you do have a fever. The aspirin is in the medicine cabinet in the hall bathroom. You should drink a glass of orange juice, too. Vitamin C will help fight off the flu. Maybe you should go back to bed and get some rest. I do hope you feel better by tomorrow."

"I do too, Grandmother. I don't know how I could have gotten the flu. I really haven't been near anyone ill."

"Sometimes there are just germs floating around in the air we breath, dear. Now, go get some rest. Oh, before you go, dear, would you mind going into the garage and getting the hammer for me. It's in the red toolbox on the shelf. I noticed that there was a nail sticking out of one of the boards of the railing on the porch. I thought I'd ask Meeno to fix it for me. I'll forget if I don't put the hammer where I can see it to remind me."

"Sure, Grandmother. I'll do it right now, before I go get the aspirin and juice."

"Thank you. You are such a dear."

After getting the hammer, Shana went to take the aspirin and downed a large glass of orange juice before heading toward the bedroom.

"I sure hope Grandmother is right about this orange juice. I sure don't want to be stuck in bed with the flu for a week."

Shana did not feel any better by the afternoon of the dinner dance. In fact, she felt worse. She had drunk enough orange juice in the last week to keep the stockholders of the Florida Orange Juice Company happy for a long, long time.

"I'm not so sure this vitamin C from orange juice is all that it's cracked up to be. It doesn't seem to have much effect on me," she said as she rolled over and covered her throbbing head with her pillow. "I guess I won't be going to any dinner dance tonight. All I want to do is sleep and get rid of this headache."

"How is Shana feeling?" asked Pearl as she sat down at the end of the table at The Jade Turtle. "I hope she's feeling better, poor dear."

"She said she still is having headaches and last night I heard her coughing all during the night. I was hoping she would be able to come tonight, but there was no way in the condition she's in. She didn't even want to eat a slice of toast this morning. I had to practically feed it to her myself. I do hope she gets better soon," said Verina.

"I know when I had the flu a couple of years ago, I felt just awful," said Bibi. "I hope I never get it again for as long as I live."

Everyone began sharing their stories about their bouts with the flu, each one trying to top the other as to the severity of their illness. After all had told flu story after flu story, they went on to tell about other illnesses and pains they had experienced over the years.

"OK. Enough of this "I was sicker than you" stuff," said Doralene. "I feel like dancing before dinner. Anyone want to shake a leg with me?" Maybe build up the old appetite?"

"OK. I'll give it a try," said Landis. "As long as it's not one of those ...what do they call it...break dancing things? My ol' legs can't take too much action these days."

"I'd like to dance...if someone would ask me," said Bibi as she looked in Owen's direction.

"OK. I get the hint, Bibi. Come on. Let's get this over with. I know you aren't going to let it rest until someone dances with you."

"Why, thank you for asking me, Owen. I would love to dance with you."

Hazel, Pearl and Verina decided they would look over the menu while the others were on the dance floor.

"I just love the desserts here, don't you?" said Pearl.

"We haven't even had the main course yet, and you are looking at the desserts, Pearl?" said Hazel.

"The desserts do look good," said Verina. "But I think we had better concentrate on the salads and the main course first. Or maybe we should be looking at the appetizers first. Yes. I think we should order appetizers for everyone. I wonder what everyone would like?"

"I love the stuffed mushrooms myself. But maybe we should wait and let everyone order what they like. We wouldn't want anybody to think we ordered poison for them," said Pearl. "Oh, sorry, Hazel. I shouldn't have said that. Please forgive me and my big stupid mouth."

"It's alright, Pearl. I knew what you meant," she smiled. "You didn't offend me. No need to watch every word you say because of me. Just relax and have a good time tonight. After all, this is the Annual Six Hundred Thousand Dollar Club Fall Festival Dinner Dance. We are here to have a good time...all of us."

"I guess you're right, Hazel. Good time it is!" said Pearl as she glanced toward the dance floor just in time to see Owen bending over Bibi in an effort to do the dip.

As the two couples returned to the table, the server approached with four more menus.

"Ah, time to eat. You are right, Doralene. Dancing did wake up my appetite. I'm starving. What's everybody ordering?" asked Landis as he looked over the menu.

"We thought we might order appetizers first," said Verina

"What would you all like?"

"Good idea," said Owen. "I'm starving too."

Stuffed mushrooms, shrimp and clams on a half shell were ordered. Doralene had asked the server if everyone could have their own cocktail sauce and dip for the mushrooms.

"With that flu bug going around, I think we should try to keep our germs to ourselves," she said when everyone looked at her at once.

Bibi decided she wanted to skip appetizers and continued to look over the main course.

While waiting for the appetizers to arrive, Bibi, Owen, Landis and Doralene decided to hit the dance floor again.

"No use letting good music go to waste," said Doralene.

Hazel looked at Pearl and said, " Hey, Pearl, is it still OK for ladies to dance together, if there aren't any men around to dance with?"

"Don't see why not. Let's do it! It's not like it's slow dance music they're playing right now. Do you remember how to do the Bop?"

"Sure do. If only my body can remember," said Hazel.

"I think I'll go call Shana while everybody's dancing," said Verina. I told Meeno to look in on her, but I'd feel better if I knew she is OK."

"Good idea, Verina. Tell her we're thinking about her and wish she could be here," said Hazel.

By the time everyone returned from the dance floor, the appetizers had arrived. Verina was just returning to the table after talking to Shana.

"Umm… this looks delicious," said Doralene. "Will someone pass one of those dips and cocktail sauces to me, please? I can't wait to dig into this."

"Here you go, Doralene. Enjoy!" said Owen as he passed the dip and sauce to her. "I'm glad you ordered one for each of us. I don't think I want to share mine with anyone. I may even have to order another one of each. I love the cocktail sauce here. It always has a little kick to it."

"Yum. This is delicious. And you're right. It does have a kick. This is really spicy hot, don't you think? Just the way I like it," said Doralene as she dipped another shrimp into the sauce.

The rest of the evening was filled with food, good conversation, dancing, more food, more conversation and more dancing. Everyone agreed that the dinner dance was a success and should be repeated next year, hopefully with all of the members of the club in attendance.

"Yes, good food indeed. Wasn't that the best cocktail sauce you have ever tasted, Doralene? A little spicy hot, was it? Too bad it will be your last. You should be feeling just how good it really was in oh…about twelve hours or so. I hadn't planned for you to be the next one to say good-bye to your friends, but that's what you get for digging into it so fast. You should have had more patience and maybe someone else would have been the unfortunate loser of the six hundred thousand dollars. Only five more to go…then I'll be declared the winner. The winner of the whole spicy hot pot, that is."

"I must be catching that flu bug that Shana has. I feel awful. Every time I throw up, my mouth burns. I hate throwing up! I'm getting so dizzy, that I think I might fall down," said Doralene to herself. "And these cramps are getting worse. I've never had such pain," she whispered as she lowered herself to the floor.

"I can't even get to the phone to call for help…help," she whispered as she closed her eyes and slid into unconsciousness.

Two days after the dinner dance, Bibi called Doralene to see if she would like to go to the movies with Pearl and herself. She had called several times, but Doralene was not answering her phone. After the fifth try, Bibi decided that maybe she and Pearl could just go by her house on their way to the movies. They would leave early enough to give Doralene time to get ready if she wanted to go along.

"I wonder why she isn't answering her phone?" asked Bibi as she rang the doorbell. "I hope she's home."

"I don't remember her saying she was going anyplace. Maybe she's just out shopping," said Pearl. "Or maybe she had a secret date. She and Landis seem to hit it off at the dinner dance, don't you think?"

"Well, that would be just great! She gets a date and I still can't get anybody to take me anywhere. I practically had to beg Owen to dance with me. Doralene...if you're in there, open this door!" Bibi shouted as she banged on the door with her fist.

When Doralene did not answer her door Pearl and Bibi returned to go to Pearl's car and headed toward the movies.

"I'll call her tomorrow, Bibi. If she had a date, I'll let you know all the details...if she will give me any."

"Good. I hope she just went shopping!"

"That's not nice, Bibi. You shouldn't begrudge Doralene happiness."

"I know. I'm sorry. I just want to have a simple date, too...with anybody. I don't care with whom. I'm not that particular at this point. As long as he's breathing...I'll accept."

No one had heard from Doralene in a week. Everyone was beginning to get worried. Landis said he did not have a date with Doralene.

"Maybe we should call the police to go check on her," said Pearl. "It's not like her to just ignore all of us. I have a bad feeling about this. I'll call the police if none of you want to."

"I think you are right. What's the worst thing that can happen? The police will go check and if she has business of her own...well, at least we'll know she's OK," said Landis. "Go ahead and call, Pearl."

"I think I'll go by her house one more time just to see if she is there first. Would you like to go along, Bibi?"

"Sure, I'll go with you. Shall we go now? Then I think we had better call the police if she doesn't answer her door."

"Has anyone talked to Fredrick? Maybe he knows something," said Verina.

"I'll call him right now," replied Owen.

Pearl and Bibi left to go check on Doralene and Owen went to call Fredrick.

As Pearl and Bibi walked up the sidewalk leading to Doralene's house Pearl stopped and looked into Doralene's mailbox.

"Hmm..., that's odd. Doralene has a whole stack of mail in her box...and here's her alimony check from Fredrick. You know she always practically knocks the postman over trying to get to her mailbox to grab that monthly check. Why would it still be in her mailbox this late in the month?" asked Pearl.

"I don't know. It sure seems fishy to me. Let's go knock on her door," said Bibi as she continued up the sidewalk.

"She's still not answering. Something must be wrong," said Pearl.

Peering through the window, Bibi said, " I can't see anyone in there. Yuck! What is that smell? I think there must be a dead cat or dog or something around here."

"Bibi, let's go!"

"Why? We haven't talked to Doralene yet. Shouldn't we knock…"

"Bibi, let's go, now! Get in the car! We have to call the police, now!" shouted Pearl.

The police report confirmed that ricin, an extremely toxin protein substance, was found in Doralene's body. How it got there was the mystery that Detective White was determined to solve. He had a hunch that someone in the Six Hundred Thousand Dollar Club had the answers he was looking for. Someone knew more about poisons than the average person. He's goal was to find out who that someone was, hopefully before another member of that club decided to unknowingly eat himself into his or her grave.

"OK, we've been through this before. I want a statement from all of you, telling me about where you all have been and what you have been doing in the past two weeks. And you, Mr. Drake, I need to know when was the last time you saw or spoke to your ex-wife and don't leave any detail out, no matter how insignificant you might think it is, understand, everybody? Now let's hear your story starting with you, Miss Preston," said Detective White as he reached for his notebook and pen.

"I suggest that you all stay as close to home as possible in the next few days. I'll be getting back to each of you. "You may want to avoid any social gatherings until we get to the bottom of this. Oh, and I'm sorry for your loss, Mr. Drake. My condolences to the rest of you too," said

Detective White as he stood to leave. "I'll let you know when and if I find out anything significant."

"I think we need to hire our own detective to help find out what's going on," said Shana to Verina as they sat on the patio sipping their tea later that night of Detective White's visit. "I'm beginning to get scared. Something weird is happening and you all could be in danger. There may be a murderer on the loose and who knows when he may strike again. You could be next, Grandmother."

"Oh, I'm sure I'm perfectly safe, dear. I don't think we need to hire anyone. Detective White said he will do all he can to solve this mystery. I'm sure he'll do his best to find out and arrest who ever…if anyone, that is, that has murdered poor Charles and Doralene. We just need to sit tight and have patience, dear."

"Detective White's best may not be enough, Grandmother. I think we need more than his expertise on this."

"Let's just wait and see, dear. Let's give him a chance to do his job, OK?"

"We'll see. Good night, Grandmother. See you in the morning," said Shana as she kissed Verina on the cheek. Going inside, she took her teacup to the kitchen sink and then slowly walked toward her bedroom.

"I need to get some sleep. I think I'll start looking for a good private investigator tomorrow. If Grandmother won't loan me the money, I'll use my savings that I was going to use to go to nursing school next year. My education can wait. Grandmother's safety is more important," she said as she turned off the light and rolled over on her side. "Yes, that's exactly what I'll do first thing tomorrow."

Chapter Twenty-Eight: Three Heads Are Better Than Two

Shana got up early the next morning. She was dressed and ready to go out the door by the time Verina came into the kitchen.

"My, you're up early, dear. Did you sleep well?"

"Yes, Grandmother. I have a couple of errands I would like to get to this morning. I had a slice of toast. Would you like for me to make breakfast for you before I go out?"

"No, dear. I'll be fine. Do you want Meeno to drive you?"

"No, thanks Grandmother. I need to put gas in my car, so I'll drive myself. I'll try to be back early, but if I'm not back by lunchtime, don't wait for me. I'll grab something in town if I'm running late. I better get going if I want to get all of my errands done today. Love you," she said as she headed out the door. She was glad she had time to look up a couple of private detectives before her grandmother got up.

"Why is it that when you are in a hurry, you can never find a parking space? Oh, wait, there's one if I can squeeze into it. It's tight, but I think I can make it," Shana said as she maneuvered into the one and only space in sight. "If I can just squeeze…Oh no, I almost took out that BMW. Oh no, I didn't see that guy in it. Boy, he looks mad. Now I'm going to get," she said as she nearly scrapped the side of it as she tried to back out of the spot. "Let me try this again," she said as the owner of the BMW came rushing around the side of her door shouting and pounding on her window.

"What is wrong with you? Can't you see my car parked here? You nearly took the side off my car! And lady, I doubt you want to have to make a claim to your insurance company to cover the cost of repairs on my BMW...if you even have insurance. By the looks of that piece of junk you're trying to squeeze into my front seat, I doubt you even have insurance."

"I'm sorry. I didn't mean to get so close to your car. I was just trying to pull into this parking space. I guess I misjudged ..."

"Never mind. I have better things to do than to argue with a woman driver who can't even park a... what is this...an "ivic"? Excuse me, I have clients waiting and I'm running late, thanks to you," he said as he retrieved his briefcase out of his trunk and headed toward his office.

"This day is not going like I planned," said Shana as she locked her car door and headed toward the office of Richard Long, Private Investigator.

"Your next appointment should be here any minute, Richard," said Tracy Eager, Richard's assistant of five years. Together they had investigated and solved more cases than they could remember. Tracy was usually the one assigned to doing the research, while Richard spent most of his time checking out the facts of each case. He had become extremely proficient in his judgment of character, which helped to recognize truth from fiction.

"Sorry I'm late. I would have been here on time, but this ...this woman tried to take the whole side off of my car in the parking lot. You should have seen the piece of crap she was trying to squeeze into the space next to me. She's probably been driving all over town not even knowing her "C" is missing on her "ivic". How embarrassing is that?" he chuckled.

Just as he was getting his last sentence out, he turned to see Shana standing in the doorway. The look on her face told him that she had heard his every word.

"Oh, no. Don't tell me you are my next client."

"No, Mr. Long, I am not! I was going to ask you to represent my case, but I can't possibly hire anyone as rude as you! And I knew my "C" was missing, thank you very much!" She spun around and grabbed for the door handle. She was so angry that she had trouble opening the door.

"So, you have problems with opening doors, too, do you Miss..."

"Miss Willow, Richard. Her name is Miss Shana Willow," said Tracy trying to hold back a snicker.

"I apologize, Miss Willow. I didn't mean to offend you..."

"You mean you didn't mean for me to hear you offending me, Mr. Long. Isn't that what you meant to say?"

Richard reached for her hand that was still resting on the doorknob.

"Why don't we start over and you can tell me what it is that you need my services for, Miss Willow? I promise I won't say another word about your parking ability nor your ivi...I mean your Civic."

"Well I was going to ask you to find out who is poisoning the members of my grandmother's club. The Six Hundred Thousand Dollar Club. But, now..."

"Wait a minute. I just read about those alleged poisonings. You say your grandmother is a member of that club?"

"She and my deceased grandfather were the founders of the club."

"I've heard about it. You have to admit, it's a most unusual club. The only one of its kind, I believe. So you think …"

"I think someone is poisoning the members and I fear for my grandmother's safety. But as I was about to say, I'll find someone else to help me, thank you, Mr. Long.

"No, wait. I'm sure we can mend our differences for the sake of your grandmother's safety, don't you?"

"Are you mocking me, now, Mr. Long? Because if you are…"

"No, no. I'm not mocking you. I'm just trying to convince you that I can probably help you out here."

"Well, I guess we can talk. I'll have to write a check for your services today and you agree to take my case, and if I agree to let you, I can make payments if you'll let me. After all, I do have to keep up with my insurance premiums," said Shana as she lowered her eyes and smiled.

"Deal. Now, will you step into my office?"

"Hey, Richard, darling, did you know there are more accidents caused by men than women?" said Tracy smiling.

"Tracy, that's not funny!" replied Richard as he guided Shana into his office.

"I'm not trying to be funny. It's right here on the Internet. Check it out yourself if you don't believe me."

"That's probably because there are more men drivers than there are women drivers on the road. And will you please give that Internet a rest? I swear you spend more time looking up trivial information than you spend working on our cases."

"The Internet is where I get most of my facts. And you just remember that the next time you ask me for information that you need, Mr. Long!" she laughed. "Hmm... what other interesting information can I look up?" she said.

"I'll need to talk to Detective White and all of the club members and...what did you say Doralene's ex's name is?" asked Richard after Shana had given him all of the details of the events since she had arrived at her grandmother's home.

"Fredrick Drake."

"And this chauffer, Meeno Max. Is there anyone else that may have connections to the club or people connected to anyone in the club?"

"No, no one I know. Oh, wait. There is the lawyer, George Imimes. He oversees the contract that the members sighed way back in 1953 when the club was formed, according to my grandmother. That's all I know of."

"OK. Well, I'll check all of this information out and let you know if I think I can accept the case."

"OK. How much do I owe you for today, Mr. Long?" Shana said as she reached in her purse to retrieve her checkbook.

"Why don't we wait on my fee until we decide if I can be of assistance. It's the least I can do to let the consultation fee ride for now since I was such a jerk to you in the parking lot. Just be careful when you pull out of that space. Remember there's a very expensive automobile parked mighty close to your...Civic."

"I will, and thank you Mr. Long for listening to my concerns. I'm sure you'll do a good job...if you take my case. I'll be waiting to hear from you. Have a good day, sir," Shana said as she got up to leave.

"I will. And I will do my best to solve this most unusual case. You can put your money on that."

Richard walked Shana to the door. He started to open it for her when she said, "I do know how to open doors, Mr. Long, whether you believe it or not."

Returning to his office, he stopped in front of Tracy's desk.

"Are you still looking up 'important facts' on that thing, Tracy?" he chuckled.

"Did you know…" is all he heard as he picked up the phone to call Detective White's office.

"So…you're no closer to finding out who poisoned these old people than you were three weeks ago, is that what you're saying, Detective White? No clues, no motives, no suspects?"

"That's exactly what I'm saying. And I've worked my tail off trying to get somewhere, anywhere, on this case. My men have been shaking every bush they can to find something to go on. Nothing. Absolutely, nothing!"

"Well, then you shouldn't mind that I've been hired to do a little bush shaking myself. If you will give me a little look- see at the reports I would greatly appreciate it."

"Only if you promise that you will stay clear of police business. Stay out of my way and make sure I know everything you come up with. I'm only doing this because we've been friends for more years than I want to think about and because you know your stuff, also because I'm in a hole right now with this case. Understood?"

"Understood."

"And that part about me being in a hole stays between us.'

"OK, OK! I get it! Now for the report?"

"I'll have a copy ready for you to pick up in a few minutes."

"Thanks, ol' pal. I appreciate it."

"You're welcome. Good luck…and remember I *will* be waiting for any and all information."

"Well, what did Detective White have to offer, Richard? Anything you might use to get started on the mystery poisoning case…or did you decide not to take it?"

"Oh, I'm taking it alright. You know I love a challenge. Here, look at the reports he gave me. See if you get anything out of them. I need to go see Mr. Drake after lunch. Did you order us lunch, by the way?"

"No, I wasn't sure when you'd return. How about I order us sandwiches from the deli down the street? What would you like?"

"The usual…pastrami on rye. And don't let them forget my pickle this time. What's a pastrami on rye without the pickle, I ask."

After lunch, Richard made a visit to see Fredrick Drake.

Finding out that Fredrick had not personally seen Doralene for months, Richard decided it was time to meet Shana's grandmother. He could only imagine what that was going to be like. Shana had already told him that her grandmother had said that they didn't need a hired private eye.

"Seems to me that she would want any help she could get to find out what's been happening to her friends," he thought.

Verina was sitting on the patio enjoying her afternoon cup of hot tea when Richard arrived. Shana led him to the patio where she introduced him to her grandmother.

"Who is it, dear? Who was at the door?"

"Grandmother, I would like to introduce Mr. Richard Long. He is a private investigator. I hired him for us..."

"What! What do you mean, you hired for us? I said we didn't need anyone. Detective White is doing his best. Why did you go behind my back and do such a thing, Shana?"

"I didn't exactly go behind your back, Grandmother. I told you I was going out to take care of a few errands, remember?"

"You did not say one of those errands was to hire a private investigator! I am truly disappointed in you, Shana."

"I'm sorry, Grandmother, but I am thinking of your safety and that of the other club members. I am sorry you disapprove, but what is done is done. We now have a private investigator and I am paying him with my own money."

"Excuse me ladies," interrupted Richard. "Maybe you need to discuss this among yourselves. I can come back later."

"No, no. I have hired you...haven't I? Go ahead and do what ever it is you do, Mr. Long," said Shana. "Please have a seat. May I get you a cup of tea or something?"

"No thank you. Maybe I should just start asking the questions I have on my list," he said looking down at the blank notebook on his lap.

"Very well, Mr. Long. Since my granddaughter insists that she has to waste her money...go ahead and start investigating us if you must."

Richard heard practically the same version of the past few weeks of events as he had already heard from Shana.

"This makes my note taking simpler," he thought. I'll just have Tracy type them up more formally for me when I get back to the office."

Shana walked him to the door after he had finished his interview with Shana and her grandmother.

"I'm sorry about my grandmother, Mr. Long. She seems to be very stubborn at times. Thank you for taking my case."

"It's OK. I guess it's just payback time for the parking lot incident. I would like to talk with the club members and the chauffer, though. Do you know when would be the best time to meet with them?"

"Well, Meeno is off today, but he will probably be here tomorrow. I think he said he was going to visit his friend someplace, but I don't remember where. As far as the club members, they usually meet weekly if you would like to meet them all at the same time. I'll have to let you know when they plan to meet again. I think they are trying to stay close to home until this is all settled. I'll give you their home information if you want to visit them individually."

"Yes. I will be visiting them individually, but maybe I should meet them all together first. Sometimes people have different reactions within a group than they do when they are alone. I like to see body and face language in different environments. You'd be surprised at the differences."

"OK. Well I'll call you with the information about the next meeting. Have a nice evening, Mr. Long."

"And to you, Miss Willow."

When Richard returned to his office, Tracy was on the Internet as usual.

"And so she sits at her computer, staring at all that wonderful information flying across the screen at lighting speed," he teased as he walked past Tracy's desk.

"Hey, wait, Mr. smart guy. You may want to take a look at this. I looked up the poisonous material that the report shows was in the bodies of Doralene Drake and Charles Rom. Both were from poisonous plants or parts of them. Look. It says here, Nerium oleander, commonly known as oleander, contains cardiac glycosides, oldendrin and nerioside. All found in Charles Rom's body. And, Ricinus communis, better know to us as the castor bean, contains one of the most toxic substances; ricin, found in our friend Mrs. Doralene Drake's body."

"You have to be kidding. How could they have consumed poison from plants? Rom had just had dinner at a restaurant and Drake…well according to the report, had dinner with the club at a dinner dance a few days before she was found dead. Most of the food content had been thrown up into the toilet at her home, but it looked like she had enjoyed a normal meal just like the rest of the club…in a restaurant…not the same restaurant where Rom met his death. I don't get it.

"Well, the oleander could have been put in water, food or any number of ways. The castor bean… Well the only way to get the poison to work effectively, I think is, someone would have had to pulverize the beans. It says here that the poison would have to be chewed well, because the hard seed coat prevents rapid absorption. I can't imagine anyone eating the beans without realizing it."

"Keep working on it, Tracy. Let me know what you find."

"Oh, now it's OK to use my Internet to get information for you. I told you, you'd be asking for my expertise sooner or later. I'll keep looking."

"So...when are you and the club meeting again, Grandmother?" asked Shana as she and Verina were having dinner.

"I'm not sure. I do wish we could get together soon. I'm even starting to miss Bibi's chatter, if you can believe that. Maybe I should call and see if the group wants get together for a meeting to discuss what's happening with the investigation."

"That sounds like a good idea, Grandmother. I know you miss seeing your friends."

"Yes, I do. We don't have that many years left on this earth and it would be a shame to be deprived of what little time we have to share our friendship. I can't believe people think one of us would do our friends in...not if they knew us all from the beginning of our club. Such a shame."

"I hope you aren't still upset with me for hiring Mr. Long, Grandmother. I really am concerned about your safety."

"I know dear. I'm not upset. I just don't know how he can do any better than Detective White. Seems to me that if too many people are trying to stir the pot, the pot will never boil and may even get knocked over, that's all."

"So, do we want to meet on Wednesday, then?" asked Verina as she called each club member to set up a meeting to discuss the situation and to make decisions about the future of the club. She was beginning to fear that the members would want to disband the club. "And then what would happen to all the money if that happens?" she wondered. "I can't remember if we had a clause about disbandment. I'll have to get my copy of the contract out and look it up, I guess, just in case the issue comes up...which, I'm hoping it won't."

"It's fine with me," said Bibi. "Only let's not have food or drink unless we bring our own. We don't really need to eat, do we?"

"That sounds fair. Let's let the others know they can bring something if they feel they need to have refreshments. I'll see you on Wednesday at the Pink Slipper, Bibi." Verina was hoping that the owners of the Pink Slipper would not ask them to leave if they weren't ordering anything.

"Mr. Long, this is Shana Willow. I'm calling to let you know that the club is meeting on Wednesday at The Pink Slipper on Southern Avenue. They plan to meet at around four o'clock. Grandmother said that everyone will be bringing their own refreshments if they want. This way, no one will be fearing another poisoning incident.'

"Oh, that should make the folks at the Pink Slipper happy. People taking up their tables and not eating or drinking, he chuckled. "How about we meet and go together? This way you can introduce me."

"OK. Do you want me to pick you up?"

"No, why don't you meet me here at my office and I'll drive."

"Why? Are you ashamed to be seen in my "ivic" ?"

"No, I just think, since you are paying me, I should at least use my gas."

"I hope your grandmother has cooled down a little by now. I wouldn't want my head to be chopped off."

"I think she's OK now. She said she wasn't upset. She just thinks Detective White can handle it."

"Hello, everybody," said Shana as she approached the table where the club was holding their meeting. "I would like you to meet Mr. Richard Long…"

"What's he doing here?" said Verina as she glared up at Richard.

"Shana told me you all might be meeting here today, so I thought it might be a good time to get to know you all and introduce myself. I'm Richard Long, Private Investigator. Shana has hired me to help solve the mystery of the deaths of your friends."

"A dick named Dick? Now that's a new one," laughed Owen.

Landis began laughing and shaking his head.

"That's not funny you two," said Shana. Mr. Long is here to help us. He doesn't need to be insulted."

"I can't help it," said Landis as he shook his head again. "It's just that I was remembering back when I was teaching and every year we teachers could hardly wait to see the list of kids on our roll. Well some of the names... well, you know how they always list the name of the kids with last name first, then the first name? We used to laugh at how funny some of them came out. You know like...Patty Rice would be Rice Patty...John Deer would be Deer John...and then there was Billy Tall...Tall Billy, who was the shortest kid in the class. Now we have Dick Long. Your teachers must have had a good laugh at that one, Mr. Long," he said as he and Owen burst out laughing again.

"I don't get it," said Bibi.

This only made Owen and Landis laugh louder.

"Stop it you two," shouted Shana. "Please excuse these men. Apparently they can't help themselves," she said as she started to walk away.

"It's OK, Shana. Let these fellows have their fun. Actually it is quite amusing. I guess I never noticed how funny my name and title could be," he laughed. "Thanks for pointing that out gentlemen."

"Glad to meet you Mr. Long. My name is Pearl Preston and these two ladies are Bibi Mercille and Hazel Rom. The two idiots over there are Landis Gray and Owen Wheeler," she said as she pointed toward the two men still trying to control their laughter. And I think you already know Verina Steris? Please have a seat. We are just about to finish up our business, then we can talk, if that is alright with you."

Shana and Richard sat down and refrained from talking until Verina called the meeting adjourned.

"Well, that was interesting," said Richard as he and Shana drove back to his office. I gotta' say, those old guys have a hilarious sense of humor. I've never had anyone laugh so hard about my name before. They almost had me joining them in their laughter.'

"Weren't you embarrassed?"

"Embarrassed? No, why should I be embarrassed? Everything they said was true," he chuckled. "I've heard worse. At least they weren't trying to shoot me like one of the cheating husbands that I was hired to follow once."

"Sorry about Owen and Landis, dear. I hope they didn't cause hard feeling between you and your friend Mr. Long," said Verina

"No, he took it pretty well ...and he's not really my friend. He's a hired private eye, remember? He actually thought they were, I think the word he used was "hilarious'. He said he almost had to laugh with them."

"Has he figured out the murders, yet? I hope he isn't just taking your money for nothing."

"No, but I think he is getting closer to figuring out the cause."

"We already know that they were poisoned, don't we dear? Detective White already told us that much...and he's not charging us an arm and a leg for it."

"To quote your words, Grandmother 'let's give him time'. I'm sure he will come up with something soon."

"Mr. Max, what can you tell me about the people of the Six Hundred Thousand Dollar Club?" asked Richard as he took out his notebook again.

"I know they are a bunch of old coots that want to get rich. But I guess you have found that out already. They probably are harmless, but still...well you know...maybe one or more of them might not be as harmless as they appear, if you know what I mean."

"Do you know of anyone of them that may have a grudge against the others?"

"No. They all seem to get along as far as old grumpy people go. They have their days, like everyone else, I guess."

"What happened to Mr. Steris? I've been told that he died in an accident. Is that true?"

"Yes. He was... well let's just say he was someplace with someone when he shouldn't have been."

"What do you mean?"

"I mean, he was with someone other than Mrs. Steris, if you get my drift."

"And who would that be, Mr. Max? I need a name, if you please."

"Well, let's just say, the lady is no longer with us. It seems she had a little too much to eat or drink a couple of weeks ago."

"You mean Mrs. Doralene Drake? Are you saying Mr. Steris and Mrs. Drake were having an affair?"

"Well, if going out dancing and dining and spending some time in sleazy motels qualifies as an affair…"

"Did Mrs. Steris know?"

"I'm not sure. I don't think so, but she may have had her suspicions. You know how wives are. They always seem to know when their husbands are going astray. It was none of my business, so I kept out of it. I'm just the chauffer, not the marriage police."

"Thank you, Mr. Max. I may have other questions for you later. If you think of anything that may be useful, please call me," said Richard as he handed Meeno his card.

"Sure thing. I'll call if I think of anything," replied Meeno as he closed the door of his barn…apartment.

Richard and Detective White met several times over the next few days to compare notes. Neither could come up with anything solid as to how, why or by whom the two victims had been poisoned. Both men were determined to find out before the next victim munched on his or her last meal.

Chapter Twenty-Nine: Tea For One

"Well, what did you think of that Six Hundred thousand Dollar Club now that you've had time to visit each of them, Richard?" asked Tracy.

"I think they are a very unusual group, that's for sure. They're quite pleasant and very entertaining, especially Landis and Owen. And there just aren't any words to describe Bibi. Hazel is a little quiet, but that's probably because of her husband's death and the mystery that surrounds it. Verina ...well, I think she still resents the fact that Shana hired me. She doesn't say much, but it shows in her eyes and body language. She definitely doesn't care much for me. Pearl doesn't seem to fit into the group."

"Why not?"

"Because she seems normal. Nothing quirky about her."

"Does that make her more of a suspect over the others?"

"No. Maybe she just had money to invest in the club and enjoys the social benefits. As I said, those old folks are entertaining enough. You probably couldn't get as much entertainment if you went to a comedy show. Of course she is paying a thousand dollars a year for that entertainment."

"Yes, but don't forget that if she outlives the others, she gets her investment plus a whole lot more."

"Yep! That's true!" said Richard as he turned to go into his office.

A few minutes later he returned to Tracy's desk.
"Tracy, I'm going out for a while. I have a couple of errands to run and then I think I'll run by to see Shana. Do you know where the nearest Civic dealership is? And where I can buy some Gorilla Glue?"
"No, but I'll look it up if you'll give me a couple of minutes."

In five minutes Richard had both Smiling Sam's Civic Honda Dealership and the name and address of the nearest hardware store carrying Gorilla Glue in his hands, thanks to Tracy's Internet skills.
"You're welcome!" said Tracy to herself as she watched Richard disappear out of the office door. "He just doesn't appreciate the value of the Internet."

"I'll get it, Grandmother," Shana shouted as she ran to answer the door.
"Now, who could that be? I hope it's not Detective White or that Mr. Long again. Don't they know we can't help either of them with solving the case of the deaths of our friends? Don't they realize that every time they come around asking questions it just takes longer for us to get over our grieving?"
"Hello, Mr. Long. Won't you come in? I'm afraid Grandmother is not in a very good mood today. She isn't appreciative of you or Detective White coming around asking questions. I guess I'm apologizing in advance."
"You don't need to apologize. Most people feel uncomfortable when they are asked questions about murder, especially when a friend is the one murdered...even worse when it's two. But, that's not why

I came by. I have something for you," he said as he opened the small bag containing his purchase from Smiling Sam's Civic Honda Dealership.

"What is this?" asked Shana as she peered into the bag. "You brought me a "C"?"

"Not only did I bring you a "C", but I brought Gorilla Glue to put it on with. Now, if you will show me where your car is, I can get to work reattaching your "C". A lady shouldn't be driving around in an "ivic" when she could be driving a Civic, now should she?"

"I guess not. Thank you for thinking of me...or are you just embarrassed to be working for a client with her "C" missing?" laughed Shana.

"I just want you and your Civic to feel complete," Richard replied with a grin. "Now can we take a look at that car?"

"Grandmother, I'll be right back. I'm showing Mr. Long where my car is. He brought me a "C". I won't be long. Do you need anything before I go out to the garage?"

"No, dear. I'm fine."

Shana opened the garage door. She and Richard walked over to the back of her car. Richard knelt down and took the "C" out of the bag.

"I'll need something to wipe the dirt off first," he said.

"Now you're saying my car is filthy?"

"No, but everybody knows that you need to wipe any potential soil off before you begin. Here, look and you'll see it written right here on the instructions on the Gorilla Glue bottle. And I'll need something to wipe any excess glue off and if it gets on one's hands, one must wipe off immediately...so says the instructions."

"Have you ever done this before?"

"No, but it should be easy…if you follow the instructions. Now something to wipe with, please?"

"OK! OK! I'm getting it!" said Shana as she went over to the workbench to look for a rag or paper towel. "Ah, here's a rag," she said to herself. She reached to pull a rag from under some tools that Meeno or someone had left on the workbench. Since she was trying to hurry, she accidentally knocked a hammer off onto the floor.

"What was that? Are you OK, over there?"

"Yes, I'm fine. I just knocked a hammer onto the floor. Here. Here's a rag. Will that do, Mr. Handyman or is this job considered a mechanic job since it's a car?"

"Thanks. And don't get smart unless you want to remain "C-less" for the rest of your ownership of this car, Missy."

Shana's Civic was back after the few minutes it took for the Gorilla Glue to dry. The double backed tape that Richard put on the back of the "C" before he put the Gorilla Glue on, helped to hold the letter in place securely.

"There. All done. You are now a proud owner of a Civic, my lady," he said as he wiped his hands on the rag Shana had brought him.

They both stood back and admired his work.

"Thank you so kindly, Sir," said Shana smiling. "Now my life is complete."

"You are quite welcome. Glad I could be of help. Now let's clean up our mess and then I need to get back to my office and get crackin' on this case.'

Shana helped him gather the bag, the Gorilla Glue and the remainder of the double-sided tape. Richard carried it all over to the workbench. He knelt down to pick up the hammer that Shana had knocked off. A white and brown substance was stuck on the head of the hammer. When he picked it up, some of it fell onto the floor of the garage.

He bent down to examine it. He held it close to his nose to see if it had a scent.

"Hey, what's this on this hammer, Shana?"

"I don't know. Probably something that got on it when Meeno hammered the loose nail on the porch the other day."

"Do you mind if I take it with me? I'd like to have it analyzed."

"Analyzed? What for?"

"I'd just like to see what's on it. I'm curious, that's all."

"Sure. I don't think anyone would mind, but I have to say, you sure have strange ideas. Is there anything else you wish to have examined from here or are you happy to get a hammer. I think you think you did so well at replacing my "C" that you figure you'll give up investigating and go into mechanics, so you are probably collecting your tools…the first being this hammer. Am I right?" she teased.

"Now you got me. How did you guess?" he teased. Do you have a couple of plastic freezer bags I could use to put this in? I don't want to lose all the whatever it is off onto my car."

"Sure, I'll run in and get a couple from the cupboard. I'll be right back," Shana said as she ran into the house to get the bags. When she returned with the two bags, she held one open so Richard could place the hammer into it. He used the other bag to pick up the hammer and any particles of the substance, by placing the bag over his hand, trying to avoid adding any more fingerprints to the hammer than were already there.

"Thanks, Shana. I'll return this in a few days. I'll let you know if it's important to the case. Now, I better get going. I want to get this to the lab as soon as possible. See you later or I'll call you if something comes up. Bye," he said as he left to get in his BMW.

"Well, I may not drive a fancy BMW, but at least I can drive a real Civic now," said Shana out loud as she headed back into the house to sit with her grandmother before dinner.

"What did Mr. Long want dear? Did he have more questions for you?"

"No, he brought a "C" to replace my missing one, remember?"

"That was nice of him, dear, or is he adding that to your bill??"

"No, I don't think so. I think he was just trying to make up to me for insulting my car when we first met. Oh, and he took the hammer that was in the garage. He said he wanted to have some stuff that was sticking to it analyzed. I told him it was probably just something that stuck to it when Meeno fixed that nail the other day. Was that alright Grandmother, that he took the hammer, I mean?"

"He took my hammer? What if I need it, dear? I don't like people taking things from my garage. The tools and things in there belonged to your grandfather. Meeno uses them to fix things around here. He should have asked me before he took the hammer."

"I'm sorry Grandmother. It's my fault. I told him it would be OK to take it. I didn't think you would mind. I'm sure he will return it in a couple of days. If he doesn't have it back by the end of the week, I'll call him and tell him to bring it back ASAP."

"Never mind. Just keep him out of my things from now on," Verina said as she whirled her wheelchair around and headed toward the patio.

"I'm glad I didn't tell her about the two freezer bags," thought Shana.

"Here are the results from the lab, Richard," said Tracy. " I'm surprised we got the results back so fast. Usually it takes several days. I guess this was easy to test, since it only took a day. Of course, my sweet-talking to the lab tech may have had something to do with it. Aren't you glad you hired me and my finesses, Richard? You get things you need so much faster."

"Well, I guess you may have a point there. Thanks for getting on this so quickly…how ever you got the information. Now let's see what this will tell us about the stuff on the hammer."

"It says that it's castor bean. Sorry, I already checked the report for you."

"Castor bean? Hmm… That's interesting. Shana said Meeno Max used this hammer to fix a nail on her grandmother's porch. So, that tells us that the poison …castor bean could have come from the Steris place or at least someone could have used this hammer to …as you put it pulverize the castor beans to feed Doralene Drake. Tracy, I just remembered…didn't you say that the poison that killed Charles Rom came from oleanders?"

"Yes, remember I was showing you what I found on poisonous plants on the Internet?"

"I just remembered that I saw oleanders growing on the side of the patio at Verina Steris's house when I first met her. How would you like to use those Internet skills of yours by printing out a few of those poisonous plants of yours and accompany me on a little field trip to the Steris estate?"

"Oh, boy! A field trip!" teased Tracy. "I'll print the information and photos of the plants if you wish."

"That's a great idea, Tracy. I think I would like for us to take a little look around to see what other kinds of plants Mrs. Verina Steris has growing on her property. We

The Six Hundred Thousand Dollar Club

might as well take the opportunity to talk to Mr. Meeno Max while we are there."

"I didn't fix any nail on the porch," said Meeno. Who told you I did that? I'm a chauffer, not a fixit man, remember?"

"So, you're saying you never used this hammer to fix the loose nail on Mr. Steris's porch?"

"I just said that, didn't I?" Got any more questions for me? If not, I need to leave. I have to pick up a few snacks before the big game tonight. I like to sit back with a nice cold beer and eat myself silly on pizza and pretzels. So, if you'll excuse me, I'll be moving along."

"Just one more thing, Mr. Max. Do you mind if we take a look around the premises?"

"Fine with me. Just don't get Mrs. Steris's feathers ruffled," he said just as his phone rang.

"Oh, great! Now Mrs. Steris wants me to do something up at the house for her. Just when I thought I was going to have a nice quiet evening enjoying the game. Well, I guess I better go see what she wants so I can get it over with if I want to watch any of that game tonight. See you people later," he said as he headed toward the house.

"I'm going to go take a peek at that porch, Tracy. Why don't you look around and see what you might find as far as plants."

"Will do, boss. And watch out for Mrs. Steris…we wouldn't want her flogging you."

Richard returned to the area behind the barn that Meeno called his apartment to find Tracy crawling on her knees looking at the over grown weeds and plants and then looking at her copies of the poisonous plants from the Internet.

"Any luck, Tracy?" asked Richard.

"Not yet. How about you? Find anything on the porch that may be of help?"

"No. As a matter of fact, I take that back. It's what I didn't find that's interesting.

"What do you mean?"

"I mean, there is not sign of any loose nails or any evidence that any nails have been touched by a hammer in years."

"Are you sure you checked every board?"

"Yes, and nothing. Not one nail has been hit. I would have seen a shiny spot or at least a clean mark of some sort where dirt or paint would be knocked off if there had been."

"Gotcha!" said Tracy as she continued to inspect the weeds and plants in front of her.

"Hey, look at this, Richard. Doesn't this look like the picture here?" she said as she held the photo of the plant next to the one growing in front of her.

"Yes, they do look similar. What is it?" asked Richard as he bent over to get a better view of the plants.

"It's called Jimsonweed. The scientific name is Datura stramonium. It has other names, too, like Devil's trumpet, thorn apple or mad apple and oh, yeah, stinkweed. It says here that it contains hyoscine and atropine. Hyoscyamine occurs in the leaves, seeds and roots. People have died by drinking tea made from it. Why would anyone be growing this plant out here?"

"I don't know, but look. Did you break this leaf off?"

"No. I see there are several missing and look at this one is bent. What do you make of it, Richard?"

"I'm not sure. Let's keep looking around. I'm going to do some snooping around the other side."

The Six Hundred Thousand Dollar Club

When he returned, Tracy had several pictures of plants marked on her copies of plants.

"Guess what else I found, Richard? Look at this. This is Hemlock. Right now there is only the remains of the plant, but by looking at this, it looks like it grew pretty well her a while back."

"Hemlock? Isn't that that plant that some guy drank and died?"

"Yes, it was Pluto. It caused his whole body to become paralyzed, including his lungs and heart causing his most unpleasant death. I wouldn't want to go that way."

"Look, what's this? It looks like some sort of tracks."

"Yeah, it looks like racks from a bike or a...no it can't be a bike. There are two wheel tracks. A bike would have different tracks."

"It almost looks like... wait a minute. Tracy! Go call Detective White and tell him to get his men out here on the double. Tell him we have our murderer. I'm going to go check on Shana and her grandmother."

"OK! I'm on it!" said Tracy as she ran to call Detective White.

After a few minutes, Richard ran back to his car.

"Detective White and the police are on their way. What did you find out, Richard?"

"I knocked and rang the bell, but no one answered, so I went around back. I could see Verina, Meeno and Shana through the patio window. It looks like Verina is pointing a pistol at Meeno and Shana. I came back to get my gun out of the glove box. I may need it. You stay here and wait for White and his boys. I'm going to see if I can get into the house. No matter what happens, you stay put, understand? I don't want to lose my number one Internet expert. I may need her again," he said with a grin as he retrieved his pistol and ran toward the back of the house.

"Good, the patio door is unlocked. Now if I can get in without being noticed, I may be able to over take old Mrs. Steris before she knows what hit her," said Richard to himself as he tried to slip through the door quietly, with his .44 Mg cocked and pointed in Verina's direction.

"Sit down, dear. Let's have a nice hot cup of tea now that we've had our breakfast. We haven't had much time to just sit and visit lately. It's time we did. Life is too short to waste on unimportant things. We should be enjoying each other's company while we have a chance, don't you agree, dear?"

"Yes, Grandmother. I do enjoy our time together," said Shana as she sat down on the over stuffed chair in the living room.

"Tell me, dear, what's been going on with you and that Mr. Long lately? Has he gotten any closer to solving his mystery?"

"I'm not sure. I know he's working hard to find out what happened to Mr. Rom and Mrs. Drake. I hope he finds out something soon."

"Don't we all, dear? By the way, has he brought my hammer back yet?"

"Not yet. I'll call him tomorrow to see if he is done with it and to let him know that you want it back as soon as possible."

"That would be a good idea, dear. I wouldn't want him to forget where he got it."

" Ok, Grandmother, I'll make sure I call him first thing tomorrow morning."

"Well don't worry about it right now, dear. Just sit back and enjoy your tea. Do you like it? It's a new herbal tea that I thought you might enjoy. We have our regular tea so often, that I thought we might like to try something new for a change."

"It is different. It sort of has a different smell than I've never noticed in other teas. What's it called, Grandmother?"

"It's a blend of several teas. It's called …Just For Your Pleasure. Don't they give some of these new teas funny names now days? Do you like it dear?"

"It's fine, Grandmother. I guess it takes a while to acquire a taste for it, but it's not bad."

"Would you like another cup, dear?"

"No thanks, Grandmother. I think I've had enough tea. I'm thinking I'd like to start checking out some of the classes offered at the university downtown. I may change my mind about going back to San Diego. I could live on campus and be close enough to you that we could still have our time together."

"No, you could live here and go to school, if that's what you want to do. No use wasting good money on some little tiny dorm when you have a perfectly nice room here."

"Thank you for offering, Grandmother, but I'm not even sure they will have the classes I need."

"Let's just wait and see, dear. They may have *all* the classes you need."

"Maybe. Well, I guess I better get moving if I'm going to get to the university office today."

"Not already? We just started to enjoy ourselves."

"Alright, Grandmother. I'll stay a while longer. I guess if I don't make the university office today, I can always go tomorrow. What did you want to talk about?"

"Well, how about you telling me what you did with your day yesterday and then I'll share my day with you?" Verona said as she filled Shana's teacup again.

"Thanks, Grandmother. I guess since I'm not going anywhere for a while, I could drink another cup of tea."

Shana and Verina spent the rest of the day taking turns sharing the events of the day before. Verina said she spent most of her day, sewing and reading. Shana spent her day driving around in her Civic. She enjoyed her time just driving through the countryside looking at the fields and listening to the country sounds. Sounds that she had never experienced while living in San Diego. She missed the ocean sometimes, but she enjoyed the country environment here best.

"Grandmother, do you mind if I go lie down for a while. I seem to have developed a terrible headache. And for some reason, I am extremely thirsty. With all the tea, I don't know how I could possibly be thirsty. I hope I'm not coming down with the flu again. My skin feels like it's on fire."

"Maybe we should call the doctor, dear."

"No. I'll be OK" she said as she started to stand up. "Wow! I feel dizzy all of a sudden." Sitting back down, Shana rubbed her eyes trying to clear away the blurriness that she was experiencing. "Grandmother, I don't feel so great right now,"

"Just sit, dear. It will most likely go away in a little while."

"I'm not so sure, Grandmother. I've never felt this bad before, not even when I... ha...d the...flu...," Shana tried to say.

"It's alright, dear. Would you like some more tea? It may help you feel better."

"No...I feel so drowsy... so... tired."

"Well, Shana, since you don't seem to be able to go very far, I have a few things to share with you besides my daily routine."

"Like...what...?"

"Well for one thing, I intend to be the last member of The Six Hundred Dollar Club. Your grandfather and I started it a long time ago, and I deserve to get our interests back."

"What do you mean?" Shana tried to understand what her grandmother was telling her, but she was having a difficult time paying attention.

"And if it takes helping the others kick the bucket, so be it."

"Are...you... telling me...you poisoned Mr. Rom and Mrs. Drake?"

"And...I hate to admit it, but your grandfather's little accident wasn't entirely an accident. You see, dear, he and Doralene were having little private meetings, shall we say? Meetings that he thought I didn't know about. A little Hemlock salad is the best cure for cheating spouses. Did you know that dear?"

"You...murdered Grandfather?"

"...And poor old Nellie Wheeler, Owen's wife? Well she did have a bad heart, but I helped her along with my rhubarb pie. So sorry, Nellie I guess I must have left a piece of the leaf in your slice of pie."

"But why Grandmother? Why would you murder your friends?"

"I told you, dear. I want to be the one to collect all the money. How difficult could that be to understand? Oh, I forgot, you aren't feeling to well right now are you, dear? It must have been the tea. My special herb tea. Too bad it must not agree with you, dear. Maybe it's because of what it's blended with."

"The...tea...? You put something in...the ...tea?" Shana could feel herself getting weaker and weaker by the minute.

"Well, let's just say, the tea is brewed with a very special kind of leaf...stinkweed, to be more precise. Or if you prefer to call it jimsonweed. Are you familiar with it, dear? You should be learning about it first hand very soon. As a matter of fact, it will probably be the last thing you learn. You can forget about those classes you were so interested in taking at the university. You will soon be joining my friends in the far beyond. I'm so glad I got to meet you before you took leave, dear."

"But why, Grandmother...why are you doing this to me, your granddaughter? I loved you. I thought you loved me, too."

"I do love you dear. But you have your mother's stubbornness. I told you not to hire that Mr. Long, but you went behind my back and did it any way. Then you gave him my hammer. The one I smashed the castor beans for Doralene's cocktail sauce with."

"Grandmother, please get help. Don't let me die. I love you."

"I know dear, but this is how it's got to be. Shush now. It won't be long. I promise. In the mean time, let me show how I did poor old Charles in." She lifted her skirt up to reveal her cotton panties with a pocket sewn on.

"You see, dear I was able to put the poison, either the crushed up castor beans or the Squeezed, or should I say, juiced, oleander in these little tube containers until the appropriate time came along to give my friends their special treat. It was easy to slip it out of my undies pocket and put it where it needed to be. It was quite simple."

"Please, Grandmother... don't do this. I'm your granddaughter. You can't just let me die...Please," Shana pleaded.

"Sorry, dear, but I have no choice. I'll call Meeno to help me get rid of your body in a little while. I'll have to do that before your Mr. Long shows up again."

"It seemed like hours before Shana heard her grandmother on the phone ordering Meeno to come to the house. Shana was feeling the effects of the poison more by the minute.

"I need to get help," she thought to herself but knowing it was impossible in her condition. She had given up any hope of escaping her fate hours ago. Now she just wanted to get it over with.

When Meeno came into the living room, he stopped abruptly.

"What's going on here?" he asked as he looked over at Shana as she slumped on the couch. "Is Shana ill?"

"Quite, I'm afraid, Meeno. You see, she's had a terrible reaction to some tea. I'm afraid she has had her last cup of tea."

"What do you mean? Shouldn't we be calling 911? She looks like she's about to die," he said as he went over to get a better look at Shana.

"Precisely, Meeno. That's what happens to a person when they drink poison tea."

"Poison tea? What are you talking about, poison tea? Shana drank poison tea? How did that happen?"

"Well, I guess, because I gave it to her. Now, Meeno, you will need to help me get rid of her body as soon as she quits breathing. Actually you will need to do it yourself. I couldn't possibly do much in this wheelchair, now can I?"

"You are crazy, old woman!" shouted Meeno. " I'm calling the police!"

"I don't think you will Meeno. You see, I have this little pistol here that says so," said Verina as she pulled her skirt up to get to a small gun she had in the second pocket of her panties. "I'm really glad I thought of sewing these pockets in my drawers. Thank you, Great Aunt Mabel. Your nutty little self has help me tremendously lately. Now, sit down Meeno and join us as we send Shana into her here after," she said as she pointed the pistol at Meeno.

"You can't do this. Shana is your granddaughter. And I'm not going to help you, you crazy old fool."

"Oh, but we've been all through that, Shana and I. She understands why I have no choice. And you will do as I say unless you want to join her."

Meeno thought about rushing Verina and grabbing the pistol, but he didn't want to take a chance on a bullet hitting Shana or himself. He didn't want to just sit by watching Shana die either. "I have to do something," he thought. "And it had better be something fast."

"Meeno, help me," whispered Shana as she tried to move. "I...I can't get up. Grandmother put something ...in...the...tea. I'm going to die. I...don't want to...die."

"I know Shana. Don't worry, I'll get you out of here," he said, hoping it wasn't a lie.

A few minutes later, Meeno thought he saw a movement in the doorway behind Verina.

"My nerves must be affecting my eyes," he thought. "No wait I saw it again...a shadow. I saw a shadow in the dining room." He looked back at Verina and then toward the shadow again, just in time to see Richard pointing a gun at Verina. He almost let out a shout, but stopped himself.

"Now that you've poisoned your granddaughter, how do you suppose you will get rid of her body, Mrs. Steris?" he asked hoping Richard would get the hint that Verina had indeed poisoned her granddaughter and that she was holding both of them hostage.

"I told you Meeno. You will be the one to take on that little task."

"But I told you I refuse to do your dirty work."

"And I told you that you have no choice. You will do as I say, or you will most definitely be joining Shana. Don't ask me to repeat it again!" she shouted as she waved her pistol at Meeno.

Just as she was about to move her wheelchair closer so she could get a better look at Shana's condition. Richard tiptoed behind her and grabbed the gun from her hand. He pushed Verina to the floor. Her wheelchair went spinning across the room as he shoved it with his foot. Meeno jumped to his feet to help Richard lift Verina into a chair. Richard handed him Verina's pistol.

"Here, Meeno. You keep this little toy pointed on our nice old grandmother here, while I check on Shana," he said as he bent down in front of Shana's lifeless form.

"She needs help fast, Mr. Long. I don't know how long Verina has been holding her here, but by the looks of her, if she doesn't get medical attention ASAP, she may not make it."

Richard grabbed the phone on the table next to where Verina had been sitting in her wheelchair and dilled 911. Rushing back to Shana, checking her pulse.

"You're right Meeno. We don't have much time. She's fading fast."

He lifted Shana's head as he began speaking softly to her.

"Help will be here soon, Shana. Just hold on."

"Help me," she whispered. "Grandmother...the ...tea..." was all Richard heard before Shana went unconscious.

Richard could hear police sirens blasting coming up the road.

"Good the troops have arrived. And now you get to take a little ride to your new home, Mrs. Steris," he said.

"And I bet they won't be serving you any of your fancy tea," said Meeno with a sneer.

Richard went to the front door to let Detective White and the police in.

"She's in here," he was saying. "Get her out of my sight, before I lose my self control. I've never had to do harm to any old woman, but this might be my first chance."

"We got it, o'l pal," said Detective White as he motioned for the police officer to handcuff Verina to her wheelchair and wheel her to the patrol car waiting to transport her to the police station down town.

" I need to get Shana to the ER, now!" said Richard as he lifted her into his arms and headed toward the door.

"Wait, I hear the paramedics coming now," shouted Meeno as he ran to open the door.

Two men and one woman rushed in carrying medical equipment nearly knocking Richard and Shana over.

"She's been poisoned. Get her to ER, now! There is no time to lose!" shouted Richard over his shoulder as he ran carrying Shana toward the EMT vehicle waiting in the driveway.

"What's happening, Richard?" asked Tracy as she came running up behind him.

"Shana's been poisoned. Quick, I'll explain on the way to the hospital."

At the hospital, Richard and Tracy waited impatiently for Doctor Laufenberg to come out and give them any news as to Shana's chances of survival. All of the club members were waiting as well. Detective White and Meeno sat side by side with stale cold coffee in Styrofoam cups in their hands. Everyone was quiet. The club members were in shock to learn that Verina was the person responsible for the deaths of Doralene, Charles. Ardon and Nellie. They were even more shocked to think she could poison her own granddaughter...the one she seemed to adore and had put on a pedestal only a few days ago.

"I just can't believe it," said Owen. "I just can't believe she murdered my beautiful wife."

"I can't believe she murdered my Charles, either, Owen," said Hazel

"We're just lucky she didn't get to the rest of us," Landis said as he shook his head.

"What's going to happen to her share of the money?" asked Bibi.

"Who cares, right now, Bibi? We need to think about Shana right now!" Pearl said as she glared at Bibi.

"So what's going to happen to Verina?" asked Hazel "I hope she's going to get what she deserves."

"Oh, she will," said Detective White. "Everything will be taken care of after she stands trial. I don't see how she has a chance in you know where of getting out of this. She's already confessed everything. And depending on what the docs say about Shana, she may be adding one more to her list of convictions."

"Let's hope that doesn't happen," said Richard as he ran his fingers through his hair. "What's taking them so long?" he said as he got up to walk the floor for the hundredth time tonight.

"Be patient, boss," said Trace as she got up to join Richard. "I'm sure they're doing all they can."

Just then Dr. Laufenberg stepped through the door. Everyone rushed over to him shouting questions about Shana.

"Hold on a minute. If you will all sit down, I'll give you the news and explain a few things."

Everyone returned to their seats. All eyes were on Dr. Laufenberg.

"I have good news. Shana pulled through. We were able to use magnesium sulphate, a purgative, to get the Jimsonweed out of her system. She's going to be a pretty sick young lady for a while. She's lucky not to have gone into convulsions or comma. That would have meant probable death. Mr. Long, it was a good thing you got medical help before it was too late. I don't recommend visitors for a while. We'll see how she's doing tomorrow. I'll let you know then if she can have visitors. In the mean time, we're going to keep a close watch on her and try to make her comfortable through the night. Any questions?"

Everyone shook their heads as Dr. Laufenberg stood to go back behind the stainless steel doors of the of the ER.

"Whew! What a relief," said Richard as he stood.

"Yeah, you can say that again," said Landis as he also stood.

One by one everybody began standing. Hugs were not in short supply as each one breathed a sigh of relief.

"Well, I say let's all go home and get some sleep. We'll want to be in good shape for our visits with Shana tomorrow," said Owen.

"I agree," said Pearl. "At least we can go home and rest easy knowing we are safe from being poisoned. That in itself will help me sleep well tonight."

The Six Hundred Thousand Dollar Club

"Amen, to that!" said Hazel.

"And I'll probably need to start looking for a new job and a new place to live tomorrow," said Meeno.

"I think you could talk to Shana when she gets to feeling better. Maybe she can help you out there. She's going to need someone to help her for a while when she gets out of the hospital," said Detective White.

"I hope so. I've become quite fond of Miss Willow," said Meeno.

"I think we all have," said Bibi " I wasn't too sure at first. I guess she really is the cutest little thing."

"Shall we all head out, then?" asked Landis.

"I'm ready. Are you Tracy?" asked Richard.

"Let's go!" she replied.

Everyone headed toward door. Pearl looked back to see Bibi still standing in the middle of the waiting room.

"Are you coming, Bibi?"

"Yes."

"Then what are you waiting for? Let's go." said Pearl.

"I was just wondering. Did any of you notice if Dr. Laufenberg was wearing a wedding ring?"

"Bibi!" everyone shouted at once.

Epilogue

With Verina in prison, and four of the original members dead and with Fredrick resigning because if his lack of financial stability, that still leaves five active members of the club. Technically, Verina is still a member since she *is* still alive. Who is to say that she still may outlive the rest? The money would still be legally hers according to George Imimes, Attorney Of Law.

"Wouldn't that be a kick in our diapers?" said Owen to everyone at their last meeting after Verina was arrested. "It would just be like that old woman to take our money and stash it under her cell cot for some thug to find later after she kicks the bucket or some Lesbian knocks her off and breaks out of jail with it all."

Age hasn't changed the desire of any of the members to outlive the others. If anything, it's made them even more eager to live. All are taking their vitamins and seeing their doctors for their regular check ups. Each one is eager to hear the doctor's report of the others at the regular meetings, hopefully finding some clue as to how long the other ones will live. Words of encouragement are shared when one is diagnosed with some minor illness or pain.

But there is still a little disappointed that the news is so good. The members have grown to truly love one another and the money isn't often mentioned, but the thought is still in the back of the minds of every member.

Who *will* be the last survivor and the sole beneficiary of the six hundred thousand dollars? Will it be Owen or Pearl? Or could it be Bibi or Landis or Hazel…or could it be Verina, who's sitting in prison awaiting her death sentence?

I hope you'll come along with this lively little group of senior citizens as they live out their remaining days, anxiously waiting for the final meeting of The Six Hundred Thousand Dollar Club. You'll find them in The Last Shall Be First…To The Bank, That Is.

A Note From The Author

The author would like to assure you that the characters in this work of fiction are completely created by her imagination. The names of businesses and locations are also fictitious. Any resemblances to living or dead persons are completely coincidental.

She has purposely left out a lot of detail, so you the reader may have the pleasure of creating the images of people and places as you see fit in order to fully enjoy your journey with the members of The Six Hundred Thousand Club.

Much research has been done however, on historical facts that are given in the story. For example the following are true and accurate to the best of the author's knowledge:

Korean War: June 25th, 1950, ending July 27th, 1953 (Ed Evanhoe)

Viet Nam War: September 26th, 1959, ending April 30th, 1975. (Wikipedia Encyclopedia)

Tupperware Parties: Began in the mid nine- teen forties. Earl Silas Tupper created Tupperware in 1945, and introduced to the public in 1946 in the United States. (Wikipedia Encyclopedia)

Swanson TV Dinners: Produced by C.A. Swanson and Sons in 1953. The full name was TV Brand Frozen Dinner. Consisted of turkey, cornbread dressing, frozen peas and sweet potatoes. The dinner came in an aluminum T.V. shaped tray and sold for ninety-eight cents. (Wikipedia Encyclopedia)

About the author

Carol S. Trevillion is an avid reader, especially of mysteries. She reads a novel a day when not writing. Finding herself running out of good mysteries to read, she decided to write her own. She lives with her husband and a German Shepherd and several turtles. She always includes something "turtlely" in her novels. It may be a street name, an establishment, a sweater or something about an actual turtle. If you look closely as you read one of her novels, you will surely find one. Did you find "turtle" anywhere in The Six Hundred Thousand Dollar Club? You can visit her at CarolTrevillion@msn.com. Subject line: The Six Hundred Thousand Dollar Club-turtle find.

Made in the USA
Lexington, KY
03 August 2011